Into The Lake

LK Chapman

To my husband Ashley and my little son Felix. When life is difficult you keep me smiling.

Natalie

1

February sunlight filtered through the front window of Verity's Events, illuminating the small wedding and party supplies shop and its treasure trove of sparkling contents, from table decorations and invitations to confetti and artificial flowers. Though the shop was pretty to look at, and many people popped in to admire the objects inside, the real heart of the business lay in planning the weddings and parties. At a round table by the window, Natalie sat and quietly read through the notes from the meeting they'd just had with a bride-to-be. Verity, beside her, tapped the paper. 'This is my favourite bit,' she said. 'A sushi bar at a wedding. That's one request I haven't had before.'

Natalie smiled. 'Sounds fun though.'

Verity stretched out her arms and then stifled a yawn. As always, the meeting had been long and in depth; Verity had an eye for detail and an incredible skill at drawing out exactly what the clients wanted, even if they didn't quite know themselves. It was fascinating to watch her work, and Natalie hoped that after a couple of years helping her out in the shop, some of her sister-in-law's skill would have rubbed off on her.

'Valentine's day soon,' Verity said, as she pushed her unruly chestnut hair away from her face. 'Have you got any plans?' She asked the question casually enough, but her eyes glinted mischievously. She was hoping for a revelation, or at least a piece of juicy gossip. Natalie had nothing to offer. 'Yoga class, then an early night with a book,' she said.

She'd meant the words to come out defiantly – to show she didn't mind her lack of plans – but they came out sounding hollow. *Did* she mind? She'd had plenty of experience spending Valentine's day alone, and it didn't usually bother her. Anticipating that Verity would start matchmaking, Natalie jumped in first to stop her. 'What about you and Rob?' she asked.

'We'll probably just have a quiet one. Isabelle and Daisy will be at home, and I don't fancy our chances of finding a babysitter—'

'I'll look after them,' Natalie said quickly.

Verity's eyes lit up. 'You wouldn't mind?'

'Of course not! Spending the evening with my lovely nieces, or a night on my own – there's no competition.'

Verity's face broke into a wide grin. She had the biggest, most infectious smile of anybody Natalie knew, and a dimple appeared in her right cheek, her hazel eyes twinkling. 'Thank you, Nat. I really appreciate it.'

Natalie nodded, but her mind had drifted elsewhere. Valentine's day was the least of her concerns, after the invitation she'd received the day before.

'Now, are you going to tell me what's been distracting you all day?' Verity asked. Natalie blinked, startled. Was it that obvious? Verity was leaning forward eagerly, leaving Natalie in no doubt that she wouldn't let it go without a satisfactory answer.

'I can't get anything past you, can I?' she said.

'Nope. And it's not like you to be so quiet.'

Before Natalie could answer her, the door opened with a gust of cold air and a young couple came in.

'Verity, you have to help us,' the bride said, her cheeks pink with emotion. 'After our meeting with you yesterday, we've had so much to think about and we were up until midnight talking about wedding favours. What do people usually do? We want something different, but not *too* different, and what do we give the kids that are coming? We don't want hundreds of kids running about on a sugar high, but what else do kids like?' She paused for a quick breath. 'Also, what do favours go in?' she continued. 'I like the idea of having little organza bags tied up with some nice ribbon, but he—' she nudged her fiancé '—says that they would look *naff*.' Abruptly she ran out of steam, and looked at them both helplessly.

Quickly getting to her feet, Natalie helped Verity take control of the situation and before long they became embroiled in a lengthy discussion about favours and table decorations. It wasn't until the end of the day, as they closed up the shop, that Natalie found a chance to speak to Verity again.

'I got an invite to a school reunion,' she said, showing her the message on her phone. 'It's nothing too formal, just a Saturday afternoon in August, so people can bring their families.'

'I'm waiting for the *but*,' Verity said.

'Well, it's one thing just going to a party,' Natalie said. 'I rarely turn down a chance to do that. But a party where everyone knew you as a teenager? I didn't even think people had school reunions nowadays – I've never heard of anyone else going to one. It's not even a proper anniversary of when we graduated or anything.'

'Who's organising it?'

'They've set up a website for the event,' Natalie said. 'It says a bit more about it on there. There were these four girls – I used to hang out with them a bit – they were good friends and all got together recently, like a little mini reunion. They started wondering how everyone else was getting on, and, well, here we are.'

'I've never known you to be worried about a party.'

Natalie read the invitation again. Verity was right, of course, she would normally be in her element. And there was nothing particularly threatening about the event itself – a big marquee in a country park on the edge of town, plenty of space for children to play, barbecue food, lawn games, and a chance to see some old photos and reminisce. What was there not to like? Yet she was filled with unease about the whole thing, and the reason was, quite literally, written all over her face.

Verity touched her arm gently. 'Is this about the accident?' she asked. 'About your injuries?'

Natalie looked round at her sister-in-law, who was watching her sympathetically. 'Yeah,' she said, 'but it's more than that. It's about having to go through it all; all the ways my life had to change, about having to give up a job I loved. They're people who used to know me. I know it's not as if they'll have been avidly following my career, but there can't be a single person in my year who didn't hear about me being spotted by that scout, so they must all know there was a chance I would be a model. Strangers don't know that. It's uncomfortable enough when strangers stare at me, but people I went to school with? People who will wonder what happened to me, and whether I can still do modelling looking the way I do. Even if they don't come straight out and ask me, they're all going to start whispering about me, stealing glances when they think I'm not looking. I *want* to go, but I'm not sure I can face explaining it to every single person I speak to.'

'You don't owe anyone an explanation.'

'But they'll be curious. People get curious about scars; they can't help it. And what do you go to a reunion for, other than to find out what happened to everybody?'

Verity nodded slowly. 'You know, I bet everyone who's been invited feels a bit weird about it, and can't make up their minds whether to go. I'm sure it's not only you.'

'Do you think so?'

'Yes, I do. Nearly everyone has something they find difficult to talk about, whether it's visible or invisible.'

'It's not that I can't bear to talk about it–'

'Well, I know that,' Verity said. 'You talk to thousands of people every week.'

'That's not the same.'

'I think it's amazing how many people subscribe to watch your videos. You're an inspiration.'

Natalie avoided Verity's eyes. She didn't feel entirely comfortable being called an inspiration. She was just doing the best she could with the hand that had been dealt to her. The fact that so many people enjoyed her fashion and party planning vlog had come as something of a surprise to her, but a welcome one. It had been easier in the early days to show her face online than to go out in public. That way she could talk about things she enjoyed, and know that people would hear her words, but she didn't have to watch their eyes drift to her scars. Sometimes in her videos she would talk about what had happened to her, how she felt about it. Other times she'd get sidetracked with stories of modelling jobs, which usually ended up quite amusing. Mostly it was a way of just expressing herself and letting people in to her world, a world that strangers apparently found interesting.

Verity was still looking at her, her eyes full of questions. Natalie lifted her hand to her face, where, partly obscured by a curtain of wavy red hair, a raised whitish-pink line curved down from her temple across her right cheek. Just above the corner of her mouth, a second, smaller scar bisected the first. When she smiled, there was a tight, pulling sensation that she could never get used to. The scars had faded considerably since the car crash, but the doctors had said she would have them for the rest of her life. Everyone assumed she gave up modelling solely because of the scars, but in fact it had as much to do with the back injuries she'd also suffered, which made it uncomfortable to stay in one position for long.

'Nat–' Verity started to say.

'I'm fortunate, really,' Natalie said. 'I came this close to dying–' she held her thumb and finger close together–' or being paralysed. I know I can't change what's happened. I've got past wishing I can change it, and going to sleep thinking that when I wake up maybe I'll just look the way I used to. I'm okay. I am. But for some reason the idea of this reunion … it's really thrown me.'

'Come back to ours for dinner,' Verity said. 'Talk it over with Rob. And you can see the girls, too. It'll make you feel better, I promise.'

2

Arriving at Verity and Rob's house, Natalie couldn't help but smile. The 1930s semi, with an arch above the front door and a generous front garden where clumps of daffodils were sprouting, readying themselves to burst into colour come the spring, was the homeliest place she could imagine. Inside, the warmth of the house wrapped around her, the hall painted sage green, cluttered with children's shoes, bags and coats, while in the living room off to the right was an area dedicated to Verity's passion for trying all manner of crafts – from card-making to crochet – which jostled for space alongside Rob's vast record collection.

Natalie followed Verity through to the large kitchen, where the smell of cooking filled the air. They found Rob stirring a saucepan while the two curly-haired girls, six-year-old Isabelle and four-year-old Daisy, were in the early stages of what looked set to be a full-blown fight over a doll. 'Auntie Nitty!' the two girls cried out, and, distracted from their squabble, they ran over to her. Natalie couldn't quite remember how she'd ended up with that nickname, but she didn't mind. In fact she quite liked it.

'What are you cooking?' she asked her brother after extricating herself from her nieces' arms.

'Chicken and tomato pasta bake,' he said. 'I've only just started. Are you staying for tea? I can whip up a veggie version for you.'

'Thank you, yes please.' She walked over to him, and he gave her a brief hug. 'Everything okay?'

'Yeah. It's not anything urgent. I'll tell you a bit later.'

***

Once Isabelle and Daisy had gone to bed, they moved from the kitchen table into the living room, where Natalie sank gratefully into the soft sofa cushions with a glass of red wine. Verity sat beside her, while Rob settled himself on the armchair near the fireplace. The contradictions about Rob always made her smile; he was an accountant, and his approach to many things was careful, methodical and with great attention to detail, yet his shoulder-length blonde hair, loud shirts, and penchant for rock music – both listening to it and playing it – made a refreshing contrast.

'Natalie offered to look after the girls on Valentine's day,' Verity said to him.

Natalie waved away his thanks. 'I'm looking forward to it,' she said. 'But I came to talk to you about something else.' She quickly outlined her dilemma about the school reunion, while Rob listened carefully.

'Personally, I wouldn't go,' he said. 'Why bother with the hassle? People only go to things like that to show off. Either that, or because they're nosy.'

'I don't think so,' Verity said. 'They just want to catch up with old friends. And anyway, there's nothing wrong with being curious. *I* would go, if I was invited to a reunion.'

Rob was drumming his fingers on his leg – not out of frustration or impatience – it was a habit he'd had as long as Natalie could remember, like he was continuously hearing different melodies inside his head. Sometimes she wondered if all of her brother's thoughts were set to music.

'I feel like I'm going to have to keep explaining myself,' she said.

'Just say you don't want to talk about it.'

'Well, there's not much point in going if I'm not going to open up to anyone.'

'Perhaps you should ask yourself what's the worst thing that can happen?' Verity suggested.

'That I have to explain about the car crash to about a hundred separate people in the space of a few hours,' Natalie said.

Verity shook her head. 'When you put it like that, it doesn't sound great. But on the up side, maybe you'll enjoy meeting, or re-meeting – if that's a word – some of them. Or at least have a laugh reminiscing. It's not like anyone is going to be outright *nasty*, is it? And it's not even far to travel. I know Eashling Park, it's just twenty minutes down the road.'

Natalie took a large mouthful of wine. 'Maybe I'll offer to help with the organising. If the questions get too much on the day, I can always make an excuse that I need to go and sort something out.' Suddenly, her resolve strengthened. What was there to worry about? Nothing could be worse than when she'd woken up in hospital after the crash, when she was told about the injuries to her face and her back, and she'd felt more terrified and alone than she ever had in her life. When they'd eventually handed her a mirror, it had been almost impossible to believe that she was really looking at her own face. If she could get through that, she could get through a reunion, couldn't she? Her life might be different to what it used to be, but it was good. She enjoyed it. If anyone asked, that was what she would say. The scars were part of her history, the narrative of her life. Her own feelings about them still varied, and her emotions weren't always easy to sit with, but she wasn't going to let fear hold her back. Yes, she was scared, but she would go. Perhaps something good would come out of it, even if it was nothing more than a few hours of fun. If she didn't go, she'd never find out.

Josh

3

'I can't believe you talked me into this,' Josh said, as he and Gareth made their way towards the marquee in the middle of a wide grassy area at Eashling park. Trees surrounded it on three sides, giving the area some privacy from the other visitors at the country park. The sound of families picnicking around the pond and children playing in the large adventure playground drifted through the trees, and for a moment Josh felt so out of place he had to fight an impulse to turn around and make a run for it.

'I guess this is it,' Gareth said as they paused to take in the huge banner on the front of the marquee, which read 'Wayfield Community School, Class of 2002'. Some guests had already arrived with their families, and children were busy running around on the lawn in front of the marquee, or playing with the giant wooden tumble tower that had been set up. A small group were playing football near the trees. 'Look, everyone has families,' Josh continued.

'No, they don't,' Gareth said. He waved in the direction of a few groups of adults near the entrance, talking together. 'They don't look like they do. Not every single person will have kids. Or be married.'

Josh looked round at his friend, who seemed perfectly at ease in what Josh was finding a pretty uncomfortable environment. But then, it was no surprise. Never had Josh met anybody who cared less than Gareth about what people thought of him. Sometimes, Josh wondered whether he realised other people even had the capacity to think anything negative about him. He certainly assumed things would go his way, and usually they did.

Compared to Gareth – who was wearing smart jeans and a simple white shirt, his black hair combed over, making him look smart and polished – Josh was aware that his own caramel-coloured hair could, at best, be described as tousled. In addition, his face almost certainly had a rabbit-caught-in-the-headlights expression, which was something of a speciality of his.

'I'm not sure I recognise anyone,' Josh said, as they approached a small group.

Before they could join the conversation, a woman emerged from the marquee and beamed at them. Her long coppery hair flowed around her shoulders, making an electrifying contrast with her emerald green dress. The loose fabric swirled around her ankles, and on her feet were a pair of flip-flops sparkling with tiny beads in assorted metallic shades. She tucked her hair behind her ear, and Josh was taken aback by a scar across her cheek. Who was she? There had been a girl in his year with long ginger hair, though her name escaped him – it began with an M, or maybe an N. But she hadn't had a scar.

'So, I'm Natalie Woodrough, in case you don't remember,' she said, looking from one to the other. 'You're Gareth …' Her eyes fell on Josh. 'It's on the tip of my tongue.'

'Josh. Sparkes,' he said, a little shyly.

'Yes, of course!' she said. 'Okay, so, we have name badges, to save everyone spending the day awkwardly having to admit they've forgotten each other's names. I'll go and get yours. I'm supposed to have one too, but it fell off somewhere. I've been trying to find it the last fifteen minutes.'

They followed her inside the marquee, where a half-empty basket of name badges sat on a table alongside a scattering of old photos. Gareth leafed through a few, while Josh looked around at the tables, which had a couple of copies of the school year book on each. Towards the back of the marquee was a large screen and a projector. Natalie followed his gaze. 'That's for later,' she said, 'we've got some activities planned.'

Josh laughed. 'I don't know how much I like the sound of that.'

'I know what you mean,' she said. 'I dread to think what the girls have managed to dig up to show later!' She leant towards him conspiratorially. 'I did hear some rumours that a couple of our old teachers might make an appearance.'

'Really? Which ones?'

She tapped the side of her nose. 'I'm sworn to secrecy.'

As she handed Josh and Gareth their name badges, a family entering the marquee caught her attention. 'Oh, sorry guys, I'd better just...' She rushed off in a waft of floral scent, just as Gareth burst out laughing. 'Oh man, look at *this*,' he said, holding up a dreadful photo of himself and Josh. Standing outside the school hall, both in jeans and t-shirts, they were staring defiantly at the camera as though they considered themselves a pair of rebels. Instead they looked moody and awkward. 'When is that from?' Josh said. 'I don't remember that.'

'It's at a school disco or something,' Gareth said. 'Look at the state of my *hair*. And your glasses.' Josh winced as he took in the horribly unfashionable frames. Nowadays he wore contacts.

'Did you ever have anything to do with Natalie?' he asked Gareth. 'I'm not sure I spoke to her back at school. She seems very friendly.'

'No, I didn't know her back then. She wasn't really part of our crowd, was she?'

'Two people isn't a crowd.'

'Fair point,' Gareth said, with a grin. 'Let's get a drink. If I've got to pretend to be interested in how people's children are getting on at school and where everyone has been on holiday this summer, I can't do it stone cold sober.'

***

'So,' Gareth said as he sat down beside Josh, 'I've managed to find out what happened to Natalie.'

Josh gave him a sharp look. Surely the last thing she wanted was everyone gossiping about her. But he had to admit he was curious.

'Don't pretend you don't want to know,' Gareth said. 'You've been staring at her every chance you get.'

Josh shifted uncomfortably. Had it been that obvious? He wasn't staring because of her scar, though; something about her just kept drawing his attention. The way her hair was like a flame across her dress, and how she was always laughing and talking animatedly to anybody and everybody. How could she just fit in so easily? He'd never been able to. He hoped he'd get a chance to speak to her again, but she was so busy, and he hadn't gathered up enough courage to approach her himself.

Gareth was smirking, and Josh's insides twisted uncomfortably. He was about to say that he didn't want to discuss Natalie's life behind her back, but Gareth had already begun to speak. 'A woman was talking on her phone and drove through a red light into the side of Natalie's car. The woman is fine now, apparently, but Natalie nearly died.'

Josh let out his breath. 'That's awful,' he said. A sickly feeling spread over him. He shouldn't have let Gareth tell him. It was her business, not a piece of juicy gossip to be passed around.

'She was a model, you know,' Gareth said. 'I'd forgotten about that. She got spotted—'

'Yeah, I remember something about that,' Josh said.

'She isn't any more.'

'Because of her scars?'

Gareth shrugged. 'Guess so,' he said.

Josh frowned. It seemed very unfair. 'What does she do now?' he asked.

'Dunno.'

Josh glanced up and his eyes fell on Natalie again. With the hem of her long dress caught up in her hand, she was joining in a game of football with some of the families.

'I can't imagine what that must have been like for her,' he said, 'being in such a bad crash.'

'Don't try to, then,' Gareth said. 'It's best not to think about stuff like that. Now, just wait till you hear what I found out about Darren…'

***

It wasn't until the evening that Josh got a chance to speak to Natalie again. Most of the families had left now that it was getting dark, and Josh sat with Gareth at a table in the corner of the marquee, Gareth proudly holding his 'most eligible bachelor' award. Josh raised an eyebrow at his own 'same hairstyle' certificate. It could have been worse, though. At least he'd dodged 'least changed' – the idea of which was vaguely depressing. Natalie caught his eye, and came over to sit down at their table. 'What a day!' she said.

'You did a great job,' Gareth said, 'you and Sophie and the others.'

'Yeah, well, they were the brains behind it all. I just helped on the day. I've been working at my sister-in-law's event planning business – that's mainly weddings, but it's a pretty similar deal – just make sure everyone is fed, watered, entertained and can find the loos.' She pointed a finger at Gareth. 'On the topic of jobs, I can't believe I didn't know that you *made* that dating site, Hearts. Olivia told me a few minutes ago. I've actually used it, and I never knew!'

Gareth shrugged, but his eyes glinted with pride. 'It's not that big a deal.'

'It's a huge deal!' Natalie said. 'How many people do you think got together because of Hearts? Do you ever hear from anybody who married someone they met on there?'

'Occasionally.'

Natalie gave him a playful slap on the arm. 'Stop being so modest! I think it's brilliant.'

Gareth smiled, the kind of smile that said he thought it was brilliant too, but he felt no need to say so. At that moment, somebody called out his name, and he turned. 'Oh, it's Emma,' he said. 'It looks like she's going, I'll just go and say goodbye.'

Natalie smiled knowingly as Gareth got up. 'He's been talking to Emma a lot,' she said. 'You know, he shouldn't really be single, should he?' she added mischievously. 'He's not a very good advert for Hearts.'

Josh laughed. 'I never thought about it that way.' He paused. 'Well, to tell you the truth I don't think he's looking to settle down.'

'Ah,' Natalie said with another glance towards Gareth, who was leaning close to Emma and saying something in her ear. 'Have you and him stayed in touch this whole time?'

'Yeah, mostly. We lost touch for a few years, but then he got in contact – he wanted my advice on Hearts when he was developing the website. We hang out quite a bit since then.'

'What made him decide to make a dating site, do you think?'

'No idea. He's done pretty well out of it, though. Especially now he's got the app as well.' He paused for a moment. 'You said that you've used Hearts…' he said tentatively.

'Oh, yeah. For a bit. I did start seeing a guy I met on there, but then it sort of fizzled out. We wanted different things. It can actually be a bit of a pain, having the job that I did at the time. Once guys found out, it seemed like they just wanted to tell their friends they were dating a model, or something. It was hard to know if they were being genuine with me.'

'I'm sorry.'

She laughed. 'Honestly, Josh, if I had a pound for every time I've had to deal with some creep of a guy–' She waved her finger around as if she was counting. 'Well, it wouldn't really come to that much, I guess. But it's happened more times than I care to remember. And I've turned up to a couple of jobs where the pictures they wanted to take were *not* the ones they were advertising for.'

'Seriously?'

'Yes,' she said. 'Seriously. Being a model is not all it's cracked up to be, believe me.'

'What did you do, when you turned up at those photo shoots?'

'Told them to stick it,' she said. 'I don't take any crap like that.'

Josh couldn't help but smile. It was quite clear that Natalie didn't take any crap.

'It sounds like you have a lot of interesting stories to tell,' he said.

Suddenly Natalie paused and pointed her finger at him. '*You* have an interesting story to tell,' she said. 'I just remembered. You got arrested, didn't you? For something unusual like…' She puzzled over it briefly … 'Hacking.'

4

Josh's cheeks grew warm. How on earth was he going to explain *that?* He tried to smile. 'Yep, you got me,' he said, but his flippant words clearly didn't fool her.

'Sorry,' she said. 'That was insensitive of me. We don't need to talk about it.' She gestured at a wine bottle left over from dinner on the table behind Josh. 'Can you grab that?' He picked it up and refilled her glass.

'Thanks. I'm not really used to drinking now. After the accident I moved away from the city back to Wayfield so I could be near my parents and brother.' She gave a short laugh. 'Bit of a shock to the system coming back to suburbia, but I needed it. It means I don't really get out so much as I used to. I feel like I'm practically a recluse nowadays!'

'I … I heard about your accident,' Josh said, a little guiltily.

'Yeah, I think everyone has.'

He took a large gulp of wine. 'I don't really know what to say,' he said. 'I'm so sorry that happened to you.'

She nodded, but didn't reply.

'I didn't really get arrested,' he added. 'I think Gareth told everyone that after it happened, to make it sound more rock'n'roll.'

'Really?'

'I actually turned myself in.'

'Oh, okay.' She looked slightly bewildered.

'Yeah, I–it's kind of hard to explain what I was doing–'

'It's okay,' she said, 'you don't need to blind me with science.'

'No, I just mean I feel really stupid about it. I was…' He paused. 'I was just messing around, seeing if I could get into the exam board's system–'

'The exam board! Were you trying to change your grades?'

He shifted uncomfortably. 'I don't know what I was trying to do. I didn't think I'd be able to get into their system at all. I was surprised I got as far as I did. But then I felt so terrible I went to the police station and told them what I'd done.'

Natalie put her hand up to her mouth to stifle a laugh. 'That's actually really sweet,' she said.

'I guess I was always the kid who worried about rules and stuff.'

'What happened to you when everyone found out?'

'Not much, really. I was having some problems. Nothing major,' he lied, 'just teenage stuff, you know? Once I'd talked things through, it was better.'

They fell into a brief silence, as Natalie digested what he'd said. 'What do you do now?' she asked. 'I feel like you must have already said, but I can't remember–'

'It's my job now,' he said. '*Stopping* hacking, that is. It's called penetration testing.'

Natalie smirked, then shook her head. 'Sorry. Once I've had a few drinks, my sense of humour takes a nosedive. Someone could say "bum" to me and I'd be in stitches.' She tried to make her face serious again. 'Do you like doing it?'

'What? Penetration?' he asked in an innocent voice. As he hoped, Natalie snorted with laughter. 'Sorry, sorry!' she said. 'I'm ridiculous.'

'It can be quite hard, sometimes,' he continued.

Natalie burst out laughing again, and Josh couldn't help but join her.

'You know,' she said eventually, 'based on our sense of humour you wouldn't think this was eighteen years after we'd left school. You'd think we were still sixteen.'

'Sometimes I feel like I've only just stopped being a teenager,' he said. 'It feels like it was really recent. Then I see an actual teenager, and suddenly I feel really old.'

'Yep. I get it. And doing a job where everything was focused around my appearance certainly made me conscious of time passing.'

'I think you look great,' he said, and then he cringed. What? Where had that come from? The words had popped out before he'd thought about them. He must have sounded like such a prat.

'A lot of people feel like they have to say that,' she said, raising her hand towards her scars. 'To reassure me. I don't need them to.'

'That's not why I said it.'

Natalie didn't reply. Was that a smile hovering around her lips? Josh's head swam. How much had he had to drink?

'Natalie!' a voice called from across the marquee. It was one of the organisers, Aisha.

'I think everyone's going,' Natalie said. 'I probably need to help clear up.'

'Don't go,' he said stupidly as she began to stand.

She looked startled.

'No, I just mean, I want to–' God, what was wrong with his head? 'Could I see you again sometime?' he managed to stammer out.

She paused for a moment, and then she smiled. 'Sure,' she said, 'give me your phone and I'll put my number in.'

He handed it over. 'You know, I almost didn't come tonight, but I'm glad I did.'

She finished typing and handed his phone back. 'Likewise,' she said.

5

He couldn't sleep. Every time he closed his eyes, there she was, holding her green dress up while she joined in the game of football; laughing at his daft jokes while the lights inside the marquee lit up her hair; talking to him through lips of the glossiest pale pink, which left a little ring of shimmering colour on the edge of her wine glass.

Josh sat up abruptly. Stop thinking about her! He cringed at the memory of their conversation. Why had he said so many stupid things? Natalie apparently hadn't minded, though. He'd made her laugh. *But was she laughing with me, or at me?* He sighed and picked up his phone to check she really had given him her number and that it wasn't all a dream. Yes. There it was. Natalie Woodrough. He put his phone back down and went to the bathroom to splash cold water on his face. It was hardly as if he could call her in the middle of the night. He had to wait until morning at least. But would first thing in the morning be too keen? Should he wait until the afternoon? Evening? The day after that, even? He shook his head. He was driving himself crazy. He wasn't going to play games like that. He'd just text her mid-morning. That would be okay.

***

'Well?' Gareth said.

'Well what?'

'You *know* what! Are you seeing her again? Natalie?'

Josh took out his phone and checked it for probably the hundredth time that day. 'I don't know yet. I texted her this morning, and she hasn't replied.'

Gareth nodded reassuringly as he joined Josh on the sofa, having finished clearing empty wine glasses from the table.

Clearly he'd continued the party at his flat after the reunion had ended. 'It's not even been a whole day yet.' He looked at Josh closely. 'Don't get too wound up about it.'

'It's a Sunday, though.'

'She might work on Sundays. If she does events it's probably not a Monday to Friday job.'

Of course! Josh gave himself a shake. Why hadn't he thought of that? 'I think I only slept for a few hours after the reunion last night,' he said, 'I should probably–'

'I just wanted to ask a few more things about the app,' Gareth said.

'Okay, fire away,' Josh said wearily, and he listened to Gareth chattering on about the changes underway for the Hearts dating app, specifically a new add-on to the main service called Hearts Ignite. He answered Gareth's questions as best he could, though Gareth must have got the message that his head wasn't in the game, as after a few minutes he said, 'Let's leave it there. Maybe you could take a look at it again another day, let me know what you think before it launches?'

Josh was about to reply when his phone vibrated. He looked at it eagerly, but his heart immediately sank.

'Not her?'

'Unless she's a parcel that's being delivered tomorrow, then no.'

Gareth laughed. 'That would make it easier.'

'I don't know what I'm more nervous about: her replying or her not replying. She was easy enough to talk to last night, but what if I meet her again and I can't think of anything to say?'

'Then you accept it's not meant to be and you move on.'

'Just like that?'

'Look, Josh, it'll be fine. Don't give yourself such a hard time. You and her found plenty to talk about last night, and when you meet up with her again–'

'You mean *if*.'

'*When*,' Gareth insisted, 'you see her again, you'll get on really well again. Sure it might be awkward for the first couple of

24

minutes, but that's to be expected. And who knows, it might not be awkward at all.'

'She might just never reply.'

'Give her a bit of time. She might be nervous, like you obviously are. Not everyone can be like me, after all.'

Josh sighed, and shifted on the sofa, his hand brushing against something scratchy stuffed down the side of the cushion. He pulled it out. 'Oh for God's sake.'

Gareth laughed and reached across to take the empty condom wrapper from him. 'Sorry,' Gareth said, though he was clearly amused as Josh hastily rubbed his fingers on his jeans as if he'd just touched something poisonous.

'Is there anything in your flat that's safe to sit on?' Josh asked. 'Last time I came here you gave me that vivid account of what happened on one of your kitchen bar stools. And how many dirty weekends have you been on this summer–'

'Well, I *am* the face of Hearts,' Gareth said. 'I have to act the part. I can't really be scared of dates.'

'I'm not scared of going on a date with Natalie–'

Gareth raised an eyebrow, but didn't argue. 'Good. Make sure you tell me how it goes. *All* the details.'

'No.'

'Some of the details.'

'Maybe.'

'It'll be fine.'

Josh nodded. Maybe it would be fine. If only Natalie would get back to him and agree to see him again. It might only have been a matter of hours since he messaged her, but each hour felt like a day to him. *I have to see her again. I just have to.*

6

'Well, I'm really glad it's working out for you,' Gareth said, leaning back in his desk chair as he glanced round at Josh. 'You deserve to have something good happen to you for once.'

Josh tried to hide the grin that sprang to his face whenever he thought about Natalie and the dates he'd been on with her. He knew Gareth would make some dig if he saw him with such a soppy expression, so he distracted himself by looking through the glass wall that separated Gareth's office from the open-plan rows of desks beyond. At this time of night the Hearts headquarters were deserted, but Gareth had insisted on meeting here, saying he enjoyed staying after hours sometimes when he could sit at his desk and take in the sight of his 'Hearts Empire'. In fact, Gareth's flat was only a couple of streets away – on the edge of this new business park that had sprung up in Wayfield several years ago along with a sprawling housing estate. When they'd been kids this part of Wayfield had been fields and woodland, and he and Gareth had sometimes cycled out here and watched the trains speeding past through the greenery, heading towards London. Something about those trains had felt impossibly exciting back then, to two kids stuck in a suburban backwater like Wayfield. Surely everything was glamorous and thrilling in the city. Surely everybody there had things all figured out.

Apparently that memory had inspired Gareth to set up his Hearts office only a stone's throw from where they used to hang out. Something about coming full circle – back to the place where they daydreamed about what they'd become one day. Gareth had certainly more than fulfilled his dreams, while Josh had ended up drifting, somewhat unwittingly, back to Wayfield after university. God knows he'd not had much happiness here, but a job had come up, and he had followed. Perhaps it had been inevitable.

Gareth's words about good things rarely happening to him finally sank in and he became defensive. 'My life hasn't been *that* bad,' he said. 'You make it sound like the whole thing has been a car crash.'

His friend raised an eyebrow, but didn't say anything, and Josh tried to change the subject. He'd been checking the new Hearts Ignite app for the final time before the launch, and though he suspected Gareth had invited him here as much to grill him about Natalie as to hear his feedback on the app, he thought he'd better deliver his conclusions. 'Anyway, Hearts Ignite looks great,' Josh said, 'and you really don't need my advice on this stuff any more. It's not like the early days when Hearts was just you and a laptop. You've got a whole team of your own now.'

'I know. Maybe it's just nostalgia. Things don't feel final until you've signed off on it.'

Josh laughed. 'Well, Ignite is good to go. I can't see any issues with it from a security point of view, and it's easy to use too.'

Gareth stretched his legs out lazily in front of him. 'You don't like the idea of it, though, do you?'

'I don't have any opinion about it. I wouldn't use it myself, but I've never used Hearts either. For one thing, I spent so long helping you make that site that I'd feel like I was working.'

Gareth gave a short laugh. 'Yeah, fair enough. But Hearts will do a lot better now you can find someone for the night as well as the long term. That was a whole load of cash we were just leaving on the table.'

'I can't argue with that.'

Gareth gave him a serious look. 'I don't know why you never accept anything from me for all the work you've done. You know Hearts wouldn't exist if it wasn't for you.'

'You know why. Hearts is your baby. You came up with all the ideas, and you went and found the users. There's no way I could have done that. I don't want to take any money from you for something I did as a favour. Besides, I enjoyed helping you. I've told you before: any money you feel compelled to give me, give it to charity instead.'

'You might feel differently in a few years. Weddings are expensive, you know. And kids.'

Josh looked round at him, startled.

'No way,' Gareth said, sitting up in his chair, 'you actually *are* thinking about it already, aren't you?'

'I don't know how you know this stuff,' Josh grumbled. 'And of course I'm not *really* thinking about it just yet. Me and Natalie have only met up a couple of times—'

'But you already know, right?'

'I don't know. She might get bored of me.'

With a sigh, Gareth reached down to the bottom drawer of his desk and pulled out a bottle.

'You keep a bottle of whisky in your desk?' Josh said.

'I do,' Gareth said, clearly pleased with himself. 'I haven't actually opened it yet. I just like to pretend I'm one of those cynical old cops you get on TV shows.'

'You like to pretend you've turned into a borderline alcoholic because of all the messed-up stuff you have to deal with every day?'

'Exactly.'

Gareth opened the bottle and took a swig before passing it to Josh, who shook his head. 'I've got to drive home in a minute.'

'You always spoil my fun.'

'You seemed like you had something you were going to say to me?'

'Yes. Why would you assume she'll get bored of you?' Gareth pointed his finger at him mischievously. 'Do you need me to give you some sex tips? Because I have plenty—'

'No,' Josh said quickly. He didn't add that he and Natalie hadn't spent the night together yet, though Gareth clearly guessed, because he said, 'So, she hasn't even sampled the goods yet and you're talking about her getting bored?'

'I didn't mean I was worried she'd get bored of *that* specifically. I was worried she'd get bored of *me*. As a person.'

Gareth screwed up his face. 'You know what this is about?'

'Enlighten me.'

'It's your fucking family again.'

'It's nothing to do with them.'

'No? When was the last time any of them, aside from your dad, gave a shit about what was going on with you? When did any of them last ask you if you were okay? Or even if you had a nice weekend?'

'It's not that easy when half of them live in Australia, and my dad's out of the country so much on business—'

'They have the internet in Australia. How hard would it be for them to at least drop you an email from time to time?'

'I don't want to get into this. I'm not exactly good at keeping in touch with them either. My family is nothing to do with Natalie.'

'Just as well, since they all fucked off to the other side of the world right when you could have done with them around. Who picks up the pieces every time you go through a break-up? I do. And why did you have those break-ups? Because they've made you feel like you shouldn't open up or get close to anyone.'

'Are you done with the psychoanalysis?' Josh said. 'And I wouldn't give up the day job if I was you, Gareth. Things haven't worked out for me because I was never that invested in anyone before. I've never met a woman who makes me feel like Natalie does. And I haven't had *that* many break-ups. You're making it sound worse than it is.'

'Okay, well, maybe you're right. But the way your family acts with you isn't because there's something wrong with you, it's because there's something wrong with them. Natalie likes you. There's no reason she wouldn't like you. You just need to believe it. And even if it's not going to last, at least have some fun for once,' Gareth added with a glint in his eye. 'The last time you got any action I'm not sure dating apps even existed.'

7

'Why do you think we never had anything to do with each other at school?' Natalie asked him, after they had both managed to get their breath back.

He looked at her face, just inches from his on the pillow. Her green eyes glowed with warmth, her hair tumbling over her bare shoulder into a flame-coloured tangle on the sheets. The attraction that had been building between them had finally reached boiling point when he turned up at her flat for dinner earlier that evening. He'd bought her a bunch of sunflowers after she'd mentioned how much she loved them, and they would clearly fit in with the riot of colour that filled her flat. Not that he'd seen all of it yet, aside from a glimpse of the living room through a doorway; he only had the boldly decorated hall and bedroom to go on. The sunflowers had soon dropped, forgotten, from her hand as she kissed him, and he'd kissed her back deeply, both of them eagerly shedding their clothes. She'd gasped when he brought his lips to her nipples, and then she'd grabbed his hand and pulled him down the hall to her bedroom. His body began to respond to the memory, and he reached across and stroked her cheek. What had she just asked him? 'I don't know,' he said as he finally remembered her question about school. 'Were we even in any of the same classes?'

'I think you were always just with Gareth,' she said. 'And I guess I was with my group. That's kind of how it goes at school, isn't it? Everyone just stays in their little bubbles.'

'Talking of Gareth,' Josh said after a pause, 'he wants us to celebrate the Hearts Ignite launch with him. He's already having a big party with people from the office, but he wants to do a smaller celebration with us, just dinner somewhere, something low key.'

Natalie propped herself up on her elbow. 'I'd rather have dinner just with you,' she said playfully. 'I want you all to myself.'

'It'll only be a couple of hours.'

She smiled and kissed him softly. 'I'm just messing around. Of course I'll come and help him celebrate. As long as I get you to myself afterwards.'

'I think I can probably agree to that,' he teased her, 'if I really have to—'

She cut off his words with another kiss, and he put his arms around her and pulled her on top of him. As Natalie lifted her body to sit astride him, his thoughts fell away, and for a while all that replaced them was bliss.

***

'Okay,' Natalie said, as she finished off her second glass of champagne and turned to face Gareth. 'Now, you have to tell me once and for all. Why a dating site? What was it that made you want to do it?'

Gareth shrugged. 'I made a dating site because I had an idea for a dating site. If I'd had an idea for something else, I would have made that instead.'

She turned to Josh. 'He's impossible.'

'All right,' Gareth said, holding his hands up, 'I'll try to explain, just for you.'

'How very gracious of you,' Natalie said with a smile.

'I just saw a need for it,' he said. 'Back when I started, there wasn't that much out there. I thought I could improve on what was on offer and I did it. I don't really have a romantic bone in my body, but it was never about that for me. *Josh* is the one who would say you and him are made for each other. *I* say, there's plenty of pairs of people out there who are compatible. I just try to make it easier for them to find each other. There's no "the one". There's just lots of possible ones, and I help put those ones together.'

Josh sat back in his chair, while Natalie leant forward eagerly, keen to debate further.

'I think you're right up to a point,' she said. 'I think it starts out that there are lots of "ones". But as a relationship builds, that's when somebody can stop being just "a one" and become "the one", don't you think?'

'All right,' Gareth said helplessly, 'enough of this now! I'm here to celebrate.' He held up his glass and said, 'Ignite,' before draining the rest of its contents. Natalie and Josh followed suit, and under the table she gave his leg a squeeze.

***

'Can we walk for a bit?' Natalie asked after they had said goodbye to Gareth. 'I need a bit of fresh air.'

They made their way down the street towards the river, where they sat on a bench, watching the water flow gently past, spangled with yellow reflections of the street lights.

'I never thought I'd come back and live in Wayfield again,' she said. 'When I was a teenager I thought it was so dull, and I couldn't wait to leave. But now it's starting to feel like home.'

Josh nodded. Wayfield was certainly nothing special. In fact the river, slipping lazily along to the north of the town centre, was probably the town's only beauty – even if it was spoilt somewhat by the oppressive seventies office blocks that loomed on the opposite bank.

'Verity's Events isn't in Wayfield, though, is it?'

'No, it's in Yetley.'

'You didn't fancy living there?' Josh asked. The little village with its narrow, higgledy-piggledy streets and quirky boutiques would suit Natalie down to the ground.

'It's expensive and hard to buy there,' she said. 'But it would be lovely. Maybe one day.'

Josh thought of Natalie's vibrant flat, festooned with house-plants and bright patterns. He'd mentioned when he was there what a happy place it was, and she'd said that you couldn't help but smile when everything around you was smiling too. He'd liked that phrase.

'I'm glad Ignite is doing well,' Natalie said. 'When did it actually launch?'

'A few days ago.'

'So, serious question,' she said, after a brief pause, 'I think it might be time for me to let my subscribers know about you. After all, I tell them about everything else. I'm beginning to feel a bit dishonest. Would that be okay, do you think?'

Josh laughed. 'As long as I don't ever have to be in any videos.'

'I think that's a deal.'

'How do you do it?' he asked her. 'Doesn't it feel a bit invasive, talking about personal stuff to strangers?'

'Is it weird to listen to it?' she said. 'I bet you've watched my channel.'

He nodded. He had watched some of her videos, but then it had started to feel like he was spying on her. And besides, although she talked about her life some of the time, most of it was about fashion and party planning, which didn't hold a great deal of interest for him. 'It's not weird,' he said. 'Well, it is a little for me because I know you, but you sound really natural. I can see why people like watching you. I just couldn't imagine having the confidence to do something like that.'

'I started doing it because I felt like all the usual ways I would express myself were closed off to me,' she said. 'I was in a lot of pain for a while, and I just felt so out of the loop. And then when I first started feeling better physically, I didn't want to leave the house, because I didn't know how people would react to seeing me. But I still wanted to be involved with the world. I still wanted to do the things I liked, even if it was in a completely different way.'

Josh swallowed hard. He could see a way to move the conversation round to his own past, and he knew he needed to say it. Gareth's comments about him being scared to open up hadn't been as inaccurate as he'd implied, and he knew it had driven a wedge through relationships in the past. He couldn't let that happen again, especially not with Natalie.

'Nat, can I ask you kind of a dark question?'

A line formed between her eyebrows, but she said, 'You can ask me anything, Josh. I'm pretty unshockable.'

'Did you ever … did it ever feel like there wasn't any hope? Like things were just never going to be okay?'

She was silent for a moment. 'Yes,' she said, 'it did feel like that sometimes. Even when I started getting better, and the injuries on my face began to settle down, I still had moments occasionally when I would get overcome with this feeling of hopelessness, and I'd wonder what the point was. I couldn't imagine what I was going to do, what my future was going to be like. Sometimes I'd wonder if I would ever be able to look in a mirror and actually feel okay. And I'm a positive person, you know? But everyone has things that push them, if not over the edge, then close to the edge. I'm just grateful I found something to hold on to. If I start drifting away, I have a dozen solid, important things to anchor me back down now. But there was a time, a scary bit of time, when I did feel like I was drifting. When I couldn't see any way back to a life I would enjoy again.'

'And Verity's shop, and the vlogging, that all helped you?'

'Massively. And spending time with my nieces, and my parents, and Rob. I've met up with friends I made during my modelling days, and some of them have been great, but others … I guess when you're hit with something this big you figure out which people in your life *really* care.'

She gave him a searching look. 'Why are you asking me about this?'

He hovered on the verge of saying there was no particular reason; that he just wanted to know more about her – which wasn't untrue. But he'd come this far. There was no pretty way of saying it, but the words were bubbling up inside him. He just wanted her to know. 'I … I tried to kill myself once. When I was sixteen. I know it's not a nice thing to talk about, and you probably don't want to know, but we've got so close, and I felt like I wanted to tell you.' He was talking faster, his words beginning to run away with him. 'I feel like you're full of light, and optimism, and you do all this amazing stuff, and sometimes – a lot of the time – I feel like I'm some sort of dark void, and one day sooner or later you'll figure that out for yourself so I might as well...' He blinked and stumbled to a halt. What was he going on about? The champagne must have really gone to his head. Though somehow his words had done an adequate job of summing up what he was thinking.

Instead of answering, Natalie took one of his hands in hers and gave it a firm squeeze. 'You're not a ... dark void,' she said. 'That's not how you seem to me at all.'

'But I gave up,' he said, 'I was weak–'

'You were a kid,' she said, her voice choked with emotion. 'And even if you weren't, stuff like that isn't about being weak or strong. You can't be hard on yourself, it doesn't help.' She paused briefly. 'How ... how did you try to do it–'

'I took an overdose.'

A breeze ruffled the water's surface, and she let it die down before she answered. 'I can't imagine how you must have been feeling.'

'I just wanted everything to stop. I was in a nightmare, and I couldn't get out of it. If anything, I thought my life was about to get even worse. I'd already been depressed and anxious for years. It got to a point where I snapped. I'd thought about dying loads of times, but all of a sudden, I just decided to make it happen.'

'Didn't your parents realise how you were feeling?'

'I didn't often see my dad because his work takes him out of the country a lot, and my mum and stepdad had no idea what was going on with me. I'd completely given up trying to talk to them by then.'

Natalie was quiet for a moment. 'But it didn't work ... what you tried to do? I mean, clearly not.'

'Toby found me.'

'Your stepbrother? He saved your life?'

Josh's stomach twisted uncomfortably. *I can't let her believe that.* 'Technically, yes, he did.'

'Surely he literally did?'

35

'I just mean, he was the source of a lot of my problems in the first place. Me and him didn't get on well. At all.' He paused. That was putting it mildly. But he couldn't face getting any deeper into it. 'The hacking I did, that I told you about at the reunion – I was trying to change Toby's grades. To make them higher, not lower. To make sure he got into uni, so that I'd not have to be around him so much.'

'That's inventive,' she said.

'Well, he got in anyway, without me needing to do that. I never actually did it, anyway. I got scared and turned myself in, and made a total idiot of myself.'

Natalie snuggled close to him and he put his arm around her. 'I'm glad you told me,' she said. 'I know it must have been difficult.'

'No more difficult than you telling me how you felt after the crash.'

She turned her head to look up at him, and he reached down to kiss her gently. 'We're a right pair, you know,' she said.

'Nat,' he said, 'I've asked you kind of a dark question; now can I ask you a more pleasant question?'

Sitting up, she smiled at him. 'If it's "can we go and curl up in bed", then the answer is yes. It's late and it's starting to get pretty chilly out–' Her words were cut off when he knelt down in front of her, clumsily pulling the ring from his jacket pocket. His heart was hammering in his chest. Was he crazy to do this? They *had* only known each other for a few weeks. *But they've been the best weeks of my life.* But would she just laugh? Or be horrified? Either way, it was too late to back out and he found himself saying the words, asking the question, his face searching Natalie's. But he needn't have worried.

'Yes,' she said, as she grabbed him and pulled him back up. 'Yes, I will marry you!'

He'd been so ready to start apologising – to say he hadn't been thinking straight, that of course she didn't want to make a decision like that yet, that he'd just got carried away – that her words completely floored him and he stared at her open mouthed. Had he heard her right?

'I said yes, Josh,' she said softly, with a smile that said she understood what he was thinking. In fact, it was as though his proposal hadn't been entirely unexpected, and his body flooded with joy, relief, elation, amazement – more feelings than he could name.

'You ... you don't seem completely surprised,' he said eventually, as Natalie studied the emerald ring with great interest, turning it this way and that so that the bright green stone sparkled.

'I chose the ring because it reminded me of when I first saw you,' he explained. 'You were wearing a green dress, and I'd never seen anyone so beautiful. That emerald jumped out at me as soon as I saw it...' he trailed off. 'If you don't like it we can change it.'

'No,' she said, 'of course I don't want to change it! It's perfect. It's all perfect. And yes, Gareth kind of dropped a hint to me, once he was pretty drunk and you'd gone to the loo. He said he thought you'd ask me soon. I didn't necessarily think he meant *this* soon–'

Josh stared at her. 'Gareth *told* you!'

'Don't be angry with him. He probably won't even remember having done it.'

'I'm not angry. I couldn't possibly be angry.' In fact, he was happier than he'd ever thought he could be. 'Do you really mean it? Are you sure? I can't believe you said yes!'

'Are you going to try to talk me out of it now?' she teased him. 'Because I still want to keep the ring.'

He couldn't help but laugh, and she laughed too. 'Josh, I mean it. I want to. I know it's quick, but I'm sure. I love you. All I want to do is to be near you, and when I'm with you I don't ever want to be apart.'

Natalie

8

'Well, that's it,' Natalie said, as she clicked upload on her latest video. 'Now it's *really* official.'

Josh smiled. 'You told your fans we're engaged?'

'I did. I mean, I had to tell them I'd moved in with you – they would have realised I was filming in a different room to usual – and if I was explaining about that, I might as well tell them about the engagement too. It was a lot of fun, actually. And they're going to want to know about everything, especially what dress I choose.' She sat back with a contented sigh. 'It's too early to think about that, though. I need a chance to take a breath after telling everyone, don't you?'

Josh nodded his agreement. They'd been doing a whirlwind tour of her friends and relatives over the past couple of weeks, and they'd been to visit his dad too.

'Oh look,' Natalie said, 'a comment already.' She quickly read it. 'Told you. She said she can't wait to see my dress.'

She turned to him. Was now a good moment to broach the subject? There had been some glaring omissions in the list of relatives they had visited. 'Josh, what are we going to do about your mum and stepdad? And Gemma? I know we can't exactly pop round to Adelaide and visit them, but it's so weird not to have even done a video call–'

'I've messaged them all.'

'You've not even spoken on the phone?'

He shrugged, and she swallowed hard. 'Josh … look, just be honest with me. Is it because you don't want them to see me? Are you scared of how they'll react?'

The expression of confusion on his face was enough to show she'd got it wrong. 'React to what?' he said.

'To my scars,' she said. 'Do you feel awkward about it?'

Now he just looked astonished. 'Nat, you don't really think–'

'No,' she said. 'No, I can see I got it wrong. *I'm* a little nervous about meeting them, though, if I'm honest, even if it is just a video call. I think I'd prefer if it happened sooner rather than later, so I don't have to think about it any more.'

Josh sighed. 'I had no idea it was upsetting you. It's nothing to do with me not wanting them to see you. It's more that I don't want you to have much to do with *them*.'

'They can't be that bad, surely? And what about your step-brother? Toby doesn't live far, we could just pop round for a cup of tea–'

'They just – it doesn't really do me good to talk to them. It took me a long time to accept that. It's hard to stop yourself caring what your family think, or wanting them to show you some sort of affection or approval. Or even to show they're interested.'

'They must have replied to your messages?'

'Yes, they did. But speaking to them, even Gemma–' A shadow passed over his face. Natalie had already guessed that the rift between him and his half-sister caused him particular distress, and he didn't finish his sentence. 'I know my mum cares about me. But she's too afraid of rocking the boat with the rest of the family. She always has been. And in the end I just say to myself, if I'm worth that little to her that she won't ever risk standing up for me, why would I bother caring any more?'

'I can see you do care, though. And I'm sorry that they treat you like that.'

'It's not usually anything you can put a finger on. But before they moved away there was always an atmosphere if I visited them. I knew it was because of me. Even if I left the room for a second, it's like they suddenly all relax and I can hear them laughing and talking normally again. I used to try so hard to be different, to make them like me. But it was taking over my life. I don't want to expose myself to that any more. I don't want *you* to be involved with it.'

'Why did they move away?' Natalie asked. 'Moving to Australia – that's a huge decision.'

'When Gemma hit her teens she started getting seasonal affective disorder really badly. Her depression was so severe in the winter it was ruining her life – it was stopping her from enjoying anything, it was just awful. My stepdad has a couple of relatives in Australia, and they went out there one year for a holiday. It made such a difference to Gemma that they decided to move permanently.'

'Did they ask if you wanted to join them?'

'Not really, but I was an adult by then. I lived on my own and I could look after myself. I had no interest in going, but it hurt a bit, especially that I found out from Toby because they told him a week before they bothered visiting me and breaking the news.' He sighed. 'I don't really even want them to come to the wedding, and I'm sure they won't want to make the trip, but I guess I'll have to invite them.'

'You don't have to. If they make you unhappy.'

'I don't know,' Josh said. 'I can't help thinking what they'll start saying if I don't – they'll think I haven't invited them out of spite. I don't want to hand them a reason to start giving me grief.'

Natalie frowned. She couldn't imagine being in the situation Josh was in. How must it feel to not want your family there on the biggest day of your life? 'Come here,' she said to Josh, and she put her arms around him. 'We're family now,' she told him. 'And I'll never make you feel the way they do.'

***

'Do you really have to work today?' Josh asked the next morning, as she lifted her head from his chest, where she'd been dozing while he stroked her hair.

'You know I do. We've got stuff to sort out for that Halloween wedding. The bride's coming in today, and she's a bit of a worrier.'

'Is she really having a Halloween wedding? Like, themed?'

Natalie laughed. 'No. God, no. Me and Verity have done a Halloween wedding in the past, though, and it was a lot of fun. The bride's dress was purple and black, and they had carved pumpkins as the table centrepieces. In fact,' she said, suppressing another laugh as she recalled one of their most bizarre requests ever, 'she wanted to have live bats released, you know like people do with doves sometimes?'

'Surely she didn't really have that?' Josh said, his face a picture of incredulity.

'No. We had to draw the line at that. But it was a great day. Me and Verity had such a laugh, and the bride and groom absolutely loved it. But I wouldn't dare mention anything like that to this bride, Yvonne. Her and her fiancé only booked the wedding a couple of days before Halloween because of work commitments – it ended up the best time for them. It is definitely *not* themed. In fact, Yvonne made a point of telling us she doesn't like Halloween. She said she's never understood why people enjoy dressing up in costumes and that horror films give her a migraine.' She sat up and looked down at him. 'I'll tell you what, if you're worried about missing me today, why don't you join me in the shower before I go?'

***

Natalie arrived at Verity's Events to find Verity on the phone, a crease between her eyebrows, but then she made a sudden exclamation of relief before she put the phone down.

'Bad news?' Natalie asked, taking in her boss's flustered appearance.

Verity straightened the bow at the neck of her green and gold floral shirt. 'Yes and no. Photographer had to cancel – she's having a family crisis. But she recommended somebody else, and he's free, I just checked. So it should be okay.'

'Yvonne's nervous enough already.'

'I know. Not particularly looking forward to telling her, but at least we've already got a solution.'

Verity paused and looked at Natalie. 'You and Josh settling in to living together?'

Natalie smiled as an image of that morning in the shower flashed through her mind, her legs wrapped tightly around Josh's body as he pressed her back against the wall. She quickly tried to rearrange her face into a more neutral expression. 'We are.'

'Have you decided what you're going to do with your flat?'

'I'm just going to rent it out for a bit.' Natalie felt a slight pang as she thought of her bright, sunny little flat on the top floor of what had originally been a single large house. Although it wasn't exactly historic, the building had some character that Josh's modern flat lacked. But it had been a practical decision – Josh's flat was bigger, and had a generous roof terrace where she'd already lined up bright planters full of flowers and herbs. 'In a few months – or maybe after the wedding – we're going to start thinking about selling my flat, and Josh's too, and buying a house together. Maybe here in Yetley,' she explained.

'You've got it all figured out,' Verity said. 'I'm really happy for you, Nat.'

Verity's face didn't seem to match her words, though. She looked distracted, even a little unhappy. 'Are you okay?' Natalie asked her. 'Are you worried about telling Yvonne about the photographer–'

'No, I'm not worried about that,' she said, and smiled. 'Just been a tiring couple of days at home, you know. Kids.' Verity didn't need to elaborate, and Natalie nodded. 'Honestly, V, if you and Rob need a night off, just call me, okay?'

Verity smiled her thanks. 'Well, enough about that,' she said. 'Have you had any thoughts about a wedding venue yet?'

'We're thinking maybe Silverdale House–'

'Really?' Verity asked, a note of surprise in her voice.

Natalie blinked, taken aback. 'What's wrong with it?'

'Oh, nothing. No, nothing. I just had visions of you some-where grand – you know, sweeping down the aisle like you're on a catwalk.'

'I didn't really do catwalks.'

'You know what I mean. You're going to look so beautiful...'
She clapped her hands together. 'I'm just so excited.'

'Well, where would you recommend to me? If I was one of your clients?'

'Firthwight Hall.'

'That place is massive! And it costs a bomb–'

'I know, I know. Look, you're my sister-in-law, I'm allowed to make a fuss of you. But if Silverdale House is what you and Josh want, we'll make sure that's what you get.'

Natalie smiled at her. Verity's enthusiasm was infectious. 'Thank you, V,' she said.

Verity smoothed down her shirt primly. 'Right, that looks like Yvonne across the street. Remember, we're all about presenting solutions, not problems. By the time she walks out of here, she needs to feel like this new photographer is the best thing that could have happened.'

9

'Nat, what's up?' Josh asked.

She paused for a moment, still reeling. Should she tell him? The comments she'd just seen on her last video were so bizarre she needed a second to process them. 'Nothing,' she said hurriedly. Putting her phone away, she sat down on the edge of the bed and Josh joined her, moving aside some of the items she'd laid out.

'What is all this stuff?' he asked, as he took in the heap of clothing, makeup, shoes and hair products.

'My autumn essentials,' Natalie said. 'I do a video every year where I reveal my favourite high street buys for wearing every day. Well, it's some essentials and then one luxury. I'm just narrowing the last couple of things down.' She picked up a pair of chunky knitted tights. 'These definitely need including, and a nice pair of boots to go with them.' She smiled at Josh's baffled expression. 'Believe it or not, some people enjoy having more than one outfit.'

'I have more than one outfit!'

'Yes, but they all look the same,' she teased him, trying to be light-hearted, though her voice fell flat as the strange comments came to mind again.

Josh looked at her closely. 'I can tell something's bothering you,' he said. 'I can hear it in your voice. You sound a bit distant.'

She swallowed hard. Her babbling about the clothes hadn't fooled him for a second. 'It's … well, it's probably better if you just look for yourself.' She took out her phone but paused before handing it to him. 'It's just a load of nonsense, though. Don't let it get to you. I'm not. Sometimes people who call themselves fans act like they're anything but.'

Josh read through the comments and a crease formed between his eyebrows. 'Natalie–'

'I know. It's a bit twisted. That's what freaks me out about it. People do say odd stuff sometimes, especially about my scars, but this is just – it's kind of sinister.'

Natalie read it again, the words sending a shiver through her.

Love everything you do Nat but you can do better than marrying a murderer.

'Some people really have issues,' she said. 'I feel sorry for whoever this is.'

Josh gave her a half-hearted smile and she put her arms around him, adding, 'I said not to let it get to you. I shouldn't have even shown you, I know you hate this kind of crap that goes on online. I don't know what happens to some people's brains when they get a bit of anonymity – I'd like to see someone say this to my face. No one even knows who I'm engaged to. It's not like I said your name.'

'It's not that hard for someone to find things out if they're determined.'

'Well, yeah, but they've clearly got it wrong.'

'Of course they have,' he said, his voice strained. 'But, Natalie—'

'Just forget it. Please. Let's go out tonight, let our hair down a bit. I'm not in the mood to do this video now anyway.'

***

By the end of the evening, Natalie had almost forgotten the comment from earlier that day, and it wasn't until she was getting into bed that she looked at her phone again.

Josh Sparkes is a murderer.

Why don't you ask him what happened all those years ago?

Ask him about Mikayla.

Ask him about the lake.

Natalie's skin prickled as Josh came into the bedroom. His hair had the floppy, messy look it usually developed by the end of the day, and he shoved it back from his forehead as he watched her. 'Hey, what's wrong?' he said. 'Have they said something else?'

She held her phone out to him, and he took it with a frown. She watched his expression carefully as he read the words. He was clearly upset, and confused. He looked up at her helplessly when he'd finished, his eyes troubled.

'Josh, I don't believe any of it,' she said before he could speak. 'But they know your name. They know this girl's name, whoever she is. You must have some idea what this is about. Why is somebody saying this?'

The day of Mikayla's death

Josh

10

The air was so hot it was like a physical wall he had to push through. His footsteps were loud in his ears; the whole area around the lake was quiet, so quiet, like everything was asleep in the drowsy heat. The small lakeside clearing, hemmed in by trees on three sides, had an odd energy to it as soon as he got there. The water was shimmering and inviting, yet sinister. It was so still, and dark. There had been a big sign in the car park where he'd been dropped off by his mum the day before, warning people not to swim in the water. He gave a shiver, in spite of the heat.

Making his way further along the path, he stopped in his tracks when he saw a small pile of fabric abandoned near the water. Clothes! A bright pink t-shirt. Was it hers? She'd been wearing something like it the day before – the pink like a bright jewel against her dark skin. He'd been mesmerised by her. His pulse raced. Surely she hadn't...

He glanced all around him. He was being ridiculous. There was some other explanation. He couldn't see her. This was probably something to do with his stepbrother, Toby. Was it a trick, to make him go into the water? He picked up the t-shirt. It *was* hers. He was sure it was hers.

'Mikayla?' he called out tentatively. Then louder. 'Mikayla? Are you okay?'

Silence.

He stared out at the lake, scanning it carefully for any signs of movement or struggle. Everywhere, it was still.

Swallowing hard, he made his way towards the shore. She probably hadn't swum far, in which case he would surely be able to find her. Filled with urgency, he pulled off his shorts and t-shirt, and stepped into the lake. Adrenalin was pumping now. Mikayla was in danger. He knew it instinctively.

He threw himself into the water. God, it was cold. Gasping, he swam out further, and then stopped for a moment to look around. No sign of her. Heat was being sapped from his body. Heart pounding, he stretched his feet down until his nose barely cleared the surface, but he couldn't touch the bottom. He tried to call her name. Fuck! What could he do? Which way should he swim? His body felt all wrong. This was bad. This was properly bad, and he was scared. He had to turn around. He had to give up.

The cold sapped the life out of his very bones. Unable to catch his breath, he thrashed uselessly in the water. Above him, the sun beat down relentlessly, the day so hot that the air shimmered, an ironic contrast to the cold that was consuming him. He had to stop. He had to give up trying to find her, or he would drown.

***

His eyes snapped open. The room was dark, Natalie breathing softly by his side. He lurched out of bed and into the en-suite, where the sudden bright light made him wince but helped to snap him back to reality. *I couldn't have looked any longer than I did. I would have died too.*

He took several deep breaths, trying to calm down.

'Josh? Are you okay?' Natalie's voice reached him, still slurred with sleep. He went back to join her in bed.

'I'm all right.'

'Is it because of what we talked about?'

She snuggled up to him and he put his arm around him. He'd told her exactly what had happened. About the weekend away at the lake with Gareth when he'd been sixteen years old. About how Toby and his friends gatecrashed, along with Mikyala and some other girls. About Mikayla's pile of clothes on the ground, and the water, and having to give up. But the pain of going through it had left a cold feeling within him – that guilt again, the feeling of not having done enough, and apparently that feeling had followed him into his dreams.

'I haven't really thought about it for years. Not in detail, anyway. I've never forgotten her, but I haven't gone through what happened that day minute by minute. I just dreamt about it, but it was like I was there. I could feel the heat on my skin as I stood in that clearing, then the way the cold water hit me and sucked the air from my body. I felt all the panic again, and the desperation.' He closed his eyes, though the room was dark anyway. Mikayla. He couldn't bring her face into his mind any more, but he could still remember the way her laugh had sounded, the way her hair flowed silkily around her shoulders. How at the time she'd seemed like the whole world to him, and her indifference had been excruciating.

'I can't believe some spiteful person dragged this up again when they must know full well her death was accidental,' Natalie said. 'There was an inquest and everything. There was no doubt about it. You tried to save her life, at risk to yourself.'

'I never even thought about the risk to myself. It was just adrenalin. I couldn't stand there and do nothing.'

'Still, you tried to save her and people started saying this horrible stuff about you.'

Josh winced as he remembered it. He'd told Natalie how the rumours had started not long after Mikayla's death, and how much they had hurt him. 'It was because I was the first person to realise anything had happened to her,' he said. 'It started out as a horrible joke, people saying it was something to do with me. But mud sticks. Even if no one official believes it. Or anyone important. Her parents thanked me for trying to help her. And they were the ones I really cared about. I cared about that even more than what the police thought. Although, I admit I was terrified about the inquest. I started thinking I was going to go to prison. That – that's a lot of the reason I tried to kill myself.'

Natalie stroked his cheek gently. 'You should never have been put in that situation,' she said. 'It was a horrible, horrible thing that you went through. And whoever is spreading these lies is clearly too spineless to ever do something as brave as what you did to try to help Mikayla. That lake is lethal – I remember going up there when we were kids sometimes – not that we ever went in the water. It's deep right from the edge and absolutely freezing. People have drowned there before; that's why they have signs telling you not to go in.'

Josh couldn't answer straight away. He'd had nightmares every night before the inquest – dreaming that somehow they'd conclude Mikayla had been murdered and that it was him. Never mind that it wasn't the truth, or that rumours about his involvement were just a cruel joke that got out of hand. He'd have stood no chance in prison. He swallowed hard and shook that old fear away before it took hold of him.

'I'm just so thankful that Toby found you in time when you took the overdose,' Natalie said. 'I know you and him didn't get on, but I can't help but feel grateful to him. If he hadn't saved you, you wouldn't be here with me. And you don't deserve any of what you've been through.'

Josh hovered on the verge of correcting her about Toby's role in his suicide attempt, but held his tongue. After all, what would it achieve? No good would come out of upsetting Natalie.

'We should go and see Toby and his family,' she continued. 'Perhaps the two of you could build some bridges. I know you're trying to accept that your family aren't great for you to be around, and yes, perhaps it isn't you who should be offering the olive branch, but someone has to be the bigger person. And you are the bigger person, Josh. You've been through stuff I could barely imagine.'

'So have you.'

'Well, yes, but what I've suffered and what you've suffered is very different. I've always had my family. It sounds like yours didn't even support you through the inquest properly – I mean, how can a sixteen-year-old be expected to deal with something like that without a huge amount of support? Let alone coping with Mikayla's death when you obviously cared about her a great deal. I think it's a miracle you got through it at all.'

Josh nodded slowly. 'I'll think about what you said about Toby. About seeing him. It'll be difficult for me, though.'

Natalie kissed him on the cheek. 'I know,' she said, 'and it's your decision. If you really can't see any good coming from meeting up with him, I won't push you.'

Josh took in a deep breath, and let it out slowly. *Toby.* Could he really bring himself to have anything to do with Toby?

11

'You can't be serious,' Gareth said, as he finished his leg-stretches and sat down on the bench. When Josh had said he wanted to meet up, Gareth had insisted he join him on his Sunday morning park run, ignoring all protests. 'Why on earth would you consider having anything to do with Toby again?'

Josh tried his best to outline Natalie's argument, while Gareth listened with obvious disapproval. 'The thing is,' he said, 'she doesn't know the full picture.'

'She's found out about Mikayla. I should have just told her from the start – she ended up finding out from some weird stuff someone posted online.'

'Why should you have told her from the start? There's nothing to tell, is there? Imagine what it would have sounded like if you'd started going on about Mikayla drowning on a first date.'

'I obviously wouldn't have done that. But it was horrible for her to find out from some troll. I wish she hadn't been put through it.'

'Who would start stirring up stuff like that?' Gareth asked. 'It's ancient history, isn't it?'

'Who knows,' Josh said, staring moodily across the park, where the trees were beginning to turn shades of yellow and orange. It was a chilly morning, and despite the fact they had just been running, he was beginning to feel the cold.

'You know, I have a good idea who would stir it up,' Gareth said suddenly, startling him. 'And you're planning on going and playing happy families with him.'

Josh stared at him. 'Toby's not a teenager any more. He wouldn't post a load of rubbish online. It's not his style.'

'Whatever you say.' Gareth sighed and sprawled back extravagantly on the bench, looking up at the cloudy sky.

'Late night last night?' Josh asked as Gareth yawned.

'Yeah, kind of.'

Josh smiled. He could tell from Gareth's tone what kind of a night it had been. 'You've met someone?'

'Josh, I'm always "meeting" people. Don't try to change the subject. I guess I should have realised this Mikayla thing was going to rear its head again. Everyone knows about everything nowadays. You can't keep secrets any more.'

'It's not a secret. There's no mystery about it.'

'I shouldn't have said secret,' he said, turning his head and fixing Josh with a firm look. 'It's not a secret. But it's private. I can see this has all started getting in your head again. Natalie doesn't know how much things affect you.'

'Well, it's done now. It's over with.'

'Except you're considering inviting Toby back into your life again. You do remember what he used to do to you, don't you?'

'Yes, I remember,' Josh snapped. 'And I can't invite someone back in who never really left. Family aren't like friends – you can't just cut them out of your life.'

'You and me will have to disagree on that,' Gareth said, 'but if you feel you have to meet up with Toby, I can't stop you. Just remember, you're not a kid any more, so he doesn't have any power over you. Maybe it'll be good for you, if you go and see him and you feel okay about it. I guess that takes a lot of guts.'

'You think so?'

'Yeah, I think so.'

Josh smiled as Gareth abruptly got to his feet again, apparently rejuvenated all of a sudden. 'And if he upsets you and Nat, just point him in my direction,' he said, with a grin. 'I'll happily break his legs for you. I hate that arrogant bastard.'

Two years before Mikayla's death

12

Josh stared at the words scrawled across the wall behind the basins in the boys' toilets. Gareth followed his gaze. 'That's your number, isn't it?'

Furiously, Josh grabbed a pen from his school bag and scribbled out his mobile number, though he left the words that appeared above it: *'For a BJ call:'*

'I can't believe he's done this *again*,' he said.

'Does anyone ever call you?'

Josh shot him a look and Gareth shrugged. 'I'm just curious.'

'No, they haven't. But that's not the point!'

'He's not going to be at the same school as us soon. He'll move on next year.'

'But he'll still be in my house!' Josh said. *And in my room*, he thought. Even if Toby was at his mum's some of the week, the days when they had to share a bedroom were like a waking nightmare.

Josh stuffed the black biro back in his bag. 'I wish he'd just—' He wanted to say die, but he couldn't quite bring himself to wish death on anyone, not out loud anyway. 'I wish he'd just go away. For good,' he said limply.

'Maybe he will,' Gareth said cheerfully. 'Accidents happen all the time.'

Josh glanced at him. 'You say some weird shit.'

***

At the sound of footsteps, Josh quickly turned, instantly on edge. Sure enough, Toby stood in the bedroom doorway, taking in the sight of Josh and Gareth playing video games. With a sigh, as though he found the whole thing very tiring, he threw his school bag down on the floor. 'Will you two wankers get out of my room?'

'It's my room too,' Josh said, but only quietly. There was no point in arguing with Toby.

'What did you say?' Toby demanded.

'He said it's his room,' Gareth said, getting to his feet. 'And you can't really call us wankers. It's just inaccurate.'

'Why? Because the two of you are fucking each other?'

'No. But I've had a ton of sex, with this girl who lives on my street. She can't get enough of it.'

Toby narrowed his eyes at Gareth, who was making his way to the door. As Josh started to follow him, Toby caught his arm. 'If I catch that fucking weird kid in my room again,' he hissed, gesturing vaguely at Gareth's back, 'I'll make you wish you were dead.'

Josh's heart sank. He shook his arm away and scurried after Gareth.

'That... was that true, what you just said to him?' Josh asked as they trudged down the stairs.

Gareth shrugged. 'Doesn't have to be true, just has to wipe the smile off of Toby's face.'

Feeling unwelcome in the house, they made their way to a small park down the street. It wasn't a particularly uplifting place – a tired old set of swings and a slide sat opposite them behind an incongruously cheerful yellow fence, and a toddler was tottering about near the seesaw, the small girl immediately rescued by her mum when she inevitably fell over. Josh smiled slightly. The little girl made him think of his sister Gemma – the one person in his house who didn't give him a hard time.

The grass where they plonked down was patchy and half made up of dandelions, but it was still one of their preferred hangouts, especially since Josh's house was getting increasingly unbearable. 'There really is a girl on my street, though,' Gareth said at length, interrupting Josh's musings. 'And I have had sex with her, but only once.'

Josh's eyes widened and all of his attention turned back to Gareth. He didn't want to act too amazed, but his curiosity overcame him. He knew a few people in their year at school had started having sex, but at fourteen it still felt way off for him. Besides, no girl had ever looked at him twice. 'What was it like?'

'Yeah, pretty good,' Gareth said casually.

'Are you and her, like, together?'

'Nah. Can't be arsed with that.'

Josh looked at him closely. Was he really being serious?

Gareth started laughing. 'Wow, it is so easy to get you to believe shit.'

'I didn't believe you,' Josh groused.

'I mean, come on. No one wants us, right? We're just a pair of freaks.'

'Speak for yourself,' Josh said, stung that Gareth had lied to him.

'Hey, look, I was just making a point. You let people in too easy. You let people twist what you think. Don't let Toby's mind games get to you. Stand up to him. Don't believe everything he says. He's not God, is he? What can he really do to you?'

'I'd rather not find out.'

Back at home that evening, Josh was startled by a scream from Gemma. His half-sister was only three, and very often a weapon that Toby used to punish him. Whenever Gemma fell over, he'd say Josh did it. Whenever a toy broke, Josh did it. Whenever Gemma was crying, Josh did it. And in the event that none of these mishaps occurred to Gemma naturally, Toby was always on hand to instigate one.

'Fluffycat!' Gemma was saying when Josh approached her room. He peeked around the door, where his mum sat on the bed beside Gemma, who had tears streaming down her cheeks. The toy in question, a pink stuffed kitten, was in two pieces, its head having been parted from its body. Josh's stomach clenched as Toby came down the hallway. He knew what was going to happen.

His mum came out and looked at the two boys. *At least ask which of us did it,* Josh willed her. *Don't just assume.*

'Josh,' his mum said. 'I can't–' She shook her head, colour rising in her cheeks. Her eyes were shiny. 'Look at what you've done to your sister,' she said. Josh peeked around the door again, where Gemma was still crying.

Please, Mum. You used to doubt these things were me. You can't really believe I did this.

'I can't – I can't even look at you right now,' she said. She disappeared back into the bedroom to comfort Gemma. In the hall, Toby grinned at him. 'I told you I don't like having that creepy friend of yours in my room,' he said. 'The two of you should go somewhere else to make out.'

'We *don't* do that!' Josh shouted. In a fit of rage, he gave Toby a shove, and Toby quickly retaliated by punching him in the arm.

'Josh! Toby!' His stepdad's voice boomed in his ears.

'Josh just started on me for no reason,' Toby said. 'He's already cut the head off of Gemma's toy cat. He's mental. I'm having to share a room with a mental patient.'

Josh shrank back against the wall. There was no point. There was just no point. If he tried to tell the truth nobody ever believed him, and Toby would always make him sorry for trying.

'Yes, all right, Toby,' Josh's stepdad snapped. 'I saw that you didn't think twice about hitting him back.'

'It was self-defence!'

'And you?' He turned back to Josh. 'Do you have anything to say?'

Josh swallowed hard. 'I'm sorry.'

'You're going to buy your sister a new toy, at the very least,' he said, 'and me and your mum will decide what else to do with you.'

As Josh turned back towards his room, tears prickling his eyes, Toby smirked at him. 'Dickhead,' he hissed, as Josh pushed past him.

Natalie

13

From the moment they stepped out of the car and began walking up the path to Toby's front door, Josh seemed tense.

'You okay?' she whispered to him.

He nodded, though it was clear he wasn't.

The door opened the second they had rung the bell, and before Natalie had a chance to speak, Toby had grasped her hand in both of his, exclaiming, 'It's so wonderful to finally meet you, Natalie. And congratulations. Welcome to the family!'

'Thank you,' she said, a little taken aback by Toby's enthusiasm. 'Although we're not married just yet.'

Toby gave a booming laugh. 'Did you hear that, Josh? Not having second thoughts already, are you?' To her surprise, Toby ruffled Josh's hair like he was a child and said, 'He might be a bit weird, but he grows on you.'

She laughed uncomfortably. 'Yes. I – he's certainly grown on me.' She looked at Josh, who was clearly mortified by the whole thing. Toby, however, was apparently unaware of how awkward he was making them feel and gestured for them to come inside. Natalie stepped into the hall, while Toby watched her, a bit too closely for her liking. A large man – he'd filled most of the doorway when he'd greeted them – Toby was smartly dressed in black trousers and a tight lilac shirt, his hair cropped short. He had the air of somebody who was used to being in charge. She met his gaze, and, realising he had been staring, he quickly said, 'Sorry, I just… wow. I can't believe Josh waited this long to show you off.'

Natalie tried to exchange a look with Josh, but he seemed to be trying to look anywhere except at her and Toby.

'Uh … thank you,' she said.

'I heard about the car accident,' Toby continued, 'and that you had a scar. But you can barely see it, honestly. I'm not sure I would even have realised.' He turned to Josh and clapped him enthusiastically on the arm, while Natalie stood motionless for a moment, dumbfounded. He was about as subtle as a foghorn, and as loud as one too.

'Well done,' Toby said to Josh. 'For the first girlfriend of yours I've ever met, I've got to hand it to you, you really pulled it out of the bag.'

Natalie took a breath and let it out slowly. This was going to be a long night.

***

'I'm so sorry,' Josh whispered to her as they followed Toby down into a modern kitchen diner, 'he's a bit–'

She squeezed his arm. 'I've dealt with worse,' she whispered back.

Inside the kitchen, a woman stood with her back to them, stirring a large saucepan. She turned as she heard their footsteps, sweeping her long, thick brown hair over her shoulder, and adjusting a pair of glasses with pink and black frames. Dressed in jeans and a striped jumper, she looked very casual and laid-back. She greeted them both warmly. 'I hope this is okay,' she said. 'It's a vegetable chilli. I don't cook vegetarian things very often; you know what Toby's like, Josh, he doesn't think it's a proper meal if something hasn't died.'

'That's not true,' Toby said, 'and you should have seen the fuss he used to make about eating anything green–'

'I'm Jodie, by the way,' she said, cutting across Toby's teasing. 'We've already heard loads about you. I've watched some of your videos. Actually, Toby has too. I caught him watching one about what you should buy for the autumn–'

'My Autumn Must-Haves,' Natalie said. 'You're into fashion, are you, Toby?'

'What, you mean that isn't obvious just by looking at me?'

Natalie raised an eyebrow, and he laughed. 'I preferred your one where you said the three best and three worst things about modelling,' he said. 'It was fascinating.'

'I'm glad you enjoyed it.'

'You've got a real talent, hasn't she, Jodie?'

'You should be on TV,' Jodie said. 'Seriously.'

'I've been on TV. In adverts, anyway, back when I was modelling.'

'You should have your own show,' Toby said. 'I'd watch it.'

'Natalie's a wedding planner,' Josh said. 'She works with her sister-in-law.'

'We can expect big things for your wedding then?'

'Nothing too crazy,' she said. Then she added mischievously, 'Maybe a little surprise or two.'

'Oh, please tell us!' Jodie said.

Natalie shook her head. 'You'll have to wait and see,' she said, mostly because she had no idea what her surprise or two would entail. Verity would help her come up with something, though. She was great at things like that.

'Are Finn and Katy in bed?' Josh asked. There was no sign of the children anywhere.

'Yeah,' Jodie said. 'Only just, but I think we got away with it. We're looking forward to having a nice, grown-up, civilised evening. Though Finn has taken to getting up about four times a night, so, we'll see how it goes.'

'How old are your children?' Natalie asked.

'Finn is three and a half. Katy had her first birthday a couple of months ago.'

'Aww, that's lovely,' Natalie said. 'I have two nieces, they're six and four. I love them to bits, they're brilliant.'

'Do you think you two will...' Toby gestured vaguely at them both.

Natalie smiled at Josh. 'It's a bit early for that—'

'Ah, well, we'll see,' Toby said.

Jodie gave him a playful shove. 'You're embarrassing them,' she said, 'leave them alone. Let them enjoy a bit of time without nappies and five a.m. wakeups. I'm kind of jealous.' She turned back to the hob. 'Right. I think this is ready. Sort some drinks out, will you, Toby?'

Toby ushered them over to the dining table, and once they sat down Josh whispered, 'He's even more full-on than I remember.'

'I'm enjoying myself,' Natalie said, surprised to find that she actually was. Yes, Toby was a bit loud, a bit tactless, and a bit too fond of teasing Josh, but there wasn't any malice behind it, not as far as she could tell. Toby and Jodie were a fun couple. Maybe it wouldn't be such a long night after all.

14

The meal passed pleasantly enough. Sat around the large rectangular dining table, lit from above by a glamorous cascade of glass pendant lights, they listened to Toby talk about his and Josh's childhood. Though Josh chipped in from time to time, and occasionally managed to force a smile at some of Toby's anecdotes, the way he pushed his food around his plate made it obvious he wasn't enjoying the conversation. Natalie was on the verge of changing the subject, when Toby abruptly did it for her.

'So how long have you been a wedding planner?' he asked.

'A few years. It's really my sister-in-law, Verity, who's the planner; I just help out. She has a little shop, so I look after that sometimes while she's out visiting venues and arranging things, and I help set up the events with her and make sure they run smoothly. After my accident I had to stop modelling, and helping V has been really good for me. I only did a few hours here and there to start with, but as her business grew and I recovered I could take on a bit more.'

Toby sat back in his chair as if considering something carefully. 'You know I work at Hartbury Hotel? We just got our licence to carry out civil marriages on the premises. In fact, I can't believe the previous manager didn't get one years ago, but then he was an incompetent old buffoon from what I can understand – I've had to spend enough time sorting out the bloody mess he made of the rest of the place.' He paused to take a large swig of wine. 'Anyway, we had to jump through all sorts of hoops. Took the council ages, of course, you know how it is.'

Natalie didn't, but nodded anyway.

'Long story short,' he concluded, 'Hartbury Hotel is open for wedding business. Should be a nice little earner.'

'Oh, brilliant,' she said, trying to rise above her distaste at him describing the biggest day of people's lives as a *nice little earner*. 'That's great news.'

'Perhaps you could come and look round? See the two room options we've got for the ceremony? I can give you a tour of the whole place, the bedrooms, the function rooms.' Toby was talking animatedly now, clearly excited at the idea. 'It would be great for us to work together. I can recommend your sister-in-law's place for planning the events, and you could send some of your couples in our direction, too.'

'I...' Natalie sipped some wine, her head spinning with Toby's enthusiasm. 'Well, yeah, I can certainly tell Verity about it.'

'Come and see it yourself! Why not? I'm sure Verity won't mind you taking a look?'

'I – yes, okay.'

'Great. When would be a good time for you?'

'Give her a chance to catch her breath!' Jodie scolded him.

'I can't think off the top of my head,' she said. 'Maybe in a week or two? We're pretty busy at the moment. I'll let you know.'

'Make sure you do,' Toby said, 'or I'll be bugging you and Josh about it.'

'I will,' she said, 'I won't forget. In the meantime, could I ask where your bathroom is?'

'In the hall, on the right.'

'Thanks.'

Out in the hall, Natalie was grateful to have a chance to take a breath. It would be good to have a new place to recommend, but Toby was an exhausting person to spend a lot of time with – by the end of the tour she'd need a lie down.

As she made her way down the hall, a huge array of photos caught her attention and she paused. Had Jodie or Toby taken all of these? There were so many, one of the pair must be a keen photographer. The ones that caught her attention particularly were family photos; there was one of Jodie with a small boy, only a toddler, who must be her son Finn, along with a young woman

Natalie didn't recognise and a middle-aged couple. Josh's family — it had to be. The young woman must be Gemma, and the couple Josh's mum and stepdad. Was the photographer Toby, then, since he didn't feature in the picture? From the bright sunshine and the summer clothes, it must have been a visit to Australia. She felt a pang. Had Josh ever been to one of these family get-togethers? She doubted it. There were others, beautiful pictures of Australian landscapes, and then many that looked like they were from decidedly closer to home: misty woodland, moody coastline. Whenever Toby's family went on a holiday or a day out, taking this amount of images must keep him pretty busy. But then, with the way he goes on, they're probably glad of something to shut him up for a few minutes, she thought to herself.

As she came out of the downstairs toilet, she was startled to spot a small child making his way down the stairs. But the child got even more of a shock, his eyes widening in surprise.

'Are you Finn?' Natalie asked. 'Come with me; we'll find Mummy and Daddy.' She held out a hand for him to take, but he simply stared at her.

'He was on his way down the stairs,' she said, as she brought the small boy into the dining room. 'I think he got a bit of a fright when he saw a stranger in the house!'

Jodie smiled and came over to give Finn a cuddle.

'Who's responsible for all the beautiful photos in the hall?' Natalie asked, glancing at Toby.

'Guilty,' he said.

'They're lovely. I really enjoyed looking at them.'

'I've got loads more upstairs,' he said. 'Some of them are from way back. I can show you if you want?'

'You know,' she said, as she caught Josh's eye, 'we should probably get going. Give you a chance to get Finn settled again. So perhaps another time.'

'You don't need to do that,' Toby said. 'Have another drink. Seriously, you'd love to see some of the others. I've got all sorts from round here. Hagney heath, before they built all those houses along the edge of it, loads of the river — some great wildlife down there sometimes – Chedford Lake…' He paused. 'Maybe not those.'

'Natalie's right,' Josh said. 'It's getting late and you need to settle Finn. I think we'd better…'

Toby looked like he was about to carry on pushing them, but Jodie discreetly shook her head at him.

'It was so great to see you both,' Toby said as they made their way towards the door. 'We won't leave it so long next time.'

'No,' Josh said, without much enthusiasm.

'And Nat, let me know about the tour, okay?'

'Yeah, of course.'

Toby gave them an appraising look as they stepped outside, and his face broke into a grin as he turned to Josh. 'Make sure you treat her right,' he said. 'You've struck gold with Natalie.'

***

'Well, that was… something,' Natalie said as they got into Josh's car, both of them glad to take a breather.

'Yeah.'

They were silent for a moment as they collected their thoughts, until finally she turned to look at him. 'You seemed a bit uncomfortable. Was it better or worse than you expected?'

'Oh, he just – he grates on me a bit. Well, kind of a lot.'

'Mm. Does he ever turn the volume down?'

'It depends which volume you mean?'

'Just, like, his personality.'

Josh laughed as he started the car, though there wasn't much humour behind it. If anything, he still seemed on edge. 'I don't know. Not that I've seen. Maybe when he's at work.'

'I guess I'll find out when I go to take a tour of the hotel.'

'Don't feel like you have to do that if you don't want to.'

'No, it's fine. Like he said, it's good to build relationships and promote each other. I'm sure I can manage an hour or so with him.'

'I'm not sure I could,' Josh said.

'Well, you just did.' She paused, and reached out to touch his cheek. 'I'm proud of you.'

As he drove, she remembered the pictures from the hallway. 'He has a lot of photos – was he into photography as a kid?'

'Yeah. Nearly always had a camera with him. It used to drive me nuts, to be honest.'

'He's certainly not modest about showing his pictures off,' she said, 'though I can't imagine you'd want to look at ones of the lake. I'm surprised he wants to look at it either.'

'It's a beautiful place,' Josh said, 'from what I remember, anyway. But I never want to set foot there again.'

Natalie leant across and gave him a quick kiss on the cheek.

'What was that for?'

'Because I know tonight was difficult for you. It wasn't that easy for me, so I can't imagine how you must have felt.'

Josh laughed uncomfortably. 'It's nothing compared to spending the whole of my adolescence with him,' he said. 'I guess if I could get through that, I can get through anything.'

Two years before Mikayla's death

Josh

15

'I've got a surprise for you!' Josh cooed as he stepped into his little sister's room. She held two chubby hands out expectantly, and Josh smiled as he presented her with her new "Fluffycat". He'd been worried that the toy shop would no longer stock the pink stuffed kittens, so he'd been filled with relief to find a heap of them still on the shelves. Soft toys were a lot more expensive than he'd realised, but even so he'd bought her an additional soft rabbit, too. He didn't have much cash left from what he'd earned cleaning neighbours' cars the past couple of weeks, and he'd have to cancel going to the cinema with Gareth that weekend, but it was more than worth it.

Gemma climbed into his lap with her new toys bundled under her arms. 'Story,' she said. Josh grabbed a book from a pile beside her bed. He was happy when it was like this. Toby was at his mum's, so nothing bad could happen. He was safe.

***

His face fell at his mum's answer. 'Are you serious?' he said. 'You won't let me outside the house with Gemma?'

'I don't think it's a good idea right now.'

Josh stared at her incredulously. He'd asked if he could take Gemma to the playground just down the road, and a line had formed across his mum's forehead, before she'd refused.

'I'll only be, like, half an hour. She wants to go.'

'I said no, okay?' His mum wouldn't meet his eye.

'What is it that you think is going to happen to her?' he said. 'I'd never hurt her. You know that.'

Now his mum snapped. 'Why can't you just go and do things normal teenage boys do?' she said. 'Most boys your age would complain about babysitting!'

Josh felt like he'd been punched. 'I like spending time with Gemma.'

'Josh,' she said, realising she'd hurt him. 'I didn't mean – Josh–'

But it was too late. He fled the room, slamming the door behind him.

***

A couple of days later, Toby returned. Josh's dread at this event always started in earnest a full twenty-four hours beforehand. His appetite – which was never good nowadays – had worsened considerably, and as they sat around the dining table, Toby stuffing cottage pie into his face without a care in the world, Josh just moved his food around the plate miserably.

'What's up with you?' his stepdad asked.

'I don't feel good.'

'It took your mum the best part of an hour to cook this.'

'It doesn't matter–' his mum started to say.

'It does matter,' his stepdad continued, his eyes boring into Josh. 'You're not ill. You just want to spoil things for everybody else.'

Josh pushed his chair back, and practically sprinted out of the room. He seemed to be doing a lot of that lately. Why was no one else in the family always fleeing from rooms, from conversations, the way he did?

Later that evening, he crept back down the stairs. His mum and stepdad were talking in the lounge, so he sat halfway down the stairs where he could just hear them through the half-open door.

'He won't even try,' his stepdad was saying. 'He's always upsetting Gemma, picking fights with Toby. I mean, Toby's only been back a few hours, and it feels like we're in a war zone again. And Toby's grades are slipping. He's distracted with everything that's going on here.'

'It's just Josh's age,' his mum said. 'I've tried talking to him, but I can't get any sense out of him. Either that or he's too busy on his computer. I'm sure it'll settle down on its own, if we give it time.'

Hot tears formed in Josh's eyes. They thought *he* was messing up *Toby's* life? For a moment he wanted to march in there and tell them the truth, but he turned at the sound of footsteps. Toby shook his head at him in a firm warning. *For God's sake! Can he hear what I'm fucking thinking now?*

He made his way up the stairs and towards his room, with Toby following. As he stepped into the bedroom, Toby pushed him into the door frame, hard enough that Josh cried out.

'That maths homework you were doing,' Toby said, 'I hope it wasn't important. It might have had a bit of an accident.'

Josh's eyes fell to the desk, which was littered with shreds of paper. Toby had torn the pages of his exercise book out and ripped them up.

'I guess you could start again,' Toby said. 'Not like you've got anything better to do, is it?'

Natalie

16

'So how was it?'

Natalie looked up from tidying a powder-pink dresser filled with samples of handmade invitations. One of Verity's close friends made them, and they were proving popular in the shop. 'How was what?'

'The meal, with Josh's stepbrother.'

Natalie sighed. 'Oh, yeah, it was…' She struggled with how to explain it. 'Interesting,' she concluded.

Verity raised an eyebrow.

'He wants us – well, me – to go and look round his hotel. He's just managed to get it approved for wedding ceremonies–'

'Hartbury?'

'That's it.'

'I can pop along there some time.'

'He particularly wanted me to go,' Natalie said awkwardly, 'I guess because I'm sort of family now. I know you usually go and visit new venues and I look after the shop–'

Verity waved her explanation away. 'No, it's fine,' she said. 'You can go, it doesn't matter which of us it is. You can tell me all about it.' She fixed her eyes on Natalie. 'Okay, now you've got to tell me what you mean by your night with Toby being "interesting",' she said. 'You can't dangle something like that in front of me and not elaborate.'

Natalie just about managed to outline the main points of the evening before the phone rang and Verity bustled away, so Natalie went back to tidying. She could hear snatches of the conversation, and it didn't sound positive.

'Well,' Verity said as she came to join her, 'I don't know what to make of that.'

'What's wrong?' Natalie said.

'Lizzie and Andrew. They don't want us to plan their wedding any more.'

Natalie looked at her in surprise. 'Lizzie and Andrew? But they were so enthusiastic! Lizzie said she was going to watch some of my videos about wedding planning–'

A shadow crossed Verity's face.

'V? What is it?' Natalie asked, a heavy feeling settling in her stomach. Although she did her best to ignore them, the comments on her videos and social media hadn't stopped. In fact, just thinking about going online made her feel sick now, as the words would start swirling in front of her eyes again no matter how much she tried to forget them.

Why are you still with him?

Josh is a murderer

Are you that desperate Natalie?

Do you think because of your scars you can't do better than a killer?

Have some self-respect!

Everyone knows Mikayla's death wasn't an accident. The inquest was a joke.

What are you teaching young girls who follow you? That violence is ok?

Who are you trying to fool Nat? You talk about confidence but you're clearly insecure to stay with josh

I used to look up to you but now you're just a joke

You're ugly inside and out

The comments and messages came in sporadic bursts: sometimes she'd get a day's respite, only to be inundated late at night, or the next morning. She'd found herself shaking once or twice when she picked up her phone, scared of what she would read next, and she wasn't sleeping well. She'd tried to keep the true extent of it hidden from Josh, as well as Rob and Verity and the rest of her family, by deleting as much of the abuse as she could, but sometimes she just wasn't quick enough, or it simply wasn't possible – not when this person seemed to be everywhere online that she was. It was inevitable that people would realise sooner or later what she was going through. But she hadn't expected it to start affecting her job, taking business away from her and Verity. Briefly, she hovered on the verge of completely breaking down – screaming, crying, she didn't know what – but she quickly composed herself. She wouldn't let herself be brought down like this. She wouldn't let them win. It was just a bunch of stupid words, it didn't mean anything. But it was so relentless.

Verity put her arm around Natalie. 'Why didn't you tell me?' she said. 'I had … I admit I have seen some of it, but I didn't know how to bring it up–'

'Did Lizzie say she didn't want us to plan her wedding because of it? Because of some stupid *bully?*'

'Well, it was the stuff about…' Verity shifted uncomfortably.

'The stuff about Josh. The rumours.'

'It's ridiculous,' Verity said, 'and besides, it obviously wasn't Josh–'

'Of course not, the police–'

'I don't mean that.' Verity lowered her voice conspiratorially. 'I heard some talk. One of my friends – you know Caitlyn Ward – her mum used to teach at the school you and Josh and Toby went to. Apparently there's always been a lot of question marks about that day. There was someone else there at the lake, some-one no one ever managed to speak to. A stranger, or maybe some friend of Josh's stepbrother or something. If you ask me, that whole business was never cleared up properly. Caitlyn's mum still talks about it, all these years later. And about what Josh did to try to save that poor girl. It could easily have ended in a double tragedy that day.'

Natalie shivered. 'I don't really like thinking about it, to be honest. And it upsets Josh. He still feels bad that he couldn't save Mikayla.'

'Well, he shouldn't. And Nat, I know it must be hard, but try to ignore this stuff.'

Natalie shook her head, thinking of Lizzie and Andrew. 'But one of our couples has changed their mind about us. We've lost business because of it.'

'I know. But there's nothing we can do about that now. We just have to move on. There are plenty of other couples.'

Natalie turned at a flash of colour outside the window. A woman was dashing across the road, pulling the hood of a fuchsia raincoat tight around her face to protect herself from the fat drops of rain that had begun to fall. It was one of their brides-to-be. 'That's Carmel coming,' Natalie said. 'I hope nothing else has gone wrong for her. She's already had that big bust-up with her sister–'

Natalie couldn't say any more as the door to the shop burst open and Carmel stepped inside, gratefully freeing her tangle of tight black curls from under her hood. 'You are still open, aren't you?' she said as she caught sight of their slightly startled faces. 'I know it's a bit late in the day, I just wanted to have a quick chat–'

Verity instantly put a smile back on as she leapt up. 'Yes. Yes, sorry Carmel. Please come in and sit down. Can I get you a tea? Coffee?'

Carmel nodded without saying which drink she wanted, and Natalie, sensing something was wrong, put a hand on her arm and looked at her sympathetically. Carmel let out a sob. 'Sorry,' she said. 'Sorry, I–' She took a moment to catch her breath. 'I don't know what I'd do without you, Natalie. And you, Verity,' she added as an afterthought. Natalie thought Verity looked slightly miffed, but she quickly hid it. 'You're better to talk to than my own family,' Carmel continued, her eyes back on Natalie. 'They think I'm being hysterical, but you get it. You know how important it is for me that everything is perfect after the year I've had…'

Natalie smiled warmly and guided Carmel over to the table in the window. 'Don't worry,' she said, 'weddings always make emotions run high. Whatever you're worried about, I'm sure it's nothing we haven't heard here before.'

***

'Tough day?' Josh asked when he arrived home from the office and found her curled up under a blanket on the sofa, holding a mug with both hands and staring listlessly at the TV.

She turned to him, and one look at his face and the kindness in his eyes made her worries ease a little. 'You could say that. One of our brides is having a wobble about her wedding dress. She's had a really difficult year and she's done so well losing a lot of weight after a health scare. She wants a dress to represent her journey, but I've got to be honest, I'm not sure she'll ever find something she's truly happy with.'

'That sounds challenging.'

'Yes, and it's not really something we can solve for her – she just wanted to chat. She's going to see her dressmaker tomorrow and talk it through.' Natalie stifled a yawn. It had been a very long day. 'She's also decided she wants bespoke ice sculptures, so we've got to try and organise that last minute. I'm kind of excited about it – we don't get asked for them very often. But I feel done in right now. I think I need to sleep for about a week.'

'I'll order a takeaway,' he said. 'You stay right there.'

She held her hand out to him. 'Josh, come here a second.'

She quickly outlined how they'd lost a customer because of the web trolling, and Josh put his hand up to his forehead. 'This is still going on?' he said. 'Nat, you haven't mentioned it. Is it still about me?'

She paused. Was it really worth upsetting him? He'd take it badly, but then, she could hardly lie. He could easily just read it all himself if he wanted to. There was far too much for her to try to hide it. 'A lot of it is,' she said honestly. 'Not all of it, but … mostly.'

He sank down onto the sofa next to her and didn't speak for a long time.

'Josh?' she said.

'I'm like a curse,' he said.

Natalie looked at him closely, taken aback by how dark he'd sounded.

'No,' she said, 'no, you're not. This idiot who's doing this, they're just twisted. Nobody believes it.'

'Your client believed it.'

'Our clients don't know you.'

Josh rested his forehead in his hand. 'I can't believe this. Why do things like this keep happening? Why can't everything just … just stop.'

'Listen to me,' she said, alarmed by his reaction. 'It's nonsense, okay. I know it's nonsense. It's not even you they're trying to hurt, it's me, and as far as I'm concerned they can just fuck off. Now let's order some food and watch a film and forget about this. Right now we're playing into their hands by getting upset–'

'That's the problem!' he said, turning to face her. 'They're trying to hurt *you*. If they were doing it to me, that would be different. But they're hurting you because of *my* past. That's what I can't handle. If they've got some axe to grind about Mikayla's death, take it up with me, for God's sake! It's nothing to do with you.'

'They're *not* hurting me,' she lied. 'I've dealt with much worse than a stupid troll. It's like water off a duck's back.'

Josh shook his head helplessly. 'Who is doing this? Why would somebody want to drag all this up again? It was bad enough at the time – why bring it up now, and why like this? Why by attacking you? I can't think why anyone would want to try and upset you.'

Natalie let out a long breath. 'I don't know either. And we might never know, but I'm sure they'll get bored soon. They can't carry on doing this forever. They want to make me doubt you, and that's not going to happen. Besides,' she said, 'when I was talking to Verity about it, she said some people still say there was someone else at the lake that day – someone nobody has ever identified. It seems to me like the whole story of what happened that day has turned into a bit of an urban legend. But still, if there's any question marks, they're surely about this stranger.'

'Who did Verity hear this from?' Josh asked.

'Her friend's mum was a teacher at our school. Mrs Ward, remember? She still seems to be holding on to some conspiracy theory about it all.'

'Well, I never heard anything about it,' Josh said, his forehead creased. 'I don't remember it coming up at the inquest.'

'Exactly. Like I said, it's just one of these weird rumours that carries on because people like a mystery.'

Josh nodded slowly, but his frown remained, and his eyes were dark and troubled.

Josh

17

'A stranger?' Gareth said slowly.

'Apparently.'

'And who on earth is saying this crap?'

Josh explained, and Gareth rolled his eyes. 'For God's sake, do people really have nothing better to do? That Mrs Ward was always so nosy.'

'Well, you tell me whether you really felt the whole thing was properly resolved? Why was Mikayla over the other side of the lake on her own? Everyone else was near the campsite—'

'You weren't,' Gareth said.

'You know what I mean.'

Gareth rubbed his temples and gave Josh a firm look. 'When you said you wanted to meet for a drink I thought you were going to tell me you and Nat were going to have a baby or something. Not this crap.'

'Babies are the last thing we're thinking about right now,' Josh said, his head beginning to pound. Why had Gareth suggested such a loud, crowded bar for them to meet in? He longed to be in the corner of a quiet pub to have a conversation like this. But that wasn't really Gareth's style. 'Planning the wedding and dealing with this troll hounding Natalie day and night, that's all we can think about. I caught her staring at her scars in the mirror this morning. She tried to pretend that's not what she was doing, but I think it's starting to affect her, having someone constantly attacking her and the decisions she's making.'

'Natalie wouldn't let stuff like that get her down,' Gareth said matter-of-factly.

'It's constant, though. And the vlogging used to be her escape. By attacking her online this person has cut off what used to be her place to be creative and be herself. It's affecting her more than she wants to let on, and it's killing me that it seems to be about what happened to Mikayla. It's happening because of me.'

'Why don't you find out who it is?' Gareth said. 'You could do it, couldn't you? Not that I'm in any doubt about who's behind it.'

'Gareth, I can't . At the very least I'd lose my job if I started spending my time hacking people's social media and got found out. I'm not doing that. Natalie wouldn't want me to do that. And it's not Toby. Why would he suddenly start this now?'

'Well, you've got to figure out who *is* doing this. Someone is going around saying you're a murderer. A *murderer*. And, what, you think it's fine for someone to do that, but it's not fine for you to defend yourself by finding out who it is and telling them to shut the fuck up?'

'That is how the world works,' Josh said helplessly.

Gareth finished his drink and pushed the glass away from him. 'Well, this evening was a real downer,' he said.

'I'm sorry I couldn't be more entertaining. But no one else is going to get it like you do. You were there – you know how weird that weekend was.'

'I don't mind talking about it, Josh, if that's really what you want to do. Yes it was weird. It was a load of hormonal teenagers, booze and no adults. Of course it was weird.'

'Someone knows more than they're letting on,' Josh said. 'Either that, or–'

'Shit!' Gareth said suddenly, as a woman knocked into him and half her drink spilt down his shirt.

'Sorry, sorry!' the woman said drunkenly as she rushed by, the remainder of her drink still sloshing around in its glass.

'Great,' he said, looking down at his shirt in disgust. 'This night is a gift that just keeps on giving.' He stared after the woman, clearly considering whether it was worth going over to her and trying his luck.

'Gareth,' Josh said. 'That's not why we're here.'

'That might not be why *you* are here,' Gareth said, 'but *I'm* not about to get married.' He fixed Josh with a look. 'If I ever somehow do end up about to get married, talk some sense into me, okay?'

Josh grabbed his friend's arm to stop him turning to look at the woman again.

'I know what it is you want to say,' Gareth said. 'And I don't want you to say it. That sort of shit is going to end up with you the wrong side of a pile of painkillers again, and I'm not going to let you go there.' He raised his voice. 'I could strangle Toby. He'd love it if he knew he'd got you second-guessing yourself like this. You might be starting to forgive him, but I am *never* going to forget what he did to you. Do not let him get inside your head again!'

'But you know it's not entirely implausible,' Josh said quietly. 'I was a mess back then. I remember ... I remember trying to save her. But memories can be wrong. Memories that are too painful can get messed up. Suppressed. Blocked out. You know Mikayla came to talk with me the night before she died, asking advice—'

'Yeah, I could hardly forget, given how cut up you were about it. I don't know what she was thinking. She knew you liked her, and it was bad enough she was going out with Toby, let alone coming to you for advice when she decided she fancied someone else. Who was it again?'

'The guy who worked with her at that pet shop where she used to go on Saturdays. She kissed him at a party, but she couldn't decide whether it really meant anything.' Josh paused. Why did it all still feel so raw? He couldn't seem to fully move on from it. 'It was horrible,' he said, 'when she was talking to me, I could almost have cried. I think I shouted at her. It all got too much for me at the lake. I wasn't thinking straight.'

'She kind of deserved to have you shout at her,' Gareth said.

'Gareth—'

'It *was* pretty insensitive, what she did. Why talk to you about it? She obviously wanted to wind you up.'

'But what if it sent me over the edge?' Josh hissed urgently, coming to the crux of the awful idea that wouldn't leave him alone. 'So that when I went to that clearing where she—'

Gareth stood up abruptly. 'I'm walking you home,' he said. 'And you are not going to say any of this to Natalie, okay? That woman loves you, you are going to get married next summer, and I am not letting you screw it up.'

'But I can't stop thinking about it.'

'Yes, you can. Because thinking about it is going to cost you Natalie. So just shut up, and sort your head out, okay?'

'You never really dealt with all your baggage either,' Josh shot back, the drinks he'd had catching up with him. 'You're hardly one to lecture me about relationships.'

'Yes,' Gareth said, casually. 'My childhood was fucked up too. I never tried to pretend it wasn't. But unlike you, I'm keeping my past and my present as two separate things.'

Six months before Mikayla's death

Gareth

18

'Wow,' Gareth said as he took in the dressing on Josh's arm. 'You weren't joking when you said he pushed you down the stairs.'

'Of course I wasn't joking.'

'No, I mean, you actually got really hurt.'

'They were concrete steps at a car park. Only a few steps, but there must have been something sharp that caught my arm as I fell.'

'Didn't your parents see?'

As Gareth predicted, Josh just shook his head. 'They were further behind us with Gemma.'

'And you didn't say anything?'

Josh didn't even dignify that with a reply. Gareth already knew the answer anyway. Josh had long since given up trying to tell anyone about Toby. All his mum and stepdad would ever say was that he should try to get on with his stepbrother. Either that, or that they thought he was exaggerating, had got it wrong, or was just downright lying. In any case, Gareth knew that Josh was too scared now to tell anyone the truth. Toby always made him pay.

'Well, he fucks off back to his mum's tomorrow for a few days, doesn't he?' Gareth said, trying to cheer him up.

'I wish he'd fuck off there forever.'

After school, Gareth and Josh walked back towards home largely in silence – both lost in their own thoughts as they trudged along under an oppressive grey sky. They spotted a group of girls on the other side of the road, just on their way out of the corner shop. Josh's head swivelled to look at them as they walked along.

'Do you know them?' Gareth asked.

'No,' Josh said quickly. 'Yes. Not really.'

Gareth watched as one of the girls peeled away from the group and crossed the road, her black hair tied in a high ponytail, and when he caught her eye he was taken aback by the directness of her gaze, her eyes large and fringed with thick dark lashes.

'That's the one,' Josh whispered to him as the girl swiftly shifted her attention away from them and carried on down the road. 'Mikayla.'

'I've gotta say,' Gareth said, 'I don't think the feeling is mutual.'

Josh gave him a little shove. 'I know that.'

Then, to his surprise, they both got a shove, and they spun angrily to find Toby, flanked by a couple of his idiotic followers. Gareth didn't know which he found more offensive: Toby himself, or the boys who would follow him, too scared themselves to not go along with whatever Toby said or did.

'I saw you last night, hanging around in the street,' Toby said to Gareth.

'And?'

'If you were hoping to meet Josh for a bit of romance, you didn't stand much chance. It was way past his bedtime.'

Gareth cocked his head to the side and considered how to answer. 'I had stuff to do.'

'Like what?'

'Like, stuff that has nothing the hell to do with you.' Gareth turned and started to walk away, but out of the corner of his eye he saw Toby grab Josh's arm. 'Are you going to let him talk to me like that?' Toby demanded.

'Gareth's going,' Josh said, 'we're both going.'

To Gareth's surprise, Toby didn't push it. He let go of Josh, but his eyes glinted darkly. 'I'll see you later then, Josh,' Toby said.

Judging by Josh's face, that was a combination of words he liked to hear less than any other.

'I guess you need to stay out of his way later,' Gareth said.

'Got any ideas how?' Josh asked, looking at him meaningfully.

Gareth shook his head. Clearly Josh wanted him to say he could stay the night at his house. But he couldn't. It was impossible. Josh could never come to his house, and that was that.

After a moment or two, Josh gave up waiting for Gareth to offer, and said instead, 'What were you doing last night, when Toby saw you?'

'I was just going to the shop.'

'For what?'

'I can't even remember.'

'Can't have been important then.'

'I guess not,' Gareth said. It wasn't important. Not the items themselves, anyway. But being at home could get pretty unbearable, and stealing from the corner shop was a rush. He shrugged to himself. He probably should pack all that in soon. And if he didn't manage to stop this week, well, next week then. He certainly couldn't tell Josh about it, either. Josh was so tightly strung already that finding out about Gareth's shoplifting habit would probably give him a heart attack.

***

Gareth swore under his breath when the front door wouldn't open wide enough for him to get inside. What fresh hell was this? He gave it an almighty shove, and tumbled into the hall, where the damp, musty atmosphere settled around him like a disgusting old coat. The hall was already stuffed with so many items that it wasn't immediately obvious what had caused the blockage, but after glancing around he spotted a couple of newer-looking cardboard boxes that must have been delivered that day. Anger flared inside him. What the fuck had she been buying now? He was on the verge of picking the boxes up and throwing them across the hall, but instead he laughed absurdly. They'd only fly through the air for a few feet before they fell on top of his mum's towers of mouldering old possessions; exactly where they would end up anyway.

'Gareth?' his mum called, 'did you have a good day?'

Should he answer? Nah. Fuck it. He'd talk to her when she stopped filling their house up with shit. He picked his way through the narrow pathway of the hall, walking sideways at times to get through, and peeked around the living room door at his mum in her armchair in front of the TV, nestled in amongst decades of junk.

'Gareth,' she said, as she spotted him, 'I asked you a question.'

'I stopped wanting to talk about what I did at school when I was about five years old.'

She started talking again, but he didn't listen, and made his way straight up the stairs to his room, closing the door with a sigh of relief. There was some excess stuff in his room – a couple of large plastic storage boxes stacked up against the wall – but she knew if she tried to sneak anything else in, he'd throw a fit. And in fact, she didn't often try. She did seem to have a tenuous sense of respect for his personal space. *But I still have to deal with her fucking hoard in every other room.* Even the bathroom was messed up – the bath was full of junk, though thankfully there was a separate shower cubicle which had so far stayed clear. *Because of her Josh has to go home and get beaten up when he could be safe here with me tonight. If I didn't live in such a hellhole.*

Suddenly, he was completely furious. He couldn't deal with this, not today. He changed out of his school uniform and dashed back down the stairs and out of the front door. He'd treat himself today – he'd give the corner shop a miss and go into town for some shoplifting. He'd stay until the shops closed. Maybe then he'd go home, or perhaps he'd stay out late, late enough that once he came back to the house he could just creep into bed, and not have to think about anything.

***

To Gareth's irritation, Josh wouldn't shut up about Mikayla all of the next week. Eventually, Gareth snapped. 'For God's sake, you're obsessed! Mikayla isn't the only girl in the world, you know.'

Josh looked at him, astonished. Please, *please* don't start saying she's the only girl in the world for you, Gareth thought. That was just the kind of soppy thing Josh would come out with.

As if by fate, they turned the corner, and there she was. But she wasn't alone. Toby and his friends were clustered on a bench at the end of the street. Along with Toby's usual crowd were three girls – and the girl sat on Toby's lap, with her arms around his neck, was Mikayla. Her black hair was tied in the same high ponytail, and she was still in school uniform. Interesting. She was their age, not Toby's, who was almost eighteen. She didn't go to the same school as Josh and Gareth, though; she went to the one on the other side of town.

'I told you,' Gareth hissed to Josh, 'you need to set your sights on someone other than Mikayla.'

Josh didn't reply. His eyes were fixed on Toby and Mikayla, and then he shook his head. 'Why … why did it have to be *him*?'

His voice was so hopeless that Gareth rounded on him. 'You know, you shouldn't let him get away with all this,' he said. 'He fucks with your life all day, every day. You should make a stand.' An image of his mum's face flashed in front of his eyes, and he blinked it away angrily. This was about Josh.

His friend looked at him in astonishment. 'What am I going to do to stop him?'

'You *know* what!' Gareth said, a plan quickly forming. 'You spend half your life at your computer. You can hack stuff, right? So do it to him. You might not be able to kick his ass physically, but you can kick it digitally.'

Josh raised an eyebrow at him. 'I cannot believe you just said that.'

'It's true, though. You could really mess him up with some of the stuff you can do. You should at least try to get something out of having skills like that.'

Josh was silent for a moment, then he shook his head, his eyes drifting over to Mikayla again. 'If I tried anything like that and Toby realised what I did, it would make it even worse.'

'It's worth considering, surely! You could come up with something that he'd never know was you, if you put your mind to it.'

Josh didn't reply, and Gareth's heart sank. It would have been so cool if Josh could think of something to really wind Toby up, but apparently he didn't have the stomach for it.

As Josh and Gareth approached Toby's group, they tried to speed up to get past them more quickly, but they had no chance.

'Don't think I don't see you staring at us,' Toby said, his hand planted firmly on Mikayla's waist. 'I guess it's the closest you two losers will ever come to getting any. Unless you really are fucking each other.'

Josh clearly wanted the ground to swallow him up as the gang of boys laughed, but Gareth was unfazed. He stopped and stood directly in front of Toby, who looked surprised at his boldness. 'So what if we are?' he said to Toby. 'You'd have a problem with that, would you?'

Toby didn't reply straight away, and the dynamic in the group shifted. With everyone's eyes on him, knowing that he was doomed whether he said yes or no, he clammed up.

'Yeah, I thought so,' Gareth said. 'Come up with something more original next time.'

Instantly, Toby was on his feet. He grabbed Gareth, and then shoved him away. Hard. Gareth almost fell, and anger pulsed through his body. He lunged at Toby and managed to plant a somewhat weak punch to the side of his face, infuriating him. With a bellow like a wild animal, Toby made a grab for Gareth, but the smaller boy was too fast. He and Josh sprinted off down the street, and when Gareth looked back over his shoulder Toby was back on the bench, Mikayla back on his lap. Toby laughed at something, trying to be casual, but it sounded forced. Gareth smiled. He'd really rattled him this time.

'You know it's me he'll take that out on,' Josh said when they finally stopped to catch their breath.

'I don't know,' Gareth said. 'He's pretty embarrassed. He might just want to forget about the whole thing.'

Josh gave him a deeply sceptical look. 'I don't want to go home. I just want to leave.'

'If you can't deal with Toby, you can't deal with the streets.'

'I don't have to be on the streets! I'd figure out something better than that. Can't I come to your house? Just for a night?'

A knot formed in Gareth's stomach. 'Josh, that's not an answer. One night at my house won't make a difference – it's not like you can just move in, is it? You want to spend your energy figuring something out, a way to make Toby leave you alone. Then you won't have to go anywhere.'

Josh

19

On the way home from school the next day, Gareth's eyes glowed with delight as Josh outlined the plan that had formed in his mind. Taking a different route to try and avoid Toby, they had gone down a narrow alleyway to a track that weaved its way along the backs of a row of terraced houses. On one side of the track they could peer into gardens over short fences and gates, while on the other a row of garages stretched out, the peeling paint on their doors shades of blue, white and grey. Although it was a slightly longer walk, it was a much more private place, out of the sight of Toby and Mikayla, and all their followers. Here they could relax a little.

'You should do it!' Gareth said, before Josh had completely finished explaining his plan. 'Make him fail all his exams!'

Josh sighed. 'I'm not going to make him *fail*,' he said. 'If I hack the exam board this summer, I can make sure he *passes*. Then I know he'll go to university. He'll be gone, for most of the time anyway.'

Gareth's eyes filled with disgust. 'You're going to do something to help him? You're going to make his life better?'

'I don't care if his life gets better, as long as mine gets better too. He has to go, I don't care how. My mum and stepdad keep talking about how Toby's grades are slipping. If they slip too far–'

'I can't believe this. If I could do what you can do, I'd use it to make Toby beg for mercy!'

Josh rolled his eyes. 'I don't want that. All I want is for him to go away. That's all I've ever wanted.' He stopped and considered for a moment. 'It's all just a fantasy, anyway. I won't really do it.

It was just a crazy idea. I probably wouldn't even be able to do it if I tried.'

Gareth just shook his head at him.

After going their separate ways at the end of the track, Josh heard a flurry of footsteps and voices behind him. He turned. Toby, flanked by a couple of friends, though Mikayla and the girls were nowhere to be seen. Shit. He hadn't managed to avoid them after all. Toby must have guessed that he and Gareth had walked this way and waited for him.

Ignore them. Just carry on.

Josh made his way towards the small bridge over the railway tracks, which he crossed every day on his way home. Unease settled in his stomach. This was his least favourite place for a run-in with Toby. Few houses overlooked the bridge, making Toby more bold. And he had nowhere else to go now except to carry on. He could turn around and try to get back to Gareth, or dart back down the track he'd emerged from, but he didn't fancy his chances at getting past Toby. Even if he did, Toby would only follow him. Prickles of foreboding spread down his spine. He really didn't want to go over the bridge. But he had no choice.

Tentatively, he made his way up the first couple of steps, and then he sped up, moving at a near run. Footsteps pounded on the path behind him, and he only just stopped himself from crying out when a pair of hands grabbed him halfway across the bridge.

'Not so brave now you're on your own,' Toby snarled into his face. 'I'm sick of you and Gareth disrespecting me. And I'm definitely sick of you looking at Mikayla. She finds it disgusting, by the way. You perving over her.'

'Leave me alone,' Josh said uselessly.

Toby's friends clustered around him, and Josh's feet left the ground as the three of them grabbed him and lifted him up against the stone wall at the edge of the bridge. Up, and then they pressed him down against the top of the wall, his head dangling into empty space. Fear gripped him, but Toby clearly wasn't satisfied as they pushed him a little further over the edge.

'Get me down!' he cried out, blinded with panic. He tried to push himself away from the edge, but it was futile, and Josh cried out as sounds began to carry from down the track. A train was coming.

'I think he gets the message,' one of Toby's friends said nervously, and one set of hands released their grip on him. But it wasn't enough for him to break free. As the train roared by beneath the bridge, he screamed.

Finally, once the train had passed, the boys pulled him back to safety, and he collapsed to the ground, shaking and trying not to cry. Toby crouched in front of him. 'What's wrong?' he asked. 'Are you scared of dying a virgin? Because that's going to happen anyway.'

Sniggering, he stood up and the three boys made off along the bridge, and disappeared down the steps at the other end. Some tears spilt from Josh's eyes. His phone vibrated and he took it from his pocket. It was a message from Toby. His finger hovered. Should he even open it? Somehow he couldn't help himself.

Do the world a favour. Jump off the bridge yourself.

He swallowed hard. A few more tears fell, and then he got unsteadily to his feet. Desperate to be away from this place, he dashed across the bridge, and made his way quickly down the steps. He was shaking all over, his pulse racing, and he felt sick. When the train went past, he'd really thought he was going to die.

Maybe that would have been better.

No. No, he refused to let his mind go down that path. He tried to recall how he felt when he'd told Gareth his crazy idea about the exam grades. He hadn't been that serious when he'd said it. But maybe…

No. It was useless. He wouldn't really do it. Knowing his luck, he'd end up ruining his own future by getting caught and Toby would get the last laugh. Again.

There's nothing I can do. Nothing. He let a couple of tears spill out – after all, there was no one around to see him. When it came down to it, he was alone. He was always alone.

Two months before Mikayla's death

Gareth

20

'Gareth!' his mum called. 'Gareth! Come in here.'

'For fuck's sake,' he mumbled under his breath as he made his way down the stairs towards the living room. His mum was pointing towards the window – or at least, towards the small sliver of glass that was visible between the towers of junk. 'Who are they?' his mum asked.

Gareth peered out of the dirty glass. What was his mum going on about? Had she just shifted up to a whole new gear of crazy? After all, they were at the end of the street. Nobody came down here except the postman and people delivering stuff his mum had ordered. Wait. A jolt of shock went through him. He recognised the figures outside; it was Toby and Mikayla.

He picked his way closer to the window. How had they found the house? *Toby must have followed me one day.* Shit. He must have been pretty distracted to not realise a great lump like Toby was following him. What were they doing out there? Toby was laughing, holding the bloody camera he had with him like he thought he was some big shot photographer, though Mikayla didn't seem to be into it.

He's showing her the house, Gareth realised. He's taking photos of it. They'd come to laugh at him, and Toby would show the photos to anyone he could get to look at them. He'd show them to *Josh.*

'Do you know them?' his mum asked.

Gareth shrugged, but inside he was fuming, his head spinning as he imagined what would happen when everyone saw.

'Are they your friends?'

'As if I'd bring friends back to this place!' he snapped. His cheeks were hot with shame. The house looked a wreck from the outside; no maintenance ever got done, and the windows were all blocked either by ancient curtains or piles of boxes, the old wooden window frames rotting. Reluctant to open the front door and risk the pair seeing inside the hall, Gareth made his way to the kitchen, where he managed to force the back door open enough to step outside. He made his way down the path at the side of the house, and stopped beside a bush where the sounds of Toby and Mikayla's voices reached him, though they were yet to spot him.

'I'm going,' Mikayla said. 'This is exactly the kind of thing I was talking about, Toby. Bringing me here to laugh at that kid's house? It's not funny. It's mean.'

She began to walk back down the street and Toby followed her, catching her arm. 'Gareth's just a little freak,' he said. 'Who cares about him? Besides, he doesn't know we're here–'

'I do, actually,' Gareth said loudly, as he stepped towards them, trying to figure out if he could make a grab for the camera. 'And I'd like you to fuck off now.'

Mikayla looked at Toby triumphantly and shook her arm free. 'See?' she said. 'He *is* here, and we shouldn't be doing this.'

She started walking again, and Toby looked between her and Gareth as if he couldn't choose which was the higher priority. At that moment, as Gareth was about to lunge towards Toby and try to wrestle the camera from him, the front door opened, and Toby, Mikayla and Gareth's eyes all fell on his mum and the contents of the hall behind her, which were clear to see.

'You heard my son,' she said, pointing her finger between Toby and Mikayla. 'Get away from here!'

Toby made a big show of looking around her into the hall. 'Wow,' he said to Gareth, raising the camera, 'your house is fucked up.' He stepped closer. 'Is your mum, like, mental or something?'

Gareth lunged at him and Mikayla ran over and tried to drag Toby away, but not before he'd managed to take a couple of shots. 'I'm sorry, um–' She looked at Gareth's mum helplessly, unsure how to refer to her. 'We're going,' she finished.

Narrowly escaping Gareth's clutches, Toby and Mikayla ran back down the street and Gareth pounded after them. He couldn't let those photos see the light of day. He'd get hold of that fucking camera if he had to prise it out of Toby's cold, dead fingers. At that moment, the pavement slammed into his cheek and his knee exploded with pain. He'd tripped over. He'd tripped over in the middle of the street and Toby was laughing as he sprinted away.

Letting out a howl of rage, Gareth struggled back to his feet, his eyes stinging with tears which he swiped at furiously. The last thing he wanted was to go back to his house, but his mum was calling his name, making a scene. For God's sake! If she carried on like this, the fucking neighbours would see inside the house next. He scurried back and glared at her furiously.

'Gareth,' his mum said, her face taking on a wobbly look around the chin. 'You fell. Are you hurt?'

'I'm fine,' he spat.

'You're bleeding.'

'Oh, what do you care?' he said, helpless with anger and shame. He *was* hurt, but the pain in his body was nothing compared to what was going on in his mind.

'That boy, he was making fun of you. I'm sorry–'

'I'm going to my room,' he said quickly.

Inside, a couple of hot tears spilt down his cheeks, stinging the cut on his face. Toby deserved to have his fucking face smashed in. Gareth swiped angrily at his tears. He wasn't going to cry over Toby. Neither would he retaliate, because Toby would only take it out on Josh. There was nothing he could do about the photos now. Toby was long gone. All he could do was steel himself for what Josh would say when he found out the truth.

This is just the way things are. I can't do anything about it. In a fit of fresh rage, he went out into the hall, where he started grabbing objects indiscriminately from a pile in the corner and throwing them at the opposite wall. Some bounced. Some smashed. His mum came tearing out of the lounge, yelling at him to stop, bounding up the stairs where she ran straight to her precious objects – not to him, though he was on the verge of tears again.

'Hello!' he said, sarcastically. 'I'm right here, Mum. I think maybe you meant to come and see if *I* was okay?'

'How could you do this?' she cried, picking up the fragments of some god-awful cat ornament. 'Look what you did!'

Furious, Gareth stamped on a large fragment of china that was still on the carpet, and his mum shrieked. 'I'm going out,' he said.

'Good. And stay out,' she said, still near-hysterical over the damage to her things. 'I don't want you to come home.'

She did, though. She sent him a text after twenty minutes when she'd calmed down, saying she never meant to say that, she was just upset. Gareth deleted the message. He would stay out. As long as he could, anyway. He'd get bored eventually.

21

'What are you doing?'

Mikayla's voice made him jump, and Gareth turned to find her standing a couple of paces from him, twirling the ends of her ponytail around her fingers and eyeing him quizzically.

'You just stole that, didn't you? I saw you take it out of your pocket.' She nodded towards the necklace in his hand, which he was doing his best to conceal. 'But why were you about to throw it away?'

For God's sake. Not only had he been stupid enough to let Toby follow him home unnoticed the previous day, now bloody Mikayla had managed to cross paths with him. She was still watching him, waiting for an answer. To his surprise she laughed, not unkindly, and said, 'Well, I guess I'd rather you were throwing it away than planning to wear it. Pink is not your colour.'

Gareth's cheeks reddened. Why wouldn't she just fuck off? She'd already seen his house, why did she have to come and bother him again? And besides, how could he explain? The rush of joy he felt at stealing things only to then throw them away. Brand new things, still in their packaging. Things that were actually *worth* something. He would imagine his mum's face as he did it. He could almost hear her now, the excuses she'd come up with for keeping this naff bit of jewellery that cost less than a tenner. *Oh, but it would go nicely with this outfit or that. It would make a nice present for somebody.* A present! Hah! Of all the justifications she came out with, that was the most ridiculous. As if she'd ever give something away as a present. Once stuff got inside the house, it never left.

His rage at her had fuelled a particularly daring spate of shoplifting today, but now Mikayla's appearance had taken the shine off of the high he'd been feeling, he fell back down to earth a little. Probably was time to pack it in for today. His luck would only stretch so far.

Gareth held out the cheap necklace with its pink heart-shaped pendant to Mikayla. 'You have it if you want.'

She shook her head. 'Could you really see me wearing something like that?'

'Suit yourself.' He reached out towards the bin, but Mikayla snatched it from his hand. 'Wait here,' she said, and she marched up the street back to the department store, popping out a few minutes later.

'What did you do?'

'I told them I found it on the pavement outside.'

'You gave it back?'

'Yes, I gave it back. My mum works in that store. You shouldn't take stuff from there. Or anywhere else.'

Gareth raised an eyebrow. How old did Mikayla think she was? She sounded like a snotty old woman. 'I don't give a shit,' he said. 'Shops like that expect some of their stuff to get nicked.'

Mikayla smiled at him kindly. 'Look, it must have been ... difficult, what happened yesterday, with me and Toby. I didn't know where he was taking me, or I wouldn't have gone with him. He just said he had something interesting to show me, but then we turned up outside your house and he was laughing and being an idiot. I've barely spoken to him since yesterday. Apart from telling him not to show those photos to anyone if he knew what was good for him.'

'Good for you,' Gareth said, though relief flickered inside him. 'Can you also stop talking to me, please?'

'I'm only trying to help–'

'I don't need *help*,' he spat. 'I'm none of your business. My house is none of your business. Just leave me alone.'

***

When he got home Gareth was astonished to find his mum in the spare bedroom upstairs. Usually it was impossible to get inside.

She'd managed to move some items out to the hall and worm her way in, and she now sat beside an open box full of old baby things.

'Are you having a clear out?' he asked. As soon as he said the words, he realised how ridiculous he was being. Of course she wasn't. This was something different, though. Interesting.

'Sit down, Gareth.'

He looked around him pointedly. 'Where?'

She shoved some stuff aside in exasperation. 'Here. Beside me.'

He did as she asked. 'So, what is it? I don't want to look at my old baby stuff.'

'It's not–' She swallowed hard. 'It's not *yours*.'

'Whose is it then?'

'Your sister's.'

'I don't have a sister. You're losing the plot, Mum. Let's put this away–'

'No. You had a sister. Her name was Holly.'

Gareth listened to her choke out the story. He couldn't seem to fully focus, but the odd word reached him: Premature. Very poorly. So tiny. 'Why didn't I know about her before?' he asked.

'Your dad didn't like talking about her, and you were only little. Then he died, and after that I couldn't see how to bring it up.'

Gareth frowned at the box of baby things. *They're not my old things. It's not even me she's sentimental over.* 'Why are you telling me now?' he asked.

'You know why,' she said, sniffing and tucking a loose strand of dark blonde hair behind her ear. 'Those kids that were here yesterday, who saw the house. You were so upset. I don't … I don't want to live like this. This isn't ever what I thought my life would be like. I don't want you to think that I think this is okay.'

'Sort it out then.'

'It's not as simple as that.'

'Yes, it is!' Gareth said. He grabbed the box of baby clothes. 'You just pick up a box, and you go and throw it out.'

She tried to snatch it back, but he held it away from her. 'These are just bits of fabric! They don't mean anything. They don't mean anything at all!'

His mum's face was a mask of sheer panic. He put the box back down. If he threw it out she'd just go and get it back out of the bin. He didn't have the stomach for it; all the drama. It was too much.

'I think about her all the time,' she went on, 'I–'

'Well, I'm glad you care about one of your children,' he snapped.

'Gareth–'

'If you cared about me, you'd sort this place out. I'd help you do it. You know I would.'

'I do care about you. More than anything. More than this stuff, I just – I can't – I try to, but–'

'Yeah. I know.' Gareth sighed. His mum's revelation didn't change anything. She couldn't change now. It was far too late.

Natalie

22

'"I hope she has a thick veil over her face on her wedding day,"' Gareth read out loud as they made their way out of the coffee shop down the street from Hearts, takeaway cups in hand. '"Who cares what dress she has, everyone will just be looking at her gross scars."' He handed her back the phone in its blue sparkly cover and turned to her. 'Natalie, this is horrendous.'

'I know.'

'So these started after you posted a video talking about ideas for your wedding dress yesterday?'

'Yeah.'

'Josh told me a little while ago that this was happening, although he said they were mainly about him.'

She sighed as they reached the end of the street. She'd asked Gareth to meet her to talk about her troll, but now it came to it, she struggled to find the words. She just felt drained. 'Which way?' she asked him.

'Left,' he said. 'There's a nice spot down here, out of the way of the offices. It's a good place to go if you need to think.'

'So,' he pressed her, as they skirted a fountain outside a smart office block, narrowly avoiding getting wet as a gust of wind caught up a spray of droplets. 'It's not just about Josh any more? They're trolling you now?'

'I guess so,' she said wearily. 'It's becoming more and more vicious.' She paused for a moment. 'I don't think this is even the same person. It seems different somehow. These are such ugly, spiteful things for someone to say.'

'So you've got *two* people attacking you now?'

'I really don't know. Maybe this new person took inspiration from the first one. How should I know what goes on in the heads of people who do this?'

Gareth looked at her sympathetically as they made their way across a large car park and found themselves on a secluded path running beside the train track. Though it was late November, the day was mild, weak sunlight brightening the sky through the bare tree branches above them. 'Are you sure you don't mind meeting me in the middle of the day like this?' she asked Gareth. 'I know you must be busy. It's just ... Josh has deteriorated so much since I told him what was happening to me. I've not mentioned it again since. He doesn't look at any of my posts or videos, because he knows I talk about ideas for my dress and I want that to be a surprise for him, but he asked me last night if it had all stopped and–' she couldn't bring herself to finish her sentence straight away '– and I lied. I told him it had. I told him no one was bothering me now.'

'Natalie–'

'I know,' she said, her voice rising a little. 'I know I shouldn't lie to him. I hate being dishonest and I never thought I'd end up in a situation like this, but I'm scared. I think – I really think he'll have a breakdown if he realises what's being said to me.'

'I saw him a few weeks ago and it didn't seem like he was dealing with the rumours very well,' Gareth said thoughtfully.

'That was probably right after I told him me and Verity lost a client because of it. He was completely crushed. That's why I'm too scared to tell him it's still happening.'

Natalie's heart ached at the thought of how Josh had been recently. Distant, distracted, upset. They'd had so much fun when they'd first got together – their lives full of laughter and delight in each other. But now Josh's preoccupation with Mikayla's death and this person who apparently had some axe to grind over it was turning him into a shadow of the man she'd fallen in love with, and seeing him in so much pain was unbearable.

'I want to help him,' she continued, 'but I don't know how. I thought maybe you would have a better idea how to get through to him. But if you need to get back—'

'It's not a problem,' he said. 'But to be honest, I've never been that great at helping him. Half the time I probably stirred things up with Toby and made it worse.'

'You don't...' The idea suddenly dawned on her. 'It couldn't be—'

'Toby? Yes, I think so. I think it's entirely plausible he could be your troll.'

They had reached their destination now, a bench at the side of the path nestled amongst the trees. She sat down beside Gareth and took a long sip of her coffee, considering his words. 'It can't be Toby,' she concluded. 'He's just – I mean, he's not that easy to get on with – but he's a pretty normal guy. He's got a family, plus he works all kinds of hours at the hotel. When would he find time to do all of this? And, even if he *was* saying the stuff about Josh, I can't imagine him making comments like that about my face.'

'Who knows what's really going on in his head. People with families aren't always happy. And he could write this crap while he's at the hotel for all you know.'

Natalie was silent for a moment, and before she could speak Gareth's phone chimed a couple of times. As he took it from his pocket she spotted the Hearts logo on the screen. She smiled. 'Have you met someone?' she said, 'on your own app?'

He laughed a little uncomfortably.

'Sorry, I've embarrassed you,' she said. 'It's none of my business. It just seems sweet, that's all.'

He put the phone away. 'Nat, I wish I could be more help. I don't really have any great insight into Josh's mind. I think because his family didn't listen to him and trivialised all his problems, he thinks that's what everyone will do. Plus he's still upset about Mikayla's death; it had a big impact on him and he's never dealt with it properly. He thinks he could have done more to save her, if he'd just got there a few minutes earlier, if he'd just looked in a different part of the lake.'

Anger suddenly flared inside her. 'I bloody hate his family sometimes.' Gareth laughed as she put her hand up to her mouth. 'I shouldn't have said that. I don't even know them.'

'Families are a nightmare,' he said. 'I swear they're like a car crash in slow motion.'

They were silent for a moment, both weighed down by the heaviness of the conversation. 'So, this is where you come to think,' she said, her voice brighter. She wanted normality. She wanted to just chat, and forget about how bleak her life was becoming.

'Yeah, sometimes, when I get a chance. Me and Josh used to come down here when we were kids, before the offices were here, and we'd go on about how shit our lives were and daydream about being anywhere else. Sometimes, when I sit here now, I wish I could reach back to my younger self and tell him that things are going to work out okay.' He shrugged and drained the last of his coffee. 'But, if I knew back then that things would work out okay, I probably wouldn't make the same choices that got me where I am. I guess the struggle and the uncertainty made me want to work hard. I wanted my life to be about something.'

'Well, you've certainly achieved a lot,' she said, and a conversation she'd had with Josh popped into her head. 'Gareth,' she said gently, 'Josh told me about your mum's hoarding. About your house when you were growing up. He said it took ages before you even told him about it.'

'He said all that?'

'I know you probably don't want to talk about it, but I just wanted to say I'm sorry you had to deal with all that. It must have been very difficult.'

He shrugged. 'No point crying about it now, is there?'

'I guess not, but still…' She paused. Gareth wasn't giving much away with his expression. Should she just drop it? He was clearly finding it painful. But she couldn't help being curious. 'How is your mum now?' she asked.

'Dead.'

'I'm so sorry, I shouldn't have brought it up–'

'No, it's fine. Honestly,' he said, seeming almost glad to talk about it now. 'She gave up on her life. I did my best to try to help her, but if somebody really doesn't want to change, there's nothing you can do.'

'How did she–'

'The house killed her in the end. It was inevitable. Josh asked me once, when we were kids, if it was safe to live in a house like that. I said something stupid about how stuff can't hurt you. It wasn't true then, and it certainly wasn't true several years later, when things had got even worse. Houses aren't meant to be lived in like that. A lot of bad stuff starts happening. Mice. Rats. Black mould. And the whole thing was a massive fire hazard. She wouldn't let anybody in, so if anything broke, it stayed broken, unless I could fix it. She never got anyone in to check the boiler or the old gas fire in the living room, and she had this ancient gas oven in the kitchen that you had to light with a match. I bought her a carbon monoxide alarm, but the next time I visited it was still just in its packaging.'

'Didn't she worry about it?'

'No. That's what I mean. She couldn't change. I know she didn't like how her life was, she'd told me as much, but you can get so used to something that change becomes scarier than sticking with how things are, no matter how nightmarish. I don't think she really cared if she died. She may even have hoped she would die.'

Natalie just shook her head. What was there to say? There weren't any words that could help.

'You'd think *I* would have been a reason for her to change,' he said. 'Not so much once I was grown up, maybe, but when I was still a kid. When I still lived there.'

'You can't think like that. I'm sure it wasn't about you.'

'Yeah. Well, in the end there was a gas leak and the house basically just exploded. And do you know the main emotion I felt when I heard about it?'

Natalie considered it. 'I think you're going to say relief,' she said.

'You don't think that's bad?' he said. 'I mean, I wasn't *happy* she was dead. I grieved for her, but at the same time, I felt kind of free. For the first time ever, I think.'

His expression was hard to read as he stared at the wire fence separating the path from the train track, back in this place he used to escape to as a kid. Was he really free? He still looked haunted, and suddenly this place he'd brought her seemed unspeakably sad to Natalie, as though the torment of these two troubled young boys was still alive here, woven through the branches of the winter trees and draped amongst the ivy. She shivered, though the air wasn't cold. Thank God Josh and Gareth had managed to escape their families in the end. Abruptly the world burst into noise as a train roared past, and she had to wait for it to pass before she could answer Gareth.

'I don't think it's bad to be relieved,' she said. 'I think it's understandable.'

'I guess focusing on Josh's problems back when I was a kid helped me in a way. If I worried about him and Toby, I didn't have to think so much about any of my shit.'

'Sometimes it can be good to face things, though.'

'In that case, what are *you* going to do? About your troll?'

Natalie sighed. Maybe she shouldn't have told Gareth about it. All she wanted right now was to bury her head in the sand. But that wasn't her style. She had to find a way through it somehow. She had to stay strong.

'Just carry on ignoring it and trying to rise above it, I guess,' she said. 'What else can I do?'

'Not a lot,' he said. 'But just remember, it's a bunch of crap. No one who really knows you would ever think those things, so you have to stop it getting inside your head. And what they said about you on your wedding day – I know for a fact that Josh will be completely blown away when he sees you. Everyone will be.'

She smiled, his words lifting her mood a little. 'Do you think so?'

'I do. And look, it's up to you how you handle all this stuff. I can see why you're torn about whether to tell Josh or not, but I think your gut instinct is right. He's better off not knowing. It's not really being dishonest if you're protecting him, is it? He's not good with stuff like this – and I know. I visited him in the hospital after what he tried to do. If letting him believe it's all stopped keeps him safe, then let him believe that. You can always talk to me about it if you need to have a rant.'

Natalie nodded. Josh's fragility truly worried her, though she still felt uneasy about deceiving him. But what Gareth had said about the risk to Josh was a stark warning. She couldn't ignore him.

'If I do find out this is Toby,' Gareth stated darkly, 'well, let's just say I'll make him regret it.'

'You'll have to get to the back of the queue, because I will be first in line. I still don't think it's him, though. I mean, why now? Why like this? I just can't see it.' She sighed. 'I've got to see him again in a couple of days. I promised I'd tour his hotel so we can recommend it to couples. I've been putting it off, but I can't really come up with any more excuses.'

Gareth raised an eyebrow. 'Good luck with that.' He stood up. 'Come on,' he said, 'let's get back. I've spent enough time here stewing in old memories. It's time to focus on the future. And Natalie, what you're going through right now, I'm sure it will resolve itself. This time next year you'll be married and looking back on this, wondering what all the worry was about.'

She smiled. 'I'm sure you're right,' she said, with more conviction that she really felt.

23

Natalie rounded the corner and caught her first glimpse of Hartbury Hotel. The main part consisted of a charming, white-painted building nestled among trees that still clung on to the last few of their autumn leaves, while to the left a modern red brick annexe stretched out, its windows overlooking the generous lawn.

Inside, the reception area was warm and welcoming, if a little old-fashioned, with a heavy dark wood desk and a red and gold patterned carpet. Tasteful Christmas decorations added sparkle, and a tall tree bedecked in gold trimmings lit up the corner of the room.

Before she could reach the desk, Toby emerged from a door, behind which she glimpsed a grand staircase, and he greeted her warmly. 'I'm so glad you finally decided to come,' he said. 'Do you want to start by having the tour? Most of the hotel has been newly renovated, though we haven't made it to the reception area yet.'

'A tour would be lovely, thank you,' she said.

She followed him back towards the stairs. 'I'll show you a couple of the rooms first,' he said, 'and then we'll move on to the function rooms and the conservatory, and we can have a chat.'

'Great,' Natalie said.

He walked quickly, almost at a jog, as though he had so much to do that even moving around was a task he had to do as efficiently as possible. Dressed in a well-fitting navy blue suit, with a pale blue tie and immaculate white shirt, Toby was clearly in his element. He greeted guests as they passed, and showed off a couple of refurbished bedrooms with obvious pride, though she could barely get a word in edgeways.

After a whirlwind tour of the dining room and the two rooms where the ceremonies could be held, they ended up in a bright hexagonal conservatory. Natalie was glad of the chance to take a breath, as Toby had been bombarding her with information and suggestions throughout the tour. The conservatory was a large, pretty room. An abundance of windows overlooked the lawn, flooding the room with light, and the space had a dreamy, peaceful feel to it. Toby pulled out a chair for her at a round table by the window before going to get coffee for them both.

'This would make a lovely room for wedding receptions,' she said on his return. 'It would work with any colour scheme. I can definitely see this room appealing to our couples.'

Toby sat down beside her, while she took a sip from her cup. 'So, what do you think of the place?' he asked her. 'And the rooms for the ceremony?'

She couldn't help but smile. 'I really like it here, Toby. It's exciting. There's loads of potential. It's nice having room options that work for larger or smaller weddings, and it's stylish, comfortable, everything we look for. You'll have to talk me through the pricing, but my initial reaction is definitely very positive.'

Toby nodded, satisfied, and she took notes as he outlined what he was thinking for the prices. 'That's what we're asking at the moment, anyway,' he said. 'I'd like to go higher, but we've only just started—'

'I wouldn't go higher yet,' Natalie said. 'It looks about right to me. You can have a rethink once you've got a few weddings under your belt and have a good feel for it.'

'Yes, of course,' he said offhandedly. 'It's best to test the waters first.' He cleared his throat. 'So, how are you and Josh getting on with your wedding plans? I can't tempt you to come here for the ceremony, can I?'

She had to bite her tongue to stop herself from saying something along the lines of 'good God, no', as visions of Toby taking over her day made her squirm. 'We already booked somewhere,' she said neutrally. 'Silverdale House.'

'And how's Josh? He must be excited. I never thought I'd see the day that he managed to settle down.'

Natalie's skin prickled with irritation. 'He's fine,' she said, in clipped tones. *It was Toby who saved his life,* she reminded herself.

The fact he was like a bull in a china shop didn't take away from that fact.

At that moment they were interrupted as a young red-haired woman came into the conservatory. 'Oh, sorry,' she said as her eyes fell on them. 'I didn't realise you were in here.'

'Chantelle, can you go and make a start on the Orchid room?' Toby said brusquely. 'We have a conference there today.'

The young woman hesitated as if she needed to ask for more details but didn't want to admit that she wasn't sure what to do.

'Look, just ask Angelique if you need to,' he said, and she scurried away, her glossy red ponytail bobbing.

'Chantelle's new,' Toby said once she'd left. Natalie could almost hear an eye-roll in his voice, as if he found new staff incredibly tiresome. It hadn't stopped him staring at Chantelle's bum as she'd left the room, though. Natalie tried to brush that observation aside. She had something she wanted to say to Toby. 'I – I get that no one really talks about this much,' she said, 'but I know Josh didn't have the easiest time as a teenager. He told me about what he tried to do, and how you saved his life—'

Toby looked startled. He swallowed his mouthful of coffee quickly, as if to stop himself spitting it out. 'He told you I saved him?'

'Well, didn't you?'

'Yes,' he said, 'I guess I did. I mean, yeah, I suppose if it wasn't for me he would have succeeded in… what he was trying to do.'

Natalie tried to conceal her frown. Why was he being so shifty?

'I think we all feel that we should have realised how much he was hurting,' Toby continued quickly. 'It shouldn't have come to that in the first place.'

'Sometimes you just can't see it,' she said. 'Especially if he was hiding it.'

'I don't know. He was on his computer most of the time; he didn't really talk to any of us.'

'Well, I'm so glad you were there.'

'So he's all good now, is he?' Toby asked. 'Over the years he's still been a bit down from time to time. But it's difficult to know how to ask about it.'

'Josh is … he's good,' she said. Was it true? It wasn't, really, but somehow she sensed telling Toby that wouldn't help anything.

He shifted uncomfortably in his seat, and Natalie took the hint and changed the subject back to the hotel. 'Thanks for showing me around, anyway,' she said. 'It's really a lovely place.'

'Do you want to ask anything?'

Natalie tried to sort through the barrage of information he'd given her as they walked round. He'd been quite thorough. 'I think you already answered pretty much everything. I'll call you if anything occurs to me.'

As she made her way back out to the car park, Natalie thought back over the exhausting meeting. What was it like for the people who worked in this place? Toby's mind seemed to go at one hundred miles per hour and he clearly didn't have much patience for staff who didn't know what they were doing. Still, the hotel was immaculate, and genuinely a nice place to hold a wedding. *It will be my turn soon,* she thought, *I'll be swishing through the halls of Silverdale House in my dress, surrounded by family and friends, with Josh – with my husband – at my side.* She still had a million things to sort out before the big day, but excited butterflies fluttered in her stomach.

At the car, she paused and reached up to her neck. Her scarf – it must still be inside, in the conservatory. She turned with a sigh. *Hopefully I won't bump into Toby and get another monologue about the hotel.* Inside, all was quiet, and she paused in the hall as she spotted some more of his photos on the wall. With a start of surprise, she leant in closer. Chedford Lake! It was a beautiful place, and there were photos of other local beauty spots, too, with labels underneath – clearly he was trying to show off the local area to guests. She looked more closely. A couple of the photos of the lake had groups of teenagers in – they were silhouetted, sitting on the grass with their backs to the camera.

There was a date next to the caption. These pictures could be from that actual weekend when Mikayla had died! Unsure what to make of it, she gave herself a little shake and made her way towards the back of the hotel and the conservatory. Why shouldn't he have photos up from that weekend, really? The water looked lovely at sunset; it was easy to see why he'd chosen to display them.

Voices in one of the function rooms drifted to her – Toby, and a woman. It sounded like the young woman who had interrupted them, Chantelle. But it didn't seem like a work conversation, and out of curiosity Natalie stepped closer and peeked around the door. Sure enough, Toby was standing close to Chantelle as she set up the table, his hand brushing her arm, as she tried to move away.

'Come on,' he said, 'one drink after work won't hurt, will it?'

Chantelle laughed nervously, and Toby moved in even closer. 'With your boyfriend in prison and two little mouths to feed, I would have thought you'd be keen to keep this job,' he said.

Natalie's breath caught in her throat. Had she heard that right? Toby's voice had been low, but his words had carried to her clearly enough. She only just managed to stop herself marching in and giving Toby a piece of her mind.

'Who told you about my family?' Chantelle asked Toby as she turned to face him, her voice rising.

'I have my ways of finding things out,' he said. 'It seems to me like you don't want to go making enemies right now.'

Initially Chantelle looked like she was going to argue back – or even give Toby a slap – but she apparently thought better of it. She edged away from Toby fearfully, muttering about needing to get some water glasses. As she approached the door, Natalie quickly darted off towards the conservatory, sickened by Toby's behaviour.

24

'So, tell me all about Hartbury Hotel,' Verity said once they'd finished their first meeting of the morning – a couple planning a big do for their tenth wedding anniversary – and they had a chance to catch their breath after a rather dizzying list of demands. 'Is it good, bad, or ugly?'

Natalie smiled. 'It's certainly not bad, or ugly,' she said. 'The refurbished rooms are all lovely, really tasteful. It's got one large formal room option for the ceremony – it would seat about one hundred and twenty people, and another smaller and more intimate room for fifty or so. Maybe sixty at a push.'

'Okay,' Verity said, making a note.

'And there's a beautiful conservatory for the reception. It's exactly the kind of thing everyone asks for. The prices are good, too, and there's a discount for winter weddings. I think it will be popular.'

'Great,' Verity said. 'I might drop round myself sometime and check it out. I'd like to see it for myself.'

'It's well run, too,' Natalie said, a little grudgingly. She was still disturbed by how Toby had treated Chantelle. And yet she couldn't deny the hotel was well kept and well organised.

'But?' Verity said, immediately picking up on Natalie's unease.

'It's just the manager … how he behaves with some of the staff, that's all.'

'This is the hotel Josh's brother manages?'

'Step-brother, yes. Toby Johnson.'

Verity was waiting for her to elaborate about her comment, and she tried to think how best to explain what she'd seen. 'He was hassling a young woman,' she said finally, 'he didn't realise I could hear their conversation. It wasn't very pleasant.'

'Nothing new there then,' Verity said, her voice bitter all of a sudden.

'V? What—'

'No, sorry. It's nothing. I'm – I'm not having the best time right now.'

'I'll make us a coffee,' Natalie said, beginning to stand. 'We can have a chat.'

Verity shut the notebook where she'd jotted down some points about Hartbury Hotel, and rested her hands on its floral cover. 'Thanks, Nat, but I don't need coffee,' she said. 'I need to talk to you about something. And it's not good news, I'm afraid.'

'Okay,' Natalie said uneasily as she sat back down in her chair.

Verity pushed a cascade of chestnut curls back from her face and then laced her fingers together on top of the notebook again. The way their chat had suddenly begun to feel official and businesslike made Natalie's hairs stand on end. What was this all about? Verity never usually behaved like this, and the change in mood was alarming.

'How is everything with you?' Verity asked. 'Are you doing okay?'

'Well, the trolling hasn't stopped, if that's what you mean,' Natalie said, wondering what she was really getting at. 'And I'm having to pretend it has to Josh because I'm not sure he could handle it otherwise.'

'I'm so sorry. I wish I could help—'

'It – I'm just getting fed up, to be honest. It feels like it will never end. I just want my life to be normal again.' She met Verity's eyes. 'Please, just say whatever it is you want to say to me. Don't keep me in suspense.'

Verity nodded sympathetically. 'So, Nat, this—' She paused. 'God, I really don't know how to say this. Believe me, if there was any other way—'

'V? What is it?' Natalie said, growing frustrated. 'Just *tell* me! It can't be that bad.'

'The business is in trouble,' Verity said. 'It has been for a while. You know they put the rent up on the shop, and I – I've made a few bad decisions. I'm not sure if I can really afford to have the shop any more. I'm thinking of cutting back, just running the events business from home.'

'I–' Natalie stared at her, stunned. 'V, I had no idea.'

'Please,' she said, holding up a hand. 'Don't be sympathetic. A lot of it's my own stupid fault.'

'Don't say that.'

'I just overstretched myself. I spent too much on things for the business that I shouldn't have done–.' Verity shook her head. 'Anyway, the thing of it is–'

'You can't afford to pay me any more,' Natalie said.

Verity's brow creased. 'I can pay you up until mid-January to cover the Christmas parties and the winter weddings we've got planned,' she said. 'But after that…'

'I need to find a new job,' Natalie said, her words coming out unsteadily as the reality hit her.

'I really am so sorry, Natalie. The timing is awful. I know you're already under pressure, and you're planning your wedding…' Verity trailed off hopelessly.

'Just give me a minute,' Natalie said, abruptly getting up from the table as her emotions began to swirl dangerously inside her. She felt like she could scream. 'I need to get some air.'

She fled from the shop, tears bubbling up, though she didn't want to shed them. She was already lying to Josh, trying to hold him together while she was falling apart – buried under the unceasing abuse. Her vlogging held little joy for her any more. Even the wedding planning was losing its shine. The one thing she had been holding on to was coming to Verity's Events, losing herself in other people's weddings and celebrations – in their dreams and plans and dramas. But come the new year, she wouldn't even have that. Her pace slowed as she passed the pretty shopfronts of Yetley's high street, glittering with Christmas sparkle, and she sank down onto a bench.

It wasn't long before Verity joined her. 'I've brought you your coat,' she said as she sat down.

Natalie took it gratefully and wrapped it around herself, a shield against the icy wind that was chilling her through her fluffy purple jumper. 'I'm sorry for running off like that,' she said. 'I'm not angry with you, or anything. I'm just overwhelmed and it was a shock.'

'It's okay,' Verity said, as Natalie let out a sob. 'Look, come round for dinner after work tonight. Spend some time with Rob and the girls. We're all still here for you, Natalie, you're not suddenly going to be on your own.'

'I'm not on my own, I have Josh.'

'You said yourself Josh isn't in a great place right now. You need your family around you. Let us make a fuss of you later.'

'How bad is it, V? The business—'

'It's salvageable, I think. I just need to downsize and then build it back up.'

Natalie nodded as a couple of tears splashed onto her cheeks. 'I just feel like my life is out of control right now,' she said, her words coming in shaky bursts.

'Like I said, it's horrible timing.' Verity put her arm around her. 'It'll be okay, though. Things will work out one way or another. Me and Rob will look out for you, okay?'

25

Natalie stepped inside Rob and Verity's house, and was almost knocked off of her feet when her two nieces launched themselves at her for cuddles. Their exuberance broke through her bleak mood and she managed a laugh as she quickly pulled off her boots and joined them in the kitchen. It was nice to be here, the house homely and comforting – it had a reassuringly permanent feel to it, when everything else kept changing.

It wasn't until after dinner, when the girls were in bed, that Natalie was able to talk about her troubles – how uncertain she felt about the future, how worried she was about Josh, and how much she was being hurt by the constant attacks on her appearance, and her relationship with Josh.

Rob and Verity listened sympathetically, until she finally stumbled to a halt. Then the couple gave each other a look.

'What?' Natalie said. 'Do you know something about it?'

'No, of course we don't,' her brother said, 'it's just...' He turned to Verity, who nodded at him. 'We were having a chat about it before you came round tonight. It's not easy for us to say this, Nat, but how well do you really know Josh?'

'What do you mean?' she asked, genuinely confused.

'Well, none of this started until the two of you were together. The allegations about Mikayla first, and now this really nasty personal stuff.'

Natalie was silent for a while as she struggled to grasp what they were getting at. 'I don't understand,' she said at last. 'Surely you don't think there's any truth to what's being said about Mikayla's death?'

'I think, *we* think, that someone somewhere has suspicions, and maybe they are on to something.'

Natalie was about to explode in anger at what Rob was implying, but he quickly held his hands up. 'I don't mean Josh hurt her, of course I don't. It's just … well.' He frowned. 'Mikayla was going out with Josh's stepbrother, wasn't she? Couldn't there have been more to that weekend than anyone is letting on? You said how weird Josh is being; he's obviously got something to hide.'

'He's hurt that anyone would think this about him, and he's angry that someone is using his past to upset me. But I've told him it's stopped, anyway, and he's less stressed now.'

'Why is he so upset, though?' Rob said. 'Unless he thinks you're going to leave him. And now the messages have turned more personal … well, maybe he wanted a way to make you stay.'

'You think *Josh* is doing it?' she said incredulously. 'You think it's him saying these things about my appearance to make me feel insecure?'

'If he's a jealous kind of guy, yeah, maybe. He was freaked out by whoever it is who knows what happened at the lake, and he's terrified you'll leave unless he makes you feel that he's the best you can do.'

'Verity, do you believe this crap?' Natalie said, turning to face her.

Verity couldn't meet her eyes. 'I am a little worried about you,' she said. 'I feel like you've changed, and it doesn't seem like a good sign when people are in a new relationship and they start to change.'

'I haven't changed! I'm stressed out, yes. I'm unsettled. *And* I've just lost my job. But I'm still me.'

Verity recoiled at the mention of the job. 'Look, I know the job's not your fault,' Natalie said. 'But I don't like what's going on here. You and Rob don't know anything about mine and Josh's relationship and yet you're making these wild claims–'

'We're just saying, be careful,' Rob said. 'We hope we're wrong, but we're just trying to look out for you. Josh is obviously troubled. He had some sort of run-in with the police, didn't he?'

'You mean when he turned himself in,' Natalie said. 'He hacked the exam board to try to change his stepbrother's grades, but he didn't actually alter them. He owned up almost straight away.'

'So you do know about the hacking.'

'Yes. He had a tricky time when he was a teenager. Everyone does, to some extent.'

Rob looked at Verity and then back to Natalie.

'Okay,' he said, 'so, the other thing. We heard Josh tried to kill himself not long after Mikayla's death. He took an overdose. You have to question the timing...'

There was a long pause. 'I know you mean well,' Natalie said, 'but I already know this. He told me he tried to kill himself.' She got to her feet, stung by the way they were treating her. 'I thought this evening would take my mind off of everything but all you've done is ambush me with a load of half-baked ideas about Josh. I'm going to leave now because I don't want to fall out with you. I love Josh, and I'd trust him with my life, okay?'

'But you've lied to him about what's happening to you!' Verity said. 'You told him the trolling has stopped, but it's worse than ever! How can you say you trust him when you don't even talk to him? I don't have any secrets from Rob.' She paused. 'And he doesn't have any from me,' she added, though the fact she said this with less certainty wasn't lost on Natalie.

'I can't ... I can't deal with this right now,' Natalie said. 'I'm going home.'

As she left, Rob caught up with her on the doorstep. 'Nat, I'm sorry,' he said. 'That didn't really go how I was hoping.'

'What did you hope for?' she said. 'That I'd be grateful?'

'I don't know.'

Natalie paused. Rob really did look upset, and she softened a little. 'Perhaps we should pretend tonight never happened,' she suggested.

'Will you tell Josh what we said?'

Natalie sighed. 'That would make for an interesting atmosphere when we're all at Mum and Dad's for Christmas dinner.'

'Nat, I'm serious,' Rob said. 'This is your whole future we're talking about here – please just think about what we've said. And now you won't have a job to go back to in the new year, I'm worried about you.'

'Well, don't be!' Natalie said, angry again. 'You and Verity, you've done more than enough today. If this is how you act when you're supposedly on my side, I'd hate to see how you treat your enemies.'

Tears stung her eyes as she walked away. She shouldn't have said that; they *had* been trying to help, even if they hadn't gone about it very well. *How can I tell Josh about this? It will kill him.* But she had to tell him. She'd lied long enough. Her troll clearly wasn't going to stop, and Josh needed to know about her job, too. As much as she hated to admit it, Verity was right that she shouldn't have secrets.

Quietly opening the front door to the flat, she sighed as she hung up her coat and scarf. She should be happy to come back to her home – but she couldn't relax here. She wasn't safe in her home. The comments didn't stop; in fact, the flat was where she usually ended up reading them. A wave of anger shook her to her core and she almost cried out. How *dare* someone make her feel like this? How dare someone take over her life this way, making her nervous to even look at her phone? And to have their nonsense get inside other people's heads too – forcing her into confrontations like the one she'd just had with Rob and Verity – it was too much. It was just too much.

She made her way towards the living room, and paused in the doorway. Josh sat on the sofa, his head in his hands. He was crying. She rushed over to him. 'Josh? Josh, what is it?'

He jumped at the sound of her voice. 'Natalie!' he said, rubbing at his face. 'I didn't hear you come in.'

'What's wrong?' she said, putting her arms around him. 'What's happened?'

'Nothing,' he said. 'Nothing. I'm fine.'

'You're not fine.'

'Has it really stopped?' he asked her after a long silence. 'Has this person really stopped saying stuff about me and Mikayla?'

Natalie let go of him. *I have to tell him the truth.* But his voice was shaky, and she could smell alcohol on his breath. Had he spent the whole evening drinking and crying?

'Tell me what you were upset about,' she said. 'Was it about Mikayla again? Because you know there's nothing more you could have done. If you'd stayed in the water any longer trying to find her, you would have drowned.'

'Sometimes I think that would have been better.'

'Stop it!' she said. 'Don't you dare say that! It wouldn't be better for me, would it?'

'I'm wrecking your life,' he said, 'I knew that I would. Wherever I go, whatever I try to do, this shit just follows me around. I can never get away from it.'

'Well, I love you,' she said, 'and you're stuck with me.'

'Has it really stopped?' he asked her. 'I could just look myself, but I know it means a lot to you that I don't see anything about your wedding dress. But I have to know.' He looked at her closely. 'It hasn't stopped, has it?'

She took out her phone. 'Here,' she said, 'I got these on my most recent post. It's not about my dress, it's just about bridal makeup. You can look at it.'

It'll take more than makeup to make you look ok
No one likes an ugly bride
I hope you're not having any wedding photos taken
Maybe you should put plastic surgery on your wedding list
why won't you wake up and face the truth – Josh Sparkes is a murderer
Everyone can see the truth but you
maybe he'll kill you next

'Josh, listen to me,' she said, as the colour drained from his face. 'This person, or people, are clearly unhinged. It doesn't mean anything.'

He handed her phone back to her without a word.

'Say something,' she said.

'Why did Rob and Verity invite you round tonight? Just you and not me?'

She rubbed at her forehead. 'They're concerned about me. They don't really know you, not like I do. They raised a few things, it was all a load of rubbish and I told them so–'

'What kind of things?'

'I don't even want to waste my breath on it.'

'They think I did it, don't they? They think I hurt Mikayla.' He stood up and strode over to the kitchen, where he planted his palms against the worktop and shook his head. 'They really think I would do that?'

'No. No, absolutely not,' she said, rushing over to him and placing her arm around him. His body was tense, filled with pent up emotion. 'They're just worried. Rob's my big brother – he wants to look out for me, that's all.'

'I can't do this, Nat,' he said.

'What do you mean?'

'I'm not good for you. It's selfish of me to let you carry on being put through this.'

'How is it selfish? Josh, I love you. I'm here because I want to be!'

'And *I* love *you*! But you're in pain, Natalie! I knew it must still be happening. I can't let this carry on, I can't drag you down with me–'

She covered his mouth with hers, and though he initially resisted, he soon started to kiss her back. 'I love you,' she said to him again, as they broke apart. 'Don't talk about leaving. Don't let this drive a wedge between us.'

He kissed her gently. 'I won't. But I don't know how much more of this I can take. I think about the lake all the time–'

'I know,' she said. 'But we're stronger if we face it together.'

He nodded, and she gave him a weak smile. 'Josh...' she started, intending to tell him about her job, too.

'What is it?' he asked, his eyes clouded with concern. His face was so drawn and tired, worry and sadness etching itself through his very skin.

She shook her head. 'Nothing,' she said. 'It'll keep.'

'I just wish I'd never suggested that we go to the lake,' he said. 'If I could somehow tell myself all those years ago not to ever suggest it, if I could make it so none of it ever happened–'

'I know,' she said, holding him close. 'I know, Josh.'

But he didn't seem to hear her.

Two months before Mikayla's death

Josh

26

'Toby's still in bed,' Josh said, as Mikayla looked up from her phone. She was standing a few paces from his and Toby's house, leaning against a lamp post, dressed in jeans and a tight white t-shirt. Her eyes fell on him, so big and wide.

She's so pretty I feel like I'm going to die.

'He's what?'

'He was asleep when I left. Was he supposed to be meeting you?'

Mikayla made a sound of disgust and put her phone away. 'His loss,' she said.

'He's an idiot.'

She looked at him closely. 'I don't like how he treats you,' she said. 'I kind of fell out with him a couple of days ago over him being a dick towards people.'

'I can handle it,' Josh said, though nothing could be further from the truth.

Mikayla seemed unsure whether to tell him something. 'Josh...' she said, 'your friend Gareth—'

'I know. He told me. He didn't want me to hear about it from Toby.'

Josh had heard all about it from Toby as well, though. He'd delighted in telling him that Gareth's mum was 'batshit crazy', and that his house was a dump. Josh had tried to ignore him, but when it became intolerable and he finally told Toby to shut up, Toby had given him a thump before saying that he should call social services and try to get Gareth taken away, the idea of which he apparently found hilarious.

'We should probably tell someone he's living like that,' Mikayla said.

Josh shuffled his feet uncomfortably. He hadn't seen inside Gareth's house yet, and he wasn't sure Gareth would let him. 'I don't want to do anything behind his back,' he said, and cast about for a change of subject. 'So, are you and Toby going to make up, do you think? I'd never just stay in bed if I was supposed to be meeting someone.'

Mikayla sighed, and started to walk down the road towards town. It wasn't where Josh wanted to go, but he fell into step with her anyway. 'I don't know,' she said finally.

'He ... I don't think he should stand you up. It's not right.'

Mikayla smiled at him. 'You're sweet.'

His face filled with heat. Stupidly, he reached out his hand and his fingers lightly brushed her arm.

'Josh, what are you–'

'I really like you,' he blurted out.

She looked at him kindly. *For God's sake. She's the same age as me, but she makes me feel like a stupid little kid.* 'I suspected you did,' she told him. 'But I'm with Toby. And even if I wasn't...' She paused. 'I didn't mean that how it sounded. You're just not my type, Josh. I'm sorry.'

Not my type. Why wasn't he her type? Was he too weird? Too ugly? Too boring? Too young? Too everything. And she was too perfect.

'I am a bit worried about Gareth,' she said. 'He was stealing stuff in town. He's going to get caught one day.'

'Yeah, he told me about that too.'

'Well, you're his friend. You should keep an eye on him.'

Josh felt a stab of irritation. Of course he'd keep an eye on Gareth. He'd been on his way to meet him right now, before he'd started following Mikayla in the wrong direction.

'I'd better...' she said.

'Yeah.' Josh's entire body was on fire with embarrassment. Why on earth had he told Mikayla how he felt? He must have sounded absolutely ridiculous. She was probably struggling to keep a straight face.

'Don't let Toby get to you,' she said. 'I don't know what goes on in his head. I'd never treat my little sister like he treats you. Yeah, she can be a pain in the arse sometimes but if anyone tried to hurt her…'

Josh didn't reply. What could he say? Toby was never going to change.

'Well, see you,' she said, and turned in a swish of shiny black hair.

He stood for a moment and watched her walk away, then made his way back towards the park where he was meeting Gareth.

***

'You *told* Mikayla you like her!' Gareth said, as they sat down on the grass. Thankfully, the council had finally decided to refurbish the depressing playground across from their spot on the grass verge, and it was closed for the moment. Josh was glad that Gemma would have a nice new place to play now – it would be fun to bring her here once the work was finished. He tried to think about that instead of his excruciating conversation with Mikayla, but Gareth wouldn't drop it. 'How did that work out?' he asked.

'Bad. Really bad,' Josh said.

Gareth nodded philosophically. 'Well, maybe it'll mean you can move on now. Perhaps you got it out of your system.'

Josh thought of Mikayla's eyes, fringed by thick dark lashes, the way she smiled, the way he'd been able to see all her curves in her tight jeans and that white t-shirt.

'I guess not, then,' Gareth said, his voice breaking through Josh's thoughts.

'What?'

'You're daydreaming about her right now.'

'Why didn't you tell me before about your house? And your mum?'

'It's … I don't know. I just couldn't.'

'You couldn't even tell *me*?'

'I kind of wanted to. I wanted to say you could stay some nights, when you were worried about going home with Toby. I felt really shit that I couldn't help.'

'Is it really that bad?'

'Whatever you're imagining, it's worse.'

'Mikayla thinks we should tell somebody about it.'

'She thinks you should do what?'

'Well, is it safe in there? In your house?'

Gareth appeared lost in thought for a moment. 'It's just stuff,' he said. 'It doesn't bite.'

Josh nodded. Leaning back on his elbows, he picked at the grass, releasing a humid green scent. For a brief second it transported him back to sunny childhood days spent playing in the buttercup and daisy studded field beside his primary school. There had been no Toby back then, nothing to hurt him. Life had been so simple. An idea popped into his head. 'Hey, so, after the exams, why don't we do something in the summer?'

'Like what?'

'There's a campsite at Chedford Lake. It might be kind of cool to go there for a couple of nights. I've got a tent at home we could take.'

'A camping trip?'

'Why not? It gets you away from your house. And me away from mine.'

'Yeah, I guess.' Gareth laughed. 'You're not going to want to show your face too much now you've confessed your love to Mikayla.'

'Shut up!'

'Come on, it'll be okay,' Gareth said. 'She's actually pretty different to what I thought. I got kind of pissed at her when she ran into me in town, and she's a bit nosy and annoying, but I think she actually cares, in a way. I think she's all right.'

Josh considered it. 'Yeah. She said she doesn't like how Toby treats people.'

'She's still going out with him, though. Even though she knows he's an arsehole.'

'Maybe not for much longer. He stood her up this morning. I don't think she'll put up with crap like that.'

***

He couldn't sleep. Toby was breathing heavily on the bed above him, while Josh writhed around, images of Mikayla haunting him. Sometimes he'd start slipping into dreams, but in his dreams she would be there; he'd be kissing her, his arms wrapped around her body. Her skin was so warm, and she was so beautiful. And then she'd take off that white t-shirt. *For God's sake, just think about something else.* But he couldn't think about anything else. His pulse thundered in his ears, and he got out of bed and crept down the hall to the bathroom.

'I hope you weren't wanking over Mikayla,' Toby said when he came back inside.

Josh froze, and Toby laughed.

'You're gross, Josh.'

'I just didn't feel well,' he mumbled. It was kind of true. He felt hot and feverish, and doing the thing Toby had just said barely seemed to have reduced the tension and frustration inside him.

'She told me what you said to her.'

Wait, what?

'We made up earlier. And it's true what they say about make-up sex being the best.'

Josh got back into bed and pulled the covers up over his head. Mikayla had *told* Toby that he'd said he liked her? After all she'd said about not liking how Toby treated him?

126

'I almost feel sorry for you that you'll never know what I'm talking about,' Toby continued. 'Almost.'

Josh rolled over onto his front and put the pillow over his head. *Shut up, Toby. Just shut up, shut up!* If there was one good thing, though, talking to Toby had broken the spell of his feverish, lustful dreams about Mikayla, and eventually he began to drift off to sleep.

Me and Gareth will get away for a few days soon. We'll leave all of this shit behind.

Natalie

27

For a brief moment, Natalie considered turning around and getting back in her car as she approached the steps of Hartbury Hotel. What had she been thinking? Could she really consider working here? But when she'd seen the job advertised – for a part time event manager, with a significant rise in salary from being Verity's assistant – she hadn't been able to resist applying. She could really spread her wings here and challenge herself. There was no way she could progress in Verity's business, and a fresh challenge would be good. Invigorating.

But now she was here, standing at the glass door beyond which she could glimpse the newly renovated reception, memories of her previous visit to the hotel flooded back. Toby was overbearing and officious – in fact, he was downright abusing his authority when it came to Chantelle, and no doubt some of his other female staff. Surely he would know better than to try anything with her – but would the environment be too toxic? *Maybe I could help, though. Perhaps with me here, keeping an eye on him, he'd rein himself in a bit.*

She reached for the door, then let her hand drop to her side again. *For God's sake! I have to make up my mind.* Josh concerned her, too. She still hadn't managed to tell him about the job. They'd had Christmas to get through, and she hadn't wanted to rock the boat. She sensed that he'd think her job loss was also his fault – especially as he knew they'd lost clients once because of the stupid allegations. It would be best to tell him once she already had a different job lined up. But was Toby's hotel really the answer?

Before she could finally make up her mind whether to go inside for her interview, the decision was made for her. Toby burst out from somewhere behind the reception desk and strode across to the door. She'd have to go in before he wondered why she was lurking around outside on a chilly January morning, sleet beginning to settle on her hair.

'Natalie,' he said. 'I wasn't sure if it could really be you when I read your application.'

'It would be a bit of a coincidence to have another Natalie Woodrough who works at Verity's Events,' she said with a laugh. She followed him inside and looked around at the new decor. The dark old-fashioned colours had been replaced with elegant sage-green walls, complemented by framed botanical prints. A huge light-fitting of curling ivory stems and leaves dominated the room and Natalie paused to admire it. 'You've really done a great job in here,' she said.

'Good, isn't it?' Toby said smugly. 'Cost a bit. And I had a few clashes with the designer–' He paused. 'Probably shouldn't say that if you're looking to work here. I'm a pussycat really. Right, Angelique?' he called over to the reception desk, where an immaculately dressed woman around Natalie's age flashed a smile. 'That's right,' she said, her voice carrying the merest hint of sarcasm along with her slight French accent. She turned back to her screen. 'A pussycat.'

'We'll talk in the conservatory, if you want?' Toby said. 'Normally I'd do interviews in my office–'

'I don't want any special favours,' Natalie said. 'Please just treat me like you would anyone else.'

'Okay, the office it is then.'

As she followed him down the corridor, the bare walls caught her attention. 'You took down your photos,' she said. 'You had pictures here of some of the local landmarks, didn't you?'

'Oh, yes,' he said dismissively. 'We took them down when the halls were painted. Not sure if I'll put them back up. I fancy a change. And besides, a lot of them were taken a while ago and are out of date. Sometimes trips down memory lane can be good, other times I don't like it so much.'

He stopped at a door with a sign reading Manager's Office and opened it for her. Inside was a small but tidy space, the things on Toby's desk lined up neatly. One of the items was a bottle of aftershave, and Natalie raised an eyebrow. Was that really for the benefit of his guests?

Toby had apparently taken her request to be treated like anyone else to heart, as he gave her a good grilling for the next thirty minutes or so, followed by another information dump about the hotel and the event manager role, leaving Natalie feeling like she'd had a mental workout by the end of it.

'Well, Nat, I think you'd be a good fit,' he said matter-of-factly. 'You don't have all the experience we're looking for, but you know events inside out and I can see you're passionate about weddings. And besides, we're family, or will be soon enough.'

'Toby, I don't want you to–'

He held a hand up. 'Honestly, Nat, the two other women I've interviewed, I couldn't see it working out. One of them had far too many opinions about how *I* should do *my* job, and the other, well, let's just say her face didn't really fit.'

Natalie stopped herself from asking what exactly he meant by this.

'The job's yours if you want it,' he said. 'I think we'd make a good team. Remind me when you finish at Verity's place?'

'Next week.'

'And what does Josh think about you applying here?' He watched her for a moment as she tried to think how to respond. 'You haven't told him?'

'I will, but there didn't seem much point until I'd had the interview.'

'Okay,' Toby said. 'Well, I would walk around the hotel with you again, explain a bit more, but my morning is jam-packed.'

'It's okay. I might just have a quick wander round by myself if you don't mind. Just re-familiarise myself with everything.'

'Great,' Toby said. 'I'll be in touch again later today, and we can have another chat and I'll let you know a few more details. Sorry it's been a bit rushed this morning.' He paused and gave her a grin. 'Well, welcome to the team!' he said. He thrust out his hand and she took it, and was treated to a firm and slightly clammy handshake, before he scuttled out of the room.

Natalie hesitated briefly outside the office door. Events Manager at Hartbury Hotel. Fizzles of excitement spread through her as she imagined it. If only the job wasn't at Toby's hotel so she didn't have to break the news to Josh that her new boss was his stepbrother.

After having a quick look at the function rooms, the dining room and the lovely conservatory again, Natalie made her way back into the reception. There were no guests around, so she walked over to the desk. It would be good to have a chat with Angelique – Natalie had sensed there was a bit more to her sarcasm about Toby's 'pussycat' comment than met the eye, and perhaps she could find out what it would really be like to work for Toby.

'Hi, I'm Natalie,' she said as she approached. 'I was just here about the event manager job.'

'Ah, yes,' Angelique said. 'It will be brilliant once we have some more help. At the moment Toby and I try to do the job between us, but now we offer wedding ceremonies it's too much for us.'

'Do you enjoy working here?' Natalie asked.

Angelique looked briefly taken aback by the question, but before she had a chance to answer, the phone rang. Natalie hovered around while she spoke to the caller. *I should have asked Toby how many weddings they already have booked for this year.* She made a mental note to ask him when he called her later. It would be good to know whether it was a trickle or if she'd be immediately snowed under.

'Sorry, what was it you asked me?' Angelique said once she'd finished her phone call.

'Oh, just if you enjoy it?' Natalie said. 'Is it busy here? A nice atmosphere?'

'Yes, it's busy. Toby likes things to run smoothly.'

Did she mean something more by that? The phone rang again so Natalie decided to take her leave. She'd hoped to find out a little more. Perhaps she could have a word with the young red-haired woman Toby had been bothering last time. Chantelle still concerned her a little, especially if she was more open to being manipulated, struggling for money with children to feed.

Natalie resolved to talk to Josh as soon as he got in from work. He'd been more settled since Christmas, and he'd be pleased that she'd found a new job that excited her. It's not like *he* would be the one seeing Toby every day, so there really wasn't anything for him to be worried about. And with all this lined up, losing her job with Verity didn't seem like a disaster any more – it was just a new step in her career. Yes. Josh would be fine about it.

Josh

28

The jangle of his phone broke Josh's concentration, and he picked it up in a bit of a daze.

'Josh?' Natalie said, her voice a little concerned. 'Where are you?'

He quickly checked the time. He would normally have been home half an hour ago, but he'd been so engrossed in helping Gareth that he'd lost track of time. 'I didn't realise it was late,' he said. 'Sorry, I should have told you.'

'Told me what?'

'There's a problem at Hearts. There was a security breach and Gareth asked if I could come and check it out after work.'

'Why you? He's got his own people, surely?'

'I know. He's just–' He lowered his voice as Gareth was sitting not too far away in his office with the door open. 'He's just a little paranoid. Hearts means so much to him, and I think he finds it reassuring to have me involved.'

'No,' Natalie said, a hint of irritation creeping into her voice and surprising him. 'He knows that you're an expert and he can get you to do it for free.' There was a pause. 'Josh, I didn't mean that. I know Gareth's not like that. I just … I really wanted you to be here tonight. I wanted to have a chat with you about something.'

'I can step outside the office for a minute and talk–'

'Not on the phone. In person.'

Josh glanced over at Gareth in his office. He'd never seen him so agitated. He'd actually said to Josh that he didn't trust anyone except him to figure out what was going on. He'd been obsessed about the privacy of the messages users had sent to each other, and though Josh had reassured him that hackers almost certainly didn't want that kind of information, it had done little to reassure him.

'Natalie, if you really need me I'll come home. Gareth will just have to make do with his own people.'

'No, I–' She was silent a moment. 'It's fine. Gareth needs you.'

'You're my priority. You know that, don't you? I *am* going to get my head straight. Nothing means more to me than you.'

'Thank you,' she said, her voice shaking a little.

'I'm coming home,' he said. 'If you're upset–'

'I'm not upset. It's absolutely fine, Josh, it's nothing bad. What I want to talk about will keep, but Gareth needs your help right now.'

A sense of unease crept through him as he put his phone back down on the desk beside him. She'd said it was nothing bad, but had something happened? Was it to do with her troll? She'd clearly been upset that she couldn't talk to him about whatever it was, and perhaps she'd just been trying to reassure him when she'd said it wasn't bad. He stood up, determined to go home to her anyway, when Gareth came out of his office.

'Any luck?' he said. 'Do you know what happened?'

'It's going to take a bit of time,' Josh said. At the concern on Gareth's face he sat back down. 'Don't worry, I'm going to check everything. It'll be okay.'

Gareth sat down at the empty desk beside him. Many of the Hearts employees had gone home, and the large open space was quiet, streetlights outside the windows lighting up the falling rain. It made Josh ache to be at home with Natalie, snuggled up on the sofa. 'You've been there for me right from the start of Hearts,' Gareth said.

'It's not a problem.'

'Did you ever think it would take off the way it has?'

'I don't know. I guess not, but not through any fault of yours.'

'I can't lose this, Josh. I can't have Hearts fucked up by this.'

Josh turned to face him. 'It won't come to that. I'm going to work out the extent of this with the help of your guys and then we'll figure out what steps to take.'

'Everyone will stop using it if they find out we got hacked–'

'Gareth, look, just don't panic. Let me work. We don't even know what happened yet.'

***

The evening wore on, and having already spent a full day at his regular job, Josh's mind at first rebelled against more work, but eventually the exhaustion gave way to a kind of restless energy. It put him in mind of all the nights he'd spent as a teenager behind a computer screen. He could have taken his life down a very different path if he'd wanted to. No one had realised quite how bloody good he was. He'd felt so powerful as he'd tested his skills those nights, pitting himself against his virtual adversaries, seeing how far he could get into their systems. He could have got whatever he wanted if he'd been willing to cross the line. But that was the thing. It was wrong. He didn't want to do anything bad or cause any harm, it was just the challenge. It was the rush, the absorption he had experienced that made the whole rest of the world fade away. There had been no Toby when he was at that keyboard. There had been no mum and stepdad, no Mikayla, no school, no anything. It had been another world completely.

I could find out who is trolling Natalie.

The thought sprang into his head and he brushed it aside. Yes, *maybe* he could.

I could make them pay. She means everything to me and I'm sitting back and letting her be tormented. I should get revenge.

He paused and took a sip from the cooling cup of coffee at his elbow. Since Gareth could do little to help with the investigation, he had taken on the role of bringing a constant stream of hot drinks. He'd also bought doughnuts with the comment it was like a police stakeout, and Josh had wondered if there was anything Gareth couldn't find some sort of humour in.

I'm just tired, he told himself. His thoughts often got weird at times like this. He was up too late, working too late, letting his thoughts run away with themselves. *I wish I could just go home and crawl into bed with Natalie.*

Natalie. Just the thought of her made him feel grounded. Safe. She was the thing he could hold on to, she was what made his life make sense and what made it worth living. *And I've been a rubbish partner to her recently.* He picked up his phone and messaged her to say he'd be back late and how much he loved her, but she didn't reply. She'd probably already gone to bed.

He finished the last of his coffee. He'd made good progress at Hearts and hopefully it wouldn't be too long now before he would be able to go home. Things would settle down soon. It was hardly surprising that Mikayla's death suddenly being brought up again after all this time would unnerve him and make him think about that unhappy part of his life, but he couldn't let it consume him. He'd hold on to Natalie, to the thought that soon they would be getting married, and he really would have a family of his own. Something stable and permanent. Somewhere he could belong, and get away from all his bad memories of Mikayla and Toby. He hadn't realised until he'd met her quite how much he needed that.

29

By the time Josh got back he was exhausted. Natalie stirred as he got into bed beside her, and then opened her eyes. 'What happened?' she asked sleepily. 'Did you sort it out?'

Josh yawned hugely. 'Well, there was some sort of breach,' he said. 'Not as bad as what Gareth feared, though. The database was accessed and it's possible the hackers may have got some information. Hearts are going to contact their users about what happened.'

'He must be upset.'

'He is, but he'll be okay, I'm sure of it.' He was silent for a moment before adding, 'It was odd, though.'

'What was odd?'

'Well, it looked like it had been hacked – I mean, the database had been accessed, but we couldn't really understand why or even how, really. I identified some security holes, but I feel kind of uneasy about it. It was a strange attack.'

Natalie was silent for a moment, and he snuggled up to her and kissed her hair. 'What did you want to talk to me about? You can tell me now–'

'It's the middle of the night,' she said, her voice already a little slurred as she drifted off again. Josh closed his eyes and tried to relax, but as he rolled over something poked into his back and he reached down to see what it was. Natalie's phone. She must have fallen asleep with it in her hand and it had dropped down into the bed. He held it in front of him, his mind racing. Should he just check it? Perhaps if he saw what she had been looking at he'd know what was bothering her. His mind made up, he traced her unlock pattern on the phone screen and was confronted with a post Natalie had made about her top five vegetarian canapés for parties, and the comments beneath it:

I wonder how Josh is going to kill you Natalie.

I hope your honeymoon isn't near any lakes
If you even live to see your honeymoon.
Josh drowned Mikayla. Face facts. Everyone knows it.
I hope he does kill you, maybe then you'll take me seriously. Except you'll be dead, lol.
If you believe in justice, do not follow Natalie Woodrough
Natalie's just as bad as her killer fiance

***

There she was: Mikayla! He thrashed through the water towards her, where she bobbed and sometimes disappeared below the surface. Her hand broke free, and she stretched it out towards him. Energy surged through him – he had to get to her!

She was beginning to sink again as he reached her; her eyes huge and dark and pleading, her jet-black hair floating around her like fine seaweed. He reached out and caught her arm, but instead of lifting her up he was pulling her down. She struggled, trying to prise his hand away, but he wouldn't relent. He would hold her there until she stopped moving. Forever. His breathing grew faster, his pulse racing as her struggles grew weaker, then horror surged through him. *No*, he tried to cry out. *No! Stop!*

He awoke to blackness. The past felt only a heartbeat away, like he could reach out and touch it, perhaps slip right back into it again. *That was real. That was a memory.*

No. No, it wasn't.

Yes, it was. That's what was real. The memory of saving her is fake.

He got out of bed and fled into the living room. The hateful comments swirled around in his head, mixing with the dream. *The memory.*

'Josh drowned Mikayla. Face facts. Everyone knows it.'

He tried to calm down. It had been a late night. He was worn out, confused, emotional. He wasn't thinking straight.

No. It's the rest of the time I'm not thinking straight. The dream was real. That dream is the only time I've been lucid since it happened.

Josh put his hands up to the sides of his head, pressing it like he could squeeze the thoughts away, and when Natalie came into the room he almost jumped out of his skin.

'Josh, what—'

'Stay away from me!' he told her, his voice high and panicked.

'What … what are you talking about?' She took a step towards him, though her eyes were frightened.

'Stay away!' he told her again. 'You're not – you're not safe here. You're not safe here with me.'

Since she showed no signs of doing what he asked, he took matters into his own hands. He fled the room, brushing past Natalie without a word. If he loved her, he had to make her safe. He had to make sure she wasn't around him.

At the lake

30

'Hey shithead!'

Josh rubbed his head where Toby had hit him, before turning to look at him, hoping he was mistaken and the voice belonged to someone else. But, no, sure enough Toby filled his vision, surrounded by a load of his stupid friends, and some girls too, including Mikayla. Josh quickly dropped his hand from his head – Mikayla would think he was pathetic just sat here licking his wounds. He should stand up for himself. For once. Anger surged through him. It had been a long time since he'd been brave enough to stand up to Toby, but having him turn up on what was supposed to be Josh's chance to get away was the last straw.

Toby must have seen the look in Josh's eyes as he laughed. 'I just wanted to see what you two lovebirds were up to, although I guess I'd rather not know the details–'

Josh leapt to his feet, all reason seeming to have left him. 'Just fuck off!' he yelled at Toby. 'Just leave us the fuck alone!'

Briefly, Toby's whole gang looked taken aback, and then they began to laugh. Painfully aware of how he must look through their eyes – his cheeks red and his eyes stinging with tears – Josh quickly turned back to Gareth. 'Come on,' he said, 'let's go.'

The laughter followed them as they disappeared into the trees, following the path around the lake.

'Josh–' Gareth started.

'Don't.'

'I was going to say you did good yelling at him. They might be laughing now, but you shut them up for a second.'

'I made a complete twat of myself.'

Gareth shrugged. 'Maybe. But let's face it, you can't really make it any worse than it already is.'

'*Mikayla* saw me.' Josh's anger rose again. 'And why the fuck are they even here?'

'You know why,' Gareth said. 'Toby wants to wind you up. So don't play into his hands. We'll just stay away from them. The lake is big enough that we don't have to go near them.'

***

The sun beat down, the heatwave that had started a couple of days before they came to the lake showing no signs of abating. Josh wiped his hand across his forehead, where a film of sweat had developed. Gareth elbowed him in the ribs. 'What?' Josh said.

Gareth rolled his eyes. 'Mikayla,' he said. 'You're staring at her. Again. I thought you were trying to get over her!'

'How can I get over her when they keep following us wherever we go!'

Their plan to stay away from Toby and his gang had proved futile. Every time they tried to move on, the others would just follow them.

Josh quickly tore his eyes away, and looked instead at his friend. Gareth was sprawled out on the grass beside him, his feet dangling into the water where it rippled against the bank. 'How can you be so calm?'

'They're obviously not going to quit following us,' Gareth said. 'We might as well make the best of it. They're not even talking to us, anyway. Just ignore them.'

Josh did his best, but his eyes kept betraying him, seeking out a glimpse of Mikayla. Right now, the party had split into three groups; Josh and Gareth, Toby with his gang, and the girls. Mikayla was sitting on top of a rock, with the other girls clustered around her, but they paled into insignificance next to her. Some were smoking, and a couple of others were vying for control of the music player in a good-natured squabble, the songs changing jarringly every minute or so. Mikayla was resplendent in denim shorts and a yellow bikini top, her pink t-shirt lying on the rock by her side. Her long black hair was loose over her shoulders, and she was laughing with her friends. Josh could feel his inadequacy next to Toby more keenly than ever; his stepbrother's gang had driven to the lake themselves and brought alcohol with them – the ground was already littered with cans and bottles where they were sitting – while Josh and Gareth had been dropped off by Josh's mum. Why on earth would Mikayla, or any of the girls, look twice at him? Especially after his ridiculous outburst earlier. She must think he was a total joke.

'Hey, Josh,' Toby yelled across, making him jump. 'Stop staring at Mikayla. Gareth will get jealous.'

'For God's sake,' Josh mumbled, turning his head away. 'Will he ever get tired of saying stuff like that about us?'

'He's coming over,' Gareth said.

Josh turned as Toby strode over to him. Toby had been drinking all afternoon – his face was red, and his steps a little unsteady. He aimed a kick at Josh, which Josh easily dodged.

'Maybe the two of you should loosen up a bit,' Toby said, smirking as if a brilliant idea had occurred to him, while an icy cold feeling spread through Josh despite the heat. At a gesture from Toby, two of his friends strolled up, holding a cheap bottle of vodka.

'Come on,' Toby said, holding out the bottle, 'drink it.'

'I don't want to.'

Toby thrust the bottle towards him, while his two idiot friends grinned. Josh snatched the bottle and took a swig, before trying to hand it back.

'More,' Toby said.

Josh drank a little more, and then before he knew what was happening the boys had grabbed him, Toby trying to force him to drink more and more of the burning liquid. There was a cacophony of laughter, and then shouting. Mikayla came and grabbed the bottle from Toby's hand. 'What the fuck are you doing?' she shouted at Toby, while Josh coughed and spluttered.

'It'll do him good,' Toby said. 'He needs to lighten up.'

'You're going to make him sick,' Mikayla said. Right on cue, Josh lurched to his feet as his stomach rejected the influx of alcohol. He just about managed to make it to a nearby bush before throwing up. Laughter erupted again, while Mikayla said, 'See?'

Toby was laughing too much to care how angry his girlfriend was. 'Oh my God, Josh,' he said, as he quickly whipped out his camera to capture the scene. 'You are pathetic. Totally pathetic.'

31

'I can't believe he's doing this!' Josh hissed to Gareth. The pair were hidden amongst the trees, spying on Toby as the evening wore on. Josh had hoped the other kids would all leave, and he'd grown increasingly despondent as it became obvious they were going to stay half the night. Maybe even until the morning. Toby and one of the girls had left the main group, and Josh was outraged when Toby put his arm around the girl's waist. 'He's already got Mikayla!' he whispered to Gareth. 'How can he—'

'Mikayla's not stupid,' Gareth said. 'She's been angry with him all afternoon – soon she'll realise what a dickhead he is and break up with him.'

'She's known for months that he's a dickhead. It's not exactly hard to see that.'

'Anyway, he'll not be around much longer,' Gareth said philosophically.

'You hope,' Josh said. 'No guarantee he'll go to uni, is there?'

Gareth nodded. 'That's true. He is pretty fucking stupid.'

They were silent for a while, as Josh stared moodily at Toby trying it on with the girl. He felt a stab of satisfaction as she rejected his advances, and eventually she stood up to leave.

'Bitch,' Toby muttered, as she disappeared back towards the lake.

'I'll make sure he goes to uni,' Josh said quietly, with more conviction than he really felt. 'He has to go.'

A slow grin crept across Gareth's face. 'You're going to do it? You're going to change his grades?'

Josh didn't answer. Was he really? He'd toyed with the idea over and over, especially as Toby had had zero interest in doing any revision before his exams, and seemed set to fail. But it was crazy, surely? And besides, he probably wouldn't be able to hack into the exam board. He could do a lot – but surely that was a step too far.

Gareth pulled his backpack closer to him, reached inside and pulled out a carrier bag. 'They're not as smart as they think they are,' he said. He opened the bag, which contained several cans of cider. 'I nicked this off them earlier.'

Gareth grinned widely, and Josh looked at him in admiration. Then he grew nervous. 'They'll flip out if they realise.'

'Nah. It'll be fine. The whole lot of them are wasted, they won't even notice.'

***

As dusk fell, Josh and Gareth retreated to their tent in the campsite for a while, keen to stay away from Toby. For the moment at least, he seemed to have forgotten about them, and they had no desire to remind him of their presence.

'What are you going to do?' Josh asked at length, as Gareth opened another can of cider. 'I ... I walked up to your house the other day. I know you didn't want me to, but I had to see it–'

'S'okay,' Gareth said, his voice slightly slurred. 'I'm sure Toby showed you the photos he took.'

'No,' Josh said, 'he took photos?'

'Yeah. I tried to break his stupid camera. Mikayla said she told him not to show anyone. I guess he listened to her.'

'You can't really live there like that, can you?'

'Funnily enough,' Gareth said, 'I said that to my mum earlier today, before we came here. I told her I'm moving out.'

'You're going to run away?'

'No. I'm going to move out. Properly. I want to make my life better, not worse. Running away and ending up on the street won't help me. I'm going to find somewhere to live.'

'Really?' Josh asked. 'Can you do that?'

'Kids can leave home when they're sixteen,' Gareth said casually, as if it was no big deal. 'I've been looking into it. It's not easy, but it's what I'm going to do.'

'What did your mum say?'

Gareth winced, and Josh was taken aback. Usually he showed about as much emotion as a rock. 'It was bad,' he said. 'Crying, hysterics. She said I was doing it to punish her. I told her it was just because of the bloody house.'

'Gareth—'

'I know it isn't her fault, but being inside that house is like living inside her head.'

Josh nodded helplessly. He couldn't imagine it. Although he did know what it was like to hate going back home.

'Is she going to let you go?'

'I don't think she can stop me. She said I won't survive a week on my own, but I will. I'm more resourceful than she thinks.'

Josh looked at him seriously. 'I'll come with you,' he said. 'When you leave, I'll leave my house too. I hate being there.'

Gareth looked at him blearily. 'This is real life, Josh. It's not like when we used to talk about getting on a train out of Wayfield and starting again. I'm sorry, but you're not cut out for this.'

'Yes, I am!' Josh insisted. 'We'll go together. I'm not letting you go on your own.'

'You're just drunk,' Gareth said. 'I'm serious about this.'

'So am I.'

32

'Josh? Can I talk to you for a second?'

He pulled the tent flap open and stared in surprise at Mikayla.

'Yeah,' he said, 'what's wrong?'

'I…' She caught sight of Gareth. 'Can I talk to you alone?'

Josh exchanged a look with Gareth, who shrugged.

'Okay,' Josh said, hope blooming inside him.

'I'm sorry Toby brought us all here this weekend,' she said, as they walked back down towards the lake. 'I didn't know you and Gareth would be here. It wasn't until he came up to you–'

'And smacked me round the head?'

'Yeah,' she said. 'I told him to leave you alone.'

For some reason, Josh found this infuriating. 'I don't need you to fight my battles for me!' he said. 'I can deal with things myself.'

'Can you?' she shot back.

Josh kicked at the ground moodily. What did Mikayla want? It obviously wasn't going to be a declaration of love. And it was getting quite dark; he wanted to get back to the campsite before they lost the light completely.

'Why do you stay with him? If you don't like the kind of person he is?'

'Josh, I just didn't want you to think I came here deliberately to mess up your weekend–'

'Whatever,' Josh said, turning round abruptly. 'I'm going back.'

'I think I've met someone else,' she said.

A stab of pain went through Josh's chest and he paused. 'Why are you telling *me*? I don't want to know about it.'

'I don't know. I guess … I'm kind of worried how Toby will react when I tell him. I thought maybe you could help to smooth things over, if he finds out and kicks off.'

Josh stared at her. She wanted him to do *what?* The infatuated part of him was ready to instantly agree to whatever she asked, but part of him was angry. She was smiling faintly, her head a little to one side. *I wonder what her hair feels like.* She smelled good, too; flowery and fresh. *I just want to lick her everywhere that scent has touched.* His cheeks flooded with heat. Where the hell had that come from? He couldn't think things like that in front of her! Her eyes were dark and glittering. *Does she know what I just thought?* His head felt thick and heavy with drink. He just wanted to go back and discuss with Gareth how they would get away from their respective parents and start a new life. Then he wanted to sleep. For a long time.

'There's this guy at my work, at the pet shop,' she said. 'But he's older. Like, twenty.'

'That's too old,' Josh said.

'Do you think so? I think he thought so, to begin with. He tries to act like he's not interested, but then, the other day we were talking, and we kissed.'

Josh felt like she'd reached in, grabbed his heart, and squeezed it. What was she trying to achieve by telling him? Did she really want his advice? Was it some sort of test? Was she enjoying tormenting him?

'He said it was a mistake. Do you think he meant it? He won't talk to me now, but I think he just doesn't want to admit how he feels.'

'Mikayla—'

'Do you think Toby is *really* that into me? I kind of want to be with the guy from work, but do I want to break up with Toby when I don't know if he's really that interested?'

'Toby was flirting with one of your friends earlier.'

Mikayla looked at him like he was a little kid. 'Everyone flirts, you know. It's not a big deal.'

Josh was almost speechless in his despair and disbelief. Why couldn't she like the one person who loved her more than anything on this earth? 'I'm in love with you,' he said stupidly, even though it was pointless. She already knew, and she didn't care.

Mikayla blinked. 'Josh–'

'You'd never have to wonder how *I* felt about you. *I* wouldn't flirt with anyone else.'

To his horror, she burst out laughing. 'Josh – sorry – Josh, it's just your face. You look so serious. We're never going to happen, I want someone mature, not someone like...' She trailed off uncomfortably.

'Not someone like me?'

'No. Sorry, Josh. It's not you–'

At her flimsy, weak attempt to reassure him, it was like something broke inside him. 'Just leave me alone!' he cried, hating how pathetic he sounded. 'Just all of you, just leave me alone!'

And with that he turned and ran back towards the campsite, without a backwards glance.

Natalie

33

'So, where is he now?' Gareth asked.

Natalie clutched the phone tightly to her ear as she went over to the kitchen window and looked down at the dark street below, huge puddles glistening in the glow of streetlights. Josh still sat inside his car, and showed no sign of getting out.

'In his car still.'

'Has he said he's going to go anywhere?'

'No. He was saying it wasn't safe for me to be around him, then he pulled on some clothes and went out to the car. I don't know whether to go down and speak to him – that's why I called you. He was with you tonight, was he okay earlier? Do you know what's happened?'

She leant against the worktop, physically and emotionally drained. It was three a.m. What the hell was going on? Why was Josh doing this?

A sob crept into Natalie's voice. 'I don't know what the hell to do. I'm scared … I'm scared he's going to do something–' Unable to finish the sentence, she slumped down into a chair at the dining table. 'Gareth, I wouldn't have called if I had any idea what to say to help him, but I don't. I know it's the middle of the night, but is there any chance you could come and talk to him? He might listen to you.'

She breathed a sigh of relief as his voice filled her ear. 'I'm on my way.'

***

The only light Natalie could see in the car was the dim gleam of Gareth's phone, which he'd left on the dashboard as he sat talking to Josh. By the time Gareth eventually came to speak to her she'd given up staring out of the window, and was curled up on the sofa with her eyes closed, though there was no chance she could sleep.

He placed his hand gently on her shoulder and she turned. 'So, I've had a long chat with him,' Gareth said.

'And?'

He sat down beside her. 'Well, it's still this business about Mikayla. He saw a load of comments tonight about him being the killer and he just can't see it clearly.'

'In what way?' Natalie asked nervously.

'He thinks that what they're saying is true,' Gareth said, after a pause. 'He's saying he wants to go to Chedford Lake and figure out what happened there once and for all.'

Natalie stared at him. This couldn't be happening. 'But he tried to save her...' she said helplessly.

'I know that. You know that. He seems to think he might have killed her and then somehow invented these memories of trying to save her—'

'But that's completely crazy!' Natalie said. 'It's just...' She paused, and had to choke out the next words as anger overwhelmed her. 'It's this fucking *idiot* writing all this nonsense online. He was absolutely fine before it started.'

Gareth nodded. 'I know. The problem is, Josh always doubts himself. After so long where he was blamed for everything that went wrong when he was still at home, he started to believe it himself. Sometimes he even feels like it was his own fault Toby bullied him. He was so fragile already when he was a kid and Toby started spreading rumours that Josh did something to Mikayla. Having that suspicion, even if only idiots believed it, just wrecked his head. And now it's all happening again. He says he needs to keep you safe and that he can't trust his own memories.'

'Gareth, what do we do? Just tell me what we can do. I'll do anything.'

'You can keep telling Josh you know he didn't do it.'

'That's not enough. I need more than that. I've been over it with him before, about how there was an inquest, about how they would have been able to tell in the post-mortem if someone had hurt her or she was trying to fight them off–'

'She had a lot of alcohol in her system,' Gareth said. 'She may not have been able to fight. Josh knows that. It doesn't matter how many facts you give him; he'll just find some way round it and argue that it could still have been him.'

'So what do I do?'

'I guess you could try to persuade him to talk to someone. This isn't exactly normal–'

'And have him start saying he thinks he killed someone?'

Gareth thought for a moment. 'Maybe that's not such a great idea.'

Natalie swallowed hard. 'I think I need to figure out exactly what happened that weekend. Verity said she heard someone else was there, maybe I can find out who–'

'Josh told me about this theory. God knows why anyone is still talking about it, let alone taking it seriously.'

'You saw Josh!' she pleaded. 'It's *killing* him, Gareth. Help me get in touch with people from that weekend. Maybe it *is* Toby we should be suspicious of, not this stranger, if they even exist. *Toby* was Mikayla's boyfriend. Maybe he pointed the finger at Josh to take the focus away from himself. Maybe he did something he shouldn't have and ended up getting away with it.'

Gareth was silent for a long time, and then he nodded. 'Well, there is something I should probably tell you both. I do know a bit more about what happened at the lake, but I had my reasons for keeping it to myself.'

Natalie's breath caught in her throat. 'Really? You know something that could help Josh?'

'I think so, yes. But first we need to get him to come back inside.'

The day of Mikayla's death

Josh

34

Once the sun had begun to rise, Josh and Gareth crept down into the trees behind the tent, keen to spy on Toby again. They were both hung-over, and after a few minutes Gareth complained that he wanted to go to sleep, but Josh shushed him. 'They're going to hear us,' he hissed.

They reached a good spot in the trees. Most of the girls had gone now; only Mikayla and one other girl had stayed overnight, along with most of the boys. Josh assumed they'd stayed up talking most of the night, and when they peeped out through the trees they saw the small group, a few of them still asleep with jackets over them, surrounded by empty bottles and cans, the rest talking quietly. Although it was early, the day already felt warm. Toby and Mikayla were nearby and from their body language they didn't seem like they were getting along too well, though Gareth and Josh couldn't hear the words.

'I guess she's still pissed off with him,' Gareth whispered.

Josh's face flushed with anger. 'If he's upset her again...'

'Come on, Josh, give it a rest. I thought you were angry with her last night, after all that stuff she was telling you about liking that other guy—'

Josh didn't reply. He didn't want to remember that conversation.

'Screw this,' Gareth said, 'I'm going back to bed. Nobody should be up this early in the morning.'

***

Josh woke up again to bright sunshine filling the inside of the tent with a yellow glow. It was hot and stuffy, and Gareth wasn't there. He groaned. He hadn't expected to fall asleep again; he'd intended to hide away in here moping until he eventually felt able to come out and face everybody.

The tent door's zip shot upwards, startling him, and Gareth came in. Sitting down heavily, he said, 'You know what, we should probably just go home. I don't want to see any more of Toby, he's pissing me off. The weekend's already ruined.'

'What's Toby doing?' Josh asked.

'I don't know where he is right now, but all the others are still down there. They don't look like they're going to move any time soon, so I can't see the point in us staying.'

Josh sighed. 'Okay.' He rubbed his face with his hands. 'I feel like shit. I need some air.'

'Yeah, it's fucking hot, isn't it?'

Outside, Josh blinked in the sunlight. It *was* fucking hot. He couldn't bear being in the campsite anymore, or near Toby, or any of them. This was supposed to be an escape. Somewhere away from Toby, and his family, and everything that made him unhappy. He kicked at the dusty ground angrily, making his way down through the trees towards the path around the lake. It wouldn't take too long to walk around it. There was a nice secluded area on the other side. He could sit down there and collect his thoughts for a while.

Natalie

35

'It was while you went back to sleep in the tent,' Gareth said to Josh.

Natalie turned to him expectantly, though Josh still seemed to be in some sort of trance. They had managed to get him to come back inside, though, which was something.

'What was?' she asked.

'Well, when we went back into the tent in the morning, I couldn't get to sleep. So I went back out and I saw Toby and Mikayla sneak off to talk in private. They were pretty angry with each other. I just thought it would be funny, to follow them and hear what they were talking about. I thought we could use it to wind Toby up. They walked down the main path, and I stayed in the trees, following them. They were talking, and I couldn't hear them. Then all of a sudden they stopped walking. They were shouting.'

'What were they saying?'

'She'd broken up with him. And he was not pleased.'

'They'd broken up?' Natalie asked. 'She broke up with him just before she died?'

'Yes,' Gareth said. 'Mikayla told him she didn't want to be with him any more, and that there was someone else, too. The guy she told Josh about, I guess.'

'Mikayla liked someone else?' she said to Josh.

He nodded listlessly.

'Josh, did you hear what Gareth said? Mikayla broke up with Toby just before she died.'

'It makes no difference.'

'It makes all the difference!' she said, wanting to grab him and shake him. But he'd gone too far inside his shell, so she turned back to Gareth.

'What did Toby say about that?'

'Toby was furious with her. He yelled at her to get away from him, and she ran off towards the clearing, where she went swimming. I turned straight around and ran back through the trees to the campsite. I was pretty angry with Toby. Mikayla was nice to us. Well, she sort of was. Either way, she didn't deserve for him to react like that. It was scary – I mean, not for me, but it would have been for someone on the receiving end of that anger. But after they argued, I didn't see where Toby went.'

Natalie curled a tendril of her hair around her fingers. 'That doesn't look great for him,' she said at length. 'It would raise a few questions, anyway.'

'Exactly,' Gareth said. 'He was Mikayla's boyfriend, and I'm sure the police talked to him—'

'They did,' Josh said, and Natalie turned at the sound of his voice. So he *was* listening and taking it in.

'But nobody knew they had broken up apart from me.'

Josh turned to look at him. 'Why didn't you tell the police?'

'Because I used it to get something I felt was more important. Me and you couldn't leave any more, like we'd planned to, not straight away anyway. We couldn't run away when there was about to be an inquest – it would have looked way too suspicious. But I knew you couldn't deal with Toby. Even if he was leaving for uni that autumn, I knew you wouldn't be able to make it through the rest of that summer. So I made a deal with him.'

'What kind of deal?'

Gareth shrugged. 'I wouldn't tell the police about the argument if he left you alone. And it worked, didn't it?'

'You – you put *me* above justice for Mikayla?'

'I had to. It wasn't easy to keep quiet, but it was too late for Mikayla. Nothing could bring her back. But Toby was making your life hell, and I had the chance to stop him. So I took it. I don't regret it. I'd do it all over again.'

'Do you … do you actually think he could have done something to her?' Natalie asked quietly, after a long pause.

'Yeah,' Gareth said. 'He was angry enough, I think. He had a nasty temper. Well, you've met him, haven't you? You know what he's like. But as I said, I didn't see where he went after the argument. He could have made his way back towards the campsite, he could have gone after Mikayla. I have no idea.'

'I can't believe you lied about this,' Josh said. 'You protected him.'

'No,' Gareth said firmly. 'No, I did not. I protected you. I couldn't care less about Toby. I would have liked to see him get what's coming to him. It was infuriating not to be able to tell the police and see him squirm, but you were more important to me than that. I didn't have anyone else apart from you. If it wasn't for you I would have completely lost my shit back then.'

***

Once Gareth had gone, Natalie put her hand over Josh's. 'You see,' she said, 'it makes no sense for it to be you.'

'I was jealous too. She told me she liked someone else the night before she died. I was angry about it.'

'Then you would have done something straight away, if you were capable of it, which you're not. You wouldn't have slept on it and then decided to kill her the next day, would you?'

'Natalie—'

'No, Josh. This troll, they're trying to get a reaction. It's not real. They probably don't really believe any of this stuff, they just want attention. It is nonsense. I don't really believe Toby did anything to her either, even if he was angry. I truly believe it was an accident. Gareth has it in for Toby, of course he's going to cast him in the worst light. But the truth is Mikayla was still drunk from the night before, went swimming in a dangerous lake and drowned. She's not the first person to do something like that and sadly she won't be the last. Deep down, you know that, Josh. You *know* that.'

She squeezed his hand, but he wouldn't meet her eye, just gazed silently across the room, lost in his own thoughts again. But then he turned to face her. 'You never did talk to me,' he said. 'You said you needed to.'

She sighed. 'It's just ... Verity has let me go, that's all.'

'You've lost your job?'

'Well, yes. But I think it might be good for me. It's time for a change.' She stopped short of mentioning Hartbury Hotel. He wouldn't be able to deal with that right now.

'When's your last day?'

'The end of this week.'

He shook his head. 'I'm so sorry, Natalie,' he said. 'I'm so sorry about all of this.'

She put her arms around him. 'I know,' she whispered. 'I know. But you are stronger than this. No matter what anyone made you believe in the past, you are stronger than this, and you are *good*, Josh. You really are.'

36

'I just wanted to come and see how you are,' Verity said as Natalie let her in to the flat. 'I don't have much on this morning, and I know it must feel really weird this week now you're not coming into the shop–'

'Honestly, V, I don't want you to worry,' Natalie said. 'Come in and sit down. I'll make you a coffee.'

Once they were sat together on the sofa, Verity smiled at Natalie's outfit. 'I'm glad you're taking it easy for a bit.'

Natalie looked down at herself – she'd forgotten she was yet to get dressed, and was currently wearing a pair of pyjama bottoms and a sleeveless pale blue t-shirt, with a large picture of a watermelon slice and the word 'Juicy!' written underneath. Tendrils of red hair escaped from the messy bun she'd piled her hair into. 'Yesterday I was bustling around sorting out wedding stuff, filming a new video, but today I feel kind of lazy.'

'I'm not surprised. You've been under a lot of pressure.'

'Well, you'll be reassured to know that I think I've found another job already,' Natalie said, as she moved a heap of wedding magazines from the coffee table so they could put their mugs down. 'I won't say too much about it because I haven't formally accepted yet, but I'm excited. So you really don't need to be concerned about me. And if you do ever need a hand with something, you can still come to me and I'll do whatever I can.'

'Thanks, Nat,' Verity said, 'I appreciate that. And that's great you've found something else. I'm so pleased for you.'

'Like I said, it's not a done deal yet. But I think it could be good for me.'

'So, what's your new video about?' Verity asked, taking a big sip of coffee and settling back against the sofa cushions.

'Bridal hair, and veils.'

Verity sat forward again eagerly. 'Oh, please tell me what you're going to have!'

'I haven't decided yet! Anyway, I need to edit the video first.' She gestured vaguely towards Josh's laptop on the coffee table. 'Josh has had to get used to me hogging his laptop all the time now. It's way better than mine.'

'I think it's great that you're still carrying on with the vlog, Nat. Considering all that's happened.'

'Well, I'm hardly going to give up just like that. Lots of people enjoy watching it, and even if it's a bit less fun for me right now, I have to believe this won't go on forever.'

***

Despite what she'd said to Verity, Natalie couldn't bring herself to edit the video straight away. Talking about veils in her video was bound to set off a whole new spate of insults about her scars and how she should hide her face, and she couldn't deal with it right now. After showering and dressing, she headed outside, hoping a walk in the fresh air would blow away some of the lethargy that was beginning to settle. It was spitting with rain, but the sun was trying to break through the clouds, and besides, she hated not being active. It felt like this after her accident, while she was recovering. In the end she walked much further than she'd originally planned, and by the time she got back to the flat her feet were aching.

'Toby!' she said, surprised by the figure she found standing outside the flat. 'What are you doing here?'

'I was going to phone you, but then I thought it would be nice to see you in person to formally offer you the event manager position.'

'Oh,' Natalie said, taken aback. 'Well, thank you. It's kind of you to come round. You'll have to excuse me, though, I've just been for a long walk and I've worn myself out–'

'Let's talk inside, then. You sit down and I'll make you a cuppa.'

Natalie sighed inwardly. There wasn't really any refusing him, not when he was about to become her new boss. And it would be good to start thinking about her new position. She wasn't exactly enjoying having time on her hands right now.

Once inside, he insisted that she sit down, despite her protests that really she should be making the drinks, and before long he handed her a mug of strong tea. She had to admit she was grateful to accept it as she made herself comfortable on the sofa.

'You look to me like you need some TLC,' Toby remarked after giving her an appraising look.

'I'm okay,' she said. 'It's been a trying few weeks, that's all.'

Toby looked around the flat. 'You've certainly put your mark on this place.'

She nodded. Josh's flat had started out modern and minimal, but she'd added a layer of colour to everything. The grey sofa – which looked like a piece of office furniture – had acquired a trio of cushions from her flat that clashed so comprehensively with it that she'd had to laugh when she'd first put them down; one was bright yellow with a flamingo on it, another hot pink and emblazoned with pineapples, while a third was blue and extremely fluffy. Equally, the high-gloss white kitchen had gained an array of bright pink, yellow and blue accessories, and a stripy pot containing a large round cactus sat in the centre of Josh's glass dining table.

'Does Josh like all this stuff?' Toby asked, his fingers resting on the blue fluffy cushion.

Is he saying my stuff is ugly? Her head started to throb. She hadn't had time to brace herself for a conversation with Toby.

'So, will you take the job?' he asked, without waiting for a reply to his dig about her home decor.

'Uh…' she faltered. Last week she'd been sure that Josh would see past the fact it was Toby's hotel and be happy for her, but now she wasn't so sure. The way he'd broken down and started to believe he'd been responsible for Mikayla's death had shaken her, and despite what she'd said to Verity about being excited and feeling the new job would be good for her, she was still uneasy about it.

'If you've got reservations because of Josh – because you think it might be a bit weird if you're working for me–'

'No,' she lied. 'It's fine.' She paused. 'Could I just let you know later today, maybe tomorrow? Would that be okay?'

An uncomfortable feeling settled in her stomach. *I have to talk to Josh about it first.* She'd talk to him that night, she promised herself. And she really would this time. She couldn't hide it from him any longer and she shouldn't be trying to. Lies and secrets were the last thing their relationship needed right now.

'That's absolutely fine, Nat. But are you sure you're okay?' he said. 'You do look a bit under the weather.'

She was forced to agree. 'I do feel tired,' she said.

'Why don't you go and lie down? Get some beauty sleep? We need you on top form if you're starting at Hartbury, after all.'

'I–'

'I'll tidy up in here if you want,' he said, glancing at the mugs on the table. 'I can load the dishwasher or something.'

'Don't you need to be at the hotel?'

'Afternoon off,' he said.

'Then surely you'd rather be doing something more exciting than tidying?'

He wouldn't take the hint, though. In the end, she admitted defeat and went to lie down. Her head was really pounding now. Surely as soon as he'd done the tidying Toby would leave her in peace.

She must have been even more tired than she realised, as when she woke it was late afternoon. There was no sign of Toby, but he'd tidied up as he promised, the dishwasher whirring away, her wedding magazines stacked neatly, and her scatter cushions plumped and arranged in a neat row on the sofa. Natalie felt refreshed, and grateful to him. It had been a kind gesture, even if the way he treated other people left a lot to be desired. Perhaps she would try to get the video edited before Josh got home from work. It would be nice to feel like she'd achieved something.

Sitting down on the sofa, she pulled Josh's laptop onto her lap and opened it. Then, after spending a minute or so trying desperately to make sense of what she was seeing on the screen, she pushed it away from her with a cry.

37

'So, I was thinking,' Josh said, as soon as he got in, 'I know I've been a nightmare recently, but you and Gareth have really helped me see sense. Maybe I could take some days off work and we can spend some time together? We could sort out some wedding stuff if you want, or maybe go away for a night or two. I want to spoil you after what an idiot I've been. What do you...'

His words trailed off when he saw her face, and she turned away from him, staring at his laptop screen. She had to be misunderstanding this. It couldn't be what she thought it was.

'How ... how did it go today?' he asked uncertainly. 'Did you get up to anything much? I know you weren't really looking forward to being at home–'

Natalie's eyes rested on the screen again. Josh. *Josh* had been the one trolling her? It couldn't be true. But right here before her eyes was an account logged in under the name of her lead attacker. Josh had been using the laptop last night; he'd clearly forgotten to close the page before he went to bed.

'Natalie?' he said, making his way across the room towards her. 'You're scaring me. What's wrong? What's happened?'

'You tell me!' she said, thrusting the laptop towards him. He took it from her and his eyes searched the screen frantically. He genuinely didn't seem to understand to begin with, but then horror spread across his face. He looked at her helplessly. 'This wasn't ... Nat, you don't think this was me, do you? I've got nothing to do with this account, I've never seen this before–'

'Then why is it on your laptop?' she exploded. 'No one else uses this, apart from me!'

Josh shook his head, panic filling his eyes. 'Natalie, I swear ... I swear on my life, I have nothing to do with this! Someone else must have done it...'

As pain began to bloom inside her at his betrayal, the realisation hit her like a bus. Of course *Josh* hadn't done it! It was obvious from his face that he hadn't, and no matter the low opinion he had of himself, she knew him better than that. It was a trick. A horrible, twisted trick.

'Natalie,' Josh said, reaching out to her desperately, 'you know me. I'm disgusted by what's been said to you! You know how beautiful I think you are, I'd never say anything bad about your scars, and as for the accusations, I'd hardly make them about myself...' He trailed off, his eyes wide and pleading, willing her to believe him.

She tried to block out his voice. *Think.* Toby had been left alone in the flat for who knew how long that afternoon. She'd fallen asleep before hearing him leave, so he'd had ample time to frame Josh. After all, there had been no need for him to offer her the job in person – it had felt odd at the time that he'd gone out of his way to come round.

'Natalie?' Josh said. 'Talk to me. Please–'

'I need to get some air,' she said.

Josh didn't try to stop her leaving, though the look in his eyes wrenched her heart. But she didn't want to say anything. Not yet. She couldn't inflame the situation between him and Toby – Josh would go mad if he knew Toby was behind it and would probably go to confront him, and she needed the job at the hotel. She couldn't sit at home twiddling her thumbs like she had to after the car crash. She couldn't go back to that.

Outside in the cool night air, she took a few deep breaths. *There has to be a way to sort this out.* Why had she shown the laptop to Josh? Why had she doubted him for even a second? The best way to solve Toby's sick games would be for her to pretend she'd never seen what he'd done. To ignore his stupid provocation.

She turned as the door opened behind her, and Josh spilled out onto the street. His demeanour had worsened significantly during the five minutes she'd been standing outside, and now he looked distraught, almost as though he was in physical pain. Had the brave face he'd put on when he got home from work all been a facade? Had he really still been crumbling inside as he suggested they spend time together? It tore her heart to see him this way.

'Maybe it *was* me,' he said. 'It could have been me.'

'Josh–'

'I was on the laptop last night, I thought … I thought I was just–'

'Stop,' she said, tears springing to her eyes at how much he doubted himself. 'Stop it, please–'

'I still have nightmares about Mikayla,' he said. 'I thought I was starting to get over it. But they're not nightmares. They're memories, just like I told you and Gareth. I killed her, Natalie. I know – I *know* I did. I must have killed her, and it must have been me who did all of this to you. It was my conscience trying to get me to remember – that's why the comments were all accusing me!' He reached out towards her. 'It all makes sense. Everyone could see it apart from me. Everyone suspected me back then, and they were right to!'

'No, they didn't,' she said. 'Hardly anyone suspected you.'

'Why are you being kind to me? You saw what I did! I don't deserve anything from you. I–' He paused, building himself up to say it, 'I'm going to turn myself in,' he said. 'I should have done it a long time ago. That's why my life has never gone right. I've just been living on borrowed time.' His voice was speeding up as his thoughts ran away with him. 'You can't live properly when you've killed someone. How could you? There comes a point when you have to wake up and accept what everyone around you is saying.'

38

'Natalie! What on earth…?'

Natalie struggled to find the right words as she stood, shaking with emotion, on Verity's doorstep. Verity's eyes were huge with concern as she took in her distraught and dishevelled state.

When Natalie made no reply, Verity stood aside to let her in, deftly moving a few stray shoes and a schoolbag out of the way before Natalie could trip over them. It was quiet inside the house, and Verity was wearing pyjama bottoms and a long grey jumper, her glossy chestnut curls hanging loose over her shoulders. 'Rob's out with some friends and the girls are in bed,' she said. 'I'll make you some tea … or do you need something stronger? You're as white as a sheet.'

'Just tea,' Natalie said, 'I need to keep my head clear. I need to think.'

She sat down gratefully at the large table in the kitchen, while Verity bustled around before placing two mugs and a plate of biscuits down on the table. For a brief, surreal moment it was as if nothing had happened and she'd just popped round for a chat, but then the mess she and Josh were in hit her like a thunderbolt.

'Right,' Verity said as she sat down, 'what exactly has been going on?'

'I – to be honest I barely know myself.'

'Is it Josh? Did you have an argument?'

Natalie put her head in her hands. She'd managed to persuade Josh not to march straight down to the police station and hand himself in, and she'd grabbed a few things and got in her car to flee to Verity's with barely another word to him. If she'd stayed, she wouldn't have been able to stop herself blurting out that it was Toby, and all hell would have broken loose. *But all hell has broken loose already. Josh is completely crushed. Will he even listen to me*

167

about not turning himself in? If he goes and confesses, who knows what will happen.

'I need to make a phone call,' she said. 'Can you just give me a second?'

Verity nodded, and Natalie slipped into the living room and closed the door behind her. Josh had stood helplessly as she'd gone back inside the flat and stuffed some clothes and toiletries into a bag. At one point he'd offered to help her. He said it was the least he could do after how he'd treated her. A tear slid down her cheek. She'd just ignored him. She hadn't been able to trust herself to speak.

Wiping away her tears, she decided against calling Josh, which had been her first instinct. Instead she called Gareth. Josh needed someone with him, but it couldn't be her right now.

Once she'd finished her call there was a soft knock on the door, and Verity came inside and placed the tea and biscuits down on the coffee table.

'Natalie?' Verity said gently, 'please talk to me.'

Natalie tried to fight her tears, but she couldn't and Verity put her arms around her. The conversation with Gareth had been dreadful. He'd accused her of giving up on Josh and leaving him when he needed her most. *And he's right.* But she couldn't tell Gareth why she'd done it. She couldn't tell anyone her suspicions about Toby, not yet. She had to let Gareth believe she'd just walked out on Josh, and she'd taken all the criticism Gareth had thrown at her. At least it showed he cared about Josh – if anyone could get through to him tonight, Gareth could.

'Natalie, you don't have to tell me what's happened,' Verity said, 'but it might help if you can talk about it?'

Natalie pulled away from her. All she wanted was to be alone. She mumbled some excuse and ran out of the house again, grabbing her coat on the way. The blast of cold air outside cleared her head a little, and she pulled her coat tightly around her before setting off down the street towards town. Toby had ample time in her flat to frame Josh. That was a fact. But why?

Did he hate his stepbrother so much that he got satisfaction from hurting him any way he could?

Gareth's words came back to her about Toby and Mikayla breaking up at the lake.

Mikayla told him she didn't want to be with him any more.

Could it be possible? Could Toby really have killed her? She jumped as a burst of laughter erupted from around the corner – a drunk couple emerged from the pub, staggering across the road. She was almost in town now, and without thinking she made her way down towards the river.

So, she said to herself, trying to be as clear-headed as she could, let's suppose, just for a moment, that Toby had killed Mikayla. If so, why draw attention to her death again? Even if his posts were accusing *Josh*, surely he'd rather no one was thinking about Mikayla at all, especially as the whole thing was over anyway and nobody was still investigating.

But who knows, maybe it *wasn't* over. Maybe someone was trying to get the case reopened. Maybe someone knew something she and Josh didn't, and Toby really did have good reason to try and turn the spotlight on Josh and away from himself. After all, it was Toby who had started the rumours that had circulated straight after her death, so he had form when it came to this sort of thing.

Natalie stopped dead when she saw it. Lit up by the yellow glow of streetlights was the bench where Josh had proposed to her. That summer night had been so beautiful, the river twinkling, the light breeze playing with her hair as she'd sat beside him. He'd told her that night about his insecurities, and about how he'd tried to take his life. They'd been so honest with each other. It had felt like together they could do anything. Now that was all in tatters.

She sat down heavily on the bench. She could almost see him there, kneeling in front of her. At that moment she missed him so much that it was a deep, crushing ache. She couldn't let him believe it was over between them! She couldn't let him blame himself. He was the victim of a cruel game Toby was playing, and she refused to let Toby win. She'd do anything for Josh – anything to get back the Josh she'd fallen in love with. The man she knew he was really, underneath this pain and the sick games Toby was playing with his head.

Toby has offered me a job at Hartbury Hotel. She stared out across the water as a plan began to form. It would be hard, dangerous even, but if she got close to Toby, perhaps she could end this whole thing. If she could prove he killed Mikayla, or at least that he was responsible for the trolling, Josh's name would be cleared once and for all.

It's crazy. You're not thinking straight.

But what if it was the only way? Josh was sure to turn himself in sooner or later, even if Gareth put him off for a day or two. He'd gone too far down the path of doubt for anyone to get through to him unless there was solid, irrefutable proof that he was not to blame. And she was in the perfect position to get it.

39

Verity was silent for a few seconds, her face frozen in shock. 'Nat, I … God, I don't even know what to say.'

'You warned me there was something off about him.'

'I–' Verity shook her head. 'I've been wanting to talk to you about that. How I behaved, ambushing you with those accusations about Josh the way I did, it wasn't right.'

'But now Josh has shown his true colours.' Natalie winced inside as she said the words. She had returned eventually from her walk to talk to Verity, but if her plan to incriminate Toby was to work, she'd have to let everyone think she and Josh were over. Worse than that, she had to let everyone think Josh was her troll. If she confessed her plan, Verity would either think she'd got the whole thing wrong, or she'd be scared for her safety and try to talk her out of it.

'I wish I *was* wrong about Josh,' Verity said. 'I'd never want any of this to happen. Are you completely sure it was him who said all these things?'

'Yes.'

'Then … then it's over?'

'Yes.' Natalie tried to separate herself emotionally from her words. She was playing a part now, and she had to do it well. If anyone realised she didn't really think Josh was her troll, it could put everything in jeopardy. Toby *had* to trust her.

Verity was silent for a while, as Natalie sat drinking her fresh cup of tea mechanically, without really tasting it. Verity watched her with concern. 'I can't believe how things have ended up for you, Nat. And your job – I'd give you your old job back if I could–'

'I'll be starting my new job soon. I was offered the position formally today and I'm going to accept.'

'That's something then. What will you be doing?'

Natalie hesitated. She didn't want to talk about it yet, but she couldn't really keep it a secret – not when she would be staying with Verity and Rob. 'Events manager at Hartbury Hotel.'

Verity's eyebrows rose. 'The hotel where Josh's stepbrother is the general manager?'

'Yes.'

'Natalie, that's a bad idea–'

'It's a good job. I'm not throwing away an opportunity like that. The only person I would hurt is myself.'

Verity was silent for a while. 'But you have your compensation money from the accident to fall back on, and the rent coming in from your flat. You don't need to start working straight away.'

'I do. I need something to occupy my time more than ever now. And I'll have to move back to my flat, I guess, once my tenants have moved on.'

'Well, you can stay here, obviously, until you get yourself sorted,' Verity said. 'Unless you'd rather go to your mum and dad's?'

'Thank you,' Natalie said, her voice sounding strange and emotionless, like something completely disconnected from her. Discussing all these arrangements with Verity was exhausting. Especially as she had no intention of moving back to her flat. Hopefully her plan with Toby wouldn't take as long as that. 'I'd like to stay here for a bit,' she told Verity.

'I can't believe what Josh has done,' Verity said. 'How could he? And why? Why would he treat you like that? It … it's sick. I've got a good mind to go round there and give him a slap!' Spots of colour appeared on her cheeks.

Natalie's stomach tightened. *I have to play along.* 'I guess I didn't really know him. And he does have issues. He went through quite a bit when he was younger. You tried to warn me.'

'Well, there's no excuse,' Verity said. 'You're better off without him.'

***

After pulling the hair brush through her curls one last time, Natalie climbed into bed. The spare room was a bit snug, but it was calming with walls of palest grey and crisp white bedding. Verity had lent her a hair brush and a set of pyjamas, which Natalie had forgotten to pack in her haste earlier. They'd talked on and off through the rest of the evening, and Josh had tried to call a couple of times but she hadn't answered.

Now she picked up her phone, and read through some of the comments again. Toby. It was sick, what he'd tried to do by framing Josh. He was a sick, sick man. *And I've got to get him to trust me.* She shivered. Could she really do it? She had to. She'd survived the car crash when all the odds were against her. She'd built a completely new life for herself. Toby was a weak, vain man. Surely it wouldn't be that difficult to get him to believe she genuinely wanted to get to know him.

She checked the time. It was late, but not *too* late. Could she call Toby now to accept the job? She wanted to do it, to get it out of the way. Otherwise by the morning she might have changed her mind.

40

At the soft knock on her door the next morning, Natalie quickly finished pulling on her jeans and jumper and opened it to find Rob outside, concern etched into his face. She'd heard him come in the night before and the murmur of him and Verity talking, but she'd stayed in her room. Verity would no doubt tell him exactly what had happened.

'Natalie,' he said, 'how are you?'

'Not great.'

'I … I don't even know what to say.'

He followed her into the spare room and they sat side by side on her bed. It would have been reassuring to confess everything to him – he always made her feel safe when they were kids, even if he'd also sometimes been incredibly annoying – but Verity was bound to have told him about her new job and he would almost certainly try to talk her out of it.

'It doesn't really cover it to say I'm sorry about what's happened,' he told her. 'When me and Verity warned you about him, I *was* concerned, but I'm not sure I ever really believed he would do this.'

Natalie stared down at the silvery grey carpet between her feet. Would Rob see right through her? *I need to get used to deceiving people. I have to deceive Toby, and the stakes couldn't be higher.*

She raised her head to look at her brother. He was dressed in jeans and a black t-shirt with a skull on the front, his long hair flopping forward over his cheek. He and Verity made a funny-looking couple sometimes – with her so smart in her silky blouses, her hair always perfect and shining like it had been polished, while Rob quite often looked like he needed a good shower. She swallowed, and tried to rearrange her face to be as convincing as possible. 'I don't really want to talk about it,' she said. 'I feel really – I feel stupid, basically. I feel stupid that I got taken in by him.'

'It's him that's the stupid one. And it's his loss. He was never good enough for you, and he knew it. That's why he tried to make you feel bad about yourself, to make sure you needed him and that you'd stay with him. Although why he brought up that girl Mikayla–'

'Rob, I really don't want to talk about it.'

'Okay,' he said. 'When … when do you start your new job?' He tried to keep his voice neutral but the disapproval crept in anyway.

'I said I'd go in later today, but I start officially tomorrow. I said I didn't want to wait.'

'Nat–'

'Don't try to talk me out of it.'

'I know, but – Toby is Josh's stepbrother.'

'I'm well aware,' Natalie said, her voice becoming defensive. *Try to hold it together.*

'Then you should be well aware that you need a clean break!' Rob said, unable to keep his opinions to himself any longer. 'You're not desperate for money, and we're not about to kick you out. You have plenty of time to look for a different job.'

'I want *this* job!' she said. 'I said the same to Verity. It's a good job, and I want to do it. Please try to respect my decision.'

Rob looked stung, and she couldn't help but soften. 'Look, I know what I'm doing,' she reassured him.

'Really? Because to me none of this makes sense. Verity told me that Josh said all this vile, sickening stuff about you, and yet this morning you don't even seem angry with him. No rage. No disgust. The Natalie I knew would be raining hell down on somebody who treated her like that.'

'Perhaps I've grown up since then. I don't want revenge. I just want to get on with my life.'

Rob was silent for a moment. 'It's not healthy to bottle all of this up. I'm sorry, Nat, but you don't seem to be dealing with this very ... normally. You need at least a bit of time to process what's happened to you.'

'I'm dealing with it exactly the way I want to!' she said, rising from the bed. 'I'd appreciate it if everyone could respect that. I know you're trying to help, but honestly, I'm okay. This happened to *me,* not you or Verity, so I'll choose how I deal with it. I am angry with Josh, but screaming and shouting about it isn't going to help. And I have things to do. I don't want to sit around talking.'

'You and Josh were about to get married,' Rob said. 'You don't get over that overnight.'

'I am not over anything!' Natalie said. 'I barely got a wink of sleep last night, I was so upset. But today I want to try to have a bit of normality, and I really, *really* want you and Verity to be on my side!'

'Nat, I'm sorry,' he said, getting up and reaching out to her. 'This has come out all wrong, I didn't mean to upset you.'

Natalie paused. She believed that. Rob could be a bit clumsy with what he said sometimes. She stepped closer to him and he put his arms around her, his head resting beside hers. For a moment, she let herself take comfort from him. He might not know exactly what was going on, but he was here. She could trust him, and he *was* on her side, she knew that without question.

Her phone jingled, and Rob let go of her. He looked at her meaningfully as Josh's name lit up the screen. With a heavy heart, she rejected the call. She had to stay strong, no matter how much it hurt. Once Rob had left, she picked up her phone and pressed it to her chest as though somehow she could send the embrace to Josh. *Just hang on a little longer,* she willed him. *It will be okay. I promise.*

***

It was all Natalie could do to sit in Toby's claustrophobic office and explain to him that she and Josh had broken up. She'd left it out of the conversation when she'd accepted the job the night before, but she had to tell him now, and she'd watch him carefully to see how he reacted.

'But why did you break up?' he asked her. 'I thought you were so good together.'

Anger surged through her. As if he didn't know! It was *him* who'd framed Josh, who'd made this whole thing happen! And now he wanted the satisfaction of listening to her talk about it, of hearing how hurt she was. Trying once more to cut herself off from her emotions, she outlined what had happened while Toby listened.

'I can't believe it!' he said. 'I can't … it's disgusting! What is wrong with him?'

Natalie's whole body was rigid with anger and she tried desperately to relax her shoulders a little. 'I'd rather not talk about it, to be honest,' she said, using the same line she'd tried with Rob. 'The whole thing is a nightmare. I feel so stupid for ever being taken in by him. I just want to throw myself into something and try to forget about it. I can't just sit in my brother's house twiddling my thumbs all day.'

'Well, there's plenty to keep you busy here, don't worry about that.'

By the end of the afternoon, Natalie had to admit he was spot on. She'd spent much of her time getting to know the other members of staff, alongside Toby talking her through things in between dealing with his other responsibilities. Natalie enjoyed spending time with Angelique, who had a wicked sense of humour, along with a great eye for detail. The details were everything when it came to parties and weddings. Not long before she left, Natalie found a chance to speak to her alone once they'd finished discussing the upcoming weddings and other functions.

'I visited a while back to look around,' she said, 'and I met a young woman called Chantelle. I was just wondering if she still works here–'

She stopped as a shadow passed across Angelique's face. 'She wasn't with us long,' Angelique said. 'Some of the young girls don't stick around. One day they're here and everything is fine, then the next day they're gone without even a goodbye.'

'Did *she* say why she was leaving? Chantelle?'

Angelique thought for a moment. 'No,' she said, 'she left without saying anything to anyone. Just like the others.'

Josh

41

'Natalie,' Josh said as he opened the door, 'I'm so glad you—' He stopped in his tracks. 'Oh, it's you.'

Gareth made a wry face. 'She called me and told me I should come and check on you.'

'She did?' He put his hand against the doorframe. He was a bit unsteady on his feet.

'You've been drowning your sorrows, then?'

'Wouldn't you be, in my situation?'

'I don't really understand your situation,' Gareth said steadily.

Josh looked at him for a moment and then said, 'Neither do I. I … did she tell you it was me? Did she tell you I was behind all that awful stuff that was—'

'Yes, she did. She also said you were going to turn yourself in for killing Mikayla.'

'She told me not to, so I haven't, not yet. I will, though.'

Gareth gave him a firm look. 'So, are you going to let me in?'

When Josh didn't move aside, Gareth said, 'You know what, I'm coming in, whether you want me to or not.' He pushed past and Josh followed him through into the living room.

'What's wrong with me, Gareth?' Josh asked, as he slumped down on the sofa.

Gareth sat down beside him. 'Just forget Natalie,' he said, with sudden venom. 'I thought she was different when the two of you got engaged, I thought she actually gave a damn about you. But she clearly doesn't. If she really loved you, she'd at least hear you out. She'd at least try and understand why you did what you did. I was disgusted when she said she'd just left you, and I told her as much.'

'Why should she hear me out?' Josh said. 'I don't deserve that. She doesn't owe me anything after what I've done, and you shouldn't have had a go at her.'

'So why did you do it?'

Josh shook his head. 'I don't know.'

'You don't know?'

'Well, I don't even remember doing it, so—'

'What?'

'I obviously do stuff like this and then block it out!' Josh said impatiently. Why was Gareth making him spell it out like this? Wasn't it obvious?

Gareth sat back against the sofa. 'For God's sake—'

'It was all there on my laptop. I did it. Don't try and tell me otherwise.'

For a moment they sat in stony silence.

'It was my conscience trying to make me realise what I'd done to Mikayla,' Josh tried to explain.

'Right,' Gareth said, his voice laced with sarcasm, 'and the posts saying her scar is gross is because your unconscious mind thinks she's ugly, is that it?'

'I'm being serious.'

'So am I! And seriously, Josh, I mean … what the fuck? Do you really believe what you're saying to me?'

'Gareth, I need you to listen. I'm not messing around – one of those trolling accounts was open on *my* laptop. What do you suggest happened?'

'I'd suggest whoever is behind it can actually *remember* doing it! But if you're so determined to think you're crazy, how can I talk you out of it? If you've given up on yourself, why should I be the one to try and give you a reason to keep going? I tried to help my mum, remember, and a fat lot of good that did. I can't help you sort this out if you don't want to sort it out. Just stay here and—' Gareth paused as he gestured towards the coffee table, and he picked up the bottle that Josh had been drinking from. Looking disgusted, he waved the bottle at Josh. 'What is this? Why are you drinking this?'

'It's the only thing I could find.'

'It's pink, for fuck's sake.'

'It's Natalie's. She likes it.'

Josh grabbed the bottle of pink gin out of Gareth's hand and tried to take a swig from it, but Gareth grabbed it back. 'No way.'

'Give it–' He made a lunge for it and Gareth held it back.

'Did you come here just to take the piss?' Josh asked furiously. 'Because–'

Gareth held his hands up. 'No. No, I didn't.'

'I just–' Josh's voice rose as the alcohol fed into his already volatile emotions. 'I just want to know what the hell is going on with me! Why am I *so* messed up? Why can't I remember stuff properly? I don't want my life to be like this, I just want to be normal. But I don't deserve that, do I? My life is … it's cursed. Because I killed Mikayla. Until I pay for that, nothing can ever be right. And Natalie … she would only have got hurt if she'd stayed with me. I would have ruined her life. It's just as well she got out while she could.'

'Okay,' Gareth said, 'okay. Here's what's going to happen. I'm going to take you out for a proper drink. Something that isn't bloody *pink*. I'll give you a free pass to go on about Natalie and this stuff all night if that's what you want to do. As long as you keep your voice down, anyway. I'll have a really boring and dreary night, but you–' he clapped Josh on the back '– you are going to feel a lot better for it.'

'I'm not going anywhere.'

'Yes you are. And tomorrow, once the hangover has cleared, perhaps you'll be able to figure this out. I'll help you figure it out, as long as you start being rational. This situation with Natalie, it could be salvageable, but you can't do anything tonight while you're in this state. You both need a chance to cool off and think clearly.'

'I don't think it'll make any difference now. She's gone.'

'Well,' Gareth said casually, 'if you're giving up as easily as that, I guess it saves me writing a best man speech.'

'Gareth, I'm not in the mood for jokes.'

'No, you're right. I wasn't ever going to write it down. I was just going to wing it on the day.'

Josh stared at him. 'Is this really a joke to you? Look, my relationship is over. I wrote horrific things to Natalie online, and I – I have to pay for what I've done. For everything I've done–'

'Fine!' Gareth snapped. He took out his phone and pressed three nines on the screen. 'Press call then,' he said, handing over the phone. Josh just stared at it. 'Or I can drive you to the police station in town if you want. Come on, what's stopping you?'

Josh handed Gareth his phone back.

'Exactly,' Gareth said. 'Deep down, you know it wasn't you. These thoughts you're getting, these doubts, they're not real. If you truly believed they were real, you'd have turned yourself in already. I'm not taking this seriously because none of it deserves to be taken seriously. You didn't do any of this, Josh, and you know you didn't. You and Natalie, you'll be back together before you know it. The world isn't ending, it's just a bump in the road, that's all.'

Josh couldn't bring himself to answer. Gareth's argument made complete sense, and yet, how had his laptop had those pages open if it wasn't him? No matter how Gareth tried to reassure him, it still didn't make sense.

'Look, let's go out,' Gareth said. 'I'm not taking no for an answer.'

42

Water lapped around his face. Icy and black, it sapped any trace of warmth from his body. It was dark this time, ripples in the water lit by the moon. He was about to turn back, to give up on finding Mikayla, when his hand caught in something floating, twisting around his fingers. Hair! He turned, and there she was, floating serenely. But she was dead; her eyes strange and milky, and she was drifting on her back staring sightlessly at the sky. He grabbed her, pushing her down, down below the surface. 'Stay dead!' he yelled at her. 'Stay dead!'

Instead of sinking, she bobbed back up to the surface, and her head turned, even though she was no longer alive. 'You did do it, Josh,' she said calmly. 'You killed me.'

'I'm so sorry,' he sobbed. 'I'm so sorry.'

She reached out at lightning speed and grabbed him by the throat. 'Then admit to it! Admit what you did! But you won't, will you? Because you're *pathetic*. Totally pathetic.'

Josh woke with a cry, his body drenched in sweat. He didn't recognise the ceiling above him. Where the hell was he? He rolled over and almost fell onto the floor. He was on a sofa in – was this Gareth's flat? Yes, it was.

'Good, you're awake,' Gareth said cheerfully, coming in with two takeaway coffees. 'I just went out for these. There's a great place round the corner.'

Josh sat up, still shaking as the dream clung to him. Gareth looked at him closely. 'You okay?'

'I ... yeah. Yeah, I'm fine.' He accepted a coffee from Gareth, and winced as he took a sip. Feeling sick, he put the cup down on the floor. 'What happened last night?' he asked. 'I can't remember.'

'You got completely wasted, told me if you didn't have Natalie there was no point in being alive, you said you were still determined to hand yourself in, you threw up in the street, and then you cried.'

'Seriously?'

'Yeah. Pretty much.' Gareth nodded. 'It was good.'

'It sounds terrible.'

'I mean it was good for you to do that. It was cathartic. I paid no attention to the "turning yourself in" bullshit, I know you'll have seen sense now.'

Josh frowned as hazy memories started to resurface. 'I need to go home.'

Gareth picked up the coffee and handed it back to him. 'You need to drink this. Then we're going out for breakfast.'

'I should call Natalie.'

'No, you shouldn't.'

'Why don't you want me to even try to make things better?' Josh asked, his voice rising. 'I just need to know she's okay, before I go to the police.'

Gareth sat down beside him. 'You need to give Nat some space. You tried to call her several times last night. We'll go for breakfast, and we'll talk about this calmly. You don't have to try to deal with this on your own, and I'm not letting you confess to something you didn't do. You are innocent, and I'm on your side. You're just … I don't know. You're not well right now. I should have taken you more seriously and seen how much pain you're in. It won't be like this forever, though. I'll make sure of it. Things *will* get better.'

Looking at his friend, Josh was flooded with relief as he saw Gareth really meant it.

'You're not a murderer, Josh,' Gareth said. 'The most likely thing is still that Mikayla drowned by accident, despite what I said about her breaking up with Toby. You must realise that. If the police had had any suspicions, they would have followed up on it. But they obviously didn't. Sometimes people just die in tragic accidents. Young people. You probably never processed her death properly at the time, and maybe getting close to Natalie triggered something and you're going through all this grief and doubt and turmoil now. You should talk to someone about it, but not until you accept it wasn't down to you. You can't go around saying that.'

Josh nodded, and then he sighed. 'I really need to speak to Nat. If I don't try to call her, she'll think I don't care about her.'

'Okay,' Gareth said, 'perhaps you're right. But just go easy on the crazy stuff.'

Josh took out his phone and called her number. It rang a few times, and then cut off as she rejected the call. Pain bloomed inside him. 'She–'

'It's not that surprising she doesn't want to answer calls from you right now. But you did what you set out to do; she knows you're thinking about her. She may well decide she wants to talk once she's had some time.'

Natalie

43

By the end of her afternoon at Hartbury Hotel, Natalie's head was spinning. Worries about Josh and her plan with Toby mingled with unease at what Angelique had told her about young female staff never staying long at the hotel. What was happening to them? Had Toby's harassment been enough to make them quit, or was he taking things a step further?

'Natty, Natty!' Daisy's little voice broke through her musings. 'I want Natty to do my reading book.'

Natalie let five-year-old Daisy climb onto her lap at the dining table, clutching her reading book. She'd started school the year before and was excited to be 'grown up' like her older sister Isabelle.

'Okay,' she said, 'you read it to me then.'

'Auntie Natty might be a bit tired—' Rob started, glancing round from filling the dishwasher, but she shook her head at him. 'It's fine,' she mouthed. But she did struggle to concentrate as she helped Daisy sound out the words. At the end, her niece said, 'Am I going to be your bridesmaid tomorrow?'

'Daisy!' Rob said. 'We've told you a hundred times Auntie Natalie's wedding isn't until July.' His voice was pained, as if he was wondering how to tell his daughter the wedding was off.

'Is it July next week?'

'No,' Rob said patiently. 'It's January at the moment. Next week it will be February, but that's still the winter—'

'Then it's spring, and *then* summer,' Natalie said.

'So it's spring tomorrow?'

Natalie looked helplessly at Rob, who came to sit down beside his daughter. 'And you know I told you that Auntie Natalie is here because she and Josh had an argument–'

Daisy's brow furrowed. 'But I'll still be a bridesmaid?'

'Well…' Rob started.

'It's a long way away yet,' Natalie said. 'Let's not worry about it all right now.'

***

'Natalie, we're going to have to tell the girls sooner or later,' Rob said as he caught her on the landing later that evening. 'The wedding is off, you can't pretend that it isn't.'

She tried to be patient. The wedding *wasn't* off, she'd have sorted things out by then – at least, she had to try to believe that. But she couldn't say that to Rob. 'I know, but, not just yet,' she said.

'They're going to keep bringing it up. Verity said Isabelle kept talking about it the whole time she drove her back from ballet class.'

'I just need to be alone for a bit,' she said, trying to get to her room. 'It's been a long day.'

'Because you shouldn't have started a new job the day after a break-up!' Rob said, blocking her path. 'This is insane, Natalie!'

'I didn't start properly. I was just meeting people and getting to know the ropes a bit–'

'But you start tomorrow. *Tomorrow.* It's way, way too soon. Toby shouldn't be making you do this.'

'He's not making me do anything. Now, please, Rob, I just need some space.'

Once she was sure Rob had gone downstairs and wasn't lurking about outside her door, she sat down on her bed and took a deep breath. Her heart heavy, she dialled Gareth's number. This was going to be an awful conversation, but she had to ask him how Josh was doing.

'So now you care?' Gareth said.

'Of course I care!'

'Then go and talk to him yourself and ask him how he is. He's gone back home now after crashing at mine last night. Go and see him.'

'I ... I can't.'

'So you *don't* care.'

Natalie had to dig her nails into her palm to stop her emotion escaping. She picked up one of the scatter cushions from her bed and hugged it to her chest as she leant her head back against the wall. It wasn't like she hadn't realised Gareth would be unpleasant towards her – Josh and Gareth's loyalty to each other ran deep. But she was drained from her afternoon at Hartbury hotel and her confrontation with Rob. She wanted nothing more than to crawl into bed. 'Josh said all those awful things to me,' she said, 'I can't just forget that–'

'Then why are you asking how he is? If you're just writing him off like that?'

'I don't want him to confess to hurting Mikayla. I know he didn't do that, no matter what else he might have done.'

'So you want *me* to clear up *your* mess, right?'

'Gareth–'

'No, it's fine,' he said sourly. 'I get it. Just walk out when things get a bit too real. Leave me to pick up the pieces. It's not like I haven't done it several times before. Let's just hope that this time I can stop him doing anything stupid, because the last time he felt this hopeless it didn't turn out so well. You might not have handed him the pills like Toby did, but–'

'What?' Natalie said. 'Toby did *what?*'

A few days after Mikayla's death

Josh

44

'Oh for fuck's sake,' Toby said, staring at him in disgust.

Josh quickly swiped at his tears with the back of his hand. He started to stand, hoping to leave, but Toby was planted firmly in the bedroom doorway so Josh sank back onto his bed. He'd been sitting there most of the morning, his thoughts bleak and frightening. Was he going mad? It felt like he was.

'She was *my* girlfriend,' Toby continued. 'So stop crying over her! She was never going to look twice at you—'

'It's not about that!' Josh yelled, startling him. 'It's about the fact she was only sixteen! She had her whole life ahead … she…' His voice broke and he stopped for a moment. 'How can she be dead?'

'Maybe because you drowned her, you little weirdo?'

Josh leapt up from the bed and gave Toby a shove, anger making him brave enough to fight back. 'I did not drown her! I tried to save her! How could you tell people that about me? How could you try to get people to believe that?'

Toby shoved him back, harder. Josh stumbled against the edge of his bed, but managed to stay on his feet. 'Why aren't you upset?' he asked Toby, 'since she was your girlfriend?'

'I don't have to explain anything to you!' Toby shouted. 'Nobody wants you, Josh! Do you know why people have no trouble believing you weren't really trying to save her? It's because everyone hates you. Everyone wishes you weren't here. I mean, what the hell have you ever done that's any good for anyone?

You're messed up in the head. You're just … I don't know. You're broken.'

'You think I don't know that?'

Toby gave him a long look. 'Just stop sitting in here crying. There'll be plenty of time for that when they lock you up.'

A heavy weight settled in his stomach. 'Toby,' he said quietly. 'You know I didn't do anything. You'll tell them at the inquest that I didn't do anything, won't you? I was just trying to save her. I found her clothes and I went in the water, but I never even saw her. You know I'm telling the truth.'

Toby shrugged.

'Toby! I know you don't really think I did it. If you really believed that, you'd be angry with me. You wouldn't let me get away with killing your girlfriend. So you must know it was an accident.'

'Look, Josh, you don't belong in the real world,' Toby said casually. 'You're made for some sort of institution.'

'I won't go,' Josh said. 'I'll kill myself.'

'Don't be so stupid.'

'I will,' Josh said. Truthfully, he'd been thinking about it on and off for quite some time. 'I will do it.'

Toby paused for a moment, and then he left the room. Josh stared after him. Was he going out? Hopefully he'd go out. Josh threw himself back down onto the bed, and was startled when Toby came back and threw a couple of small boxes down beside him. 'Go on then,' Toby said as Josh picked up the packs of painkillers. 'I'll believe it when I see it. You don't have the balls.'

One week later

Natalie

45

'Nat, could I speak to you in a minute? Once you're finished in here?'

Natalie nodded, her skin crawling. Toby was a murderer. There was no doubt in her mind now. He might have been the one to call an ambulance for Josh, but he'd given him the pills in the first place. He might as well have been the one stuffing them down Josh's throat. It was barely a stretch now to believe he'd killed Mikayla, and every time she was near him her body filled with ice. She didn't know if she was more angry, or more scared, but she knew she hated him with every fibre of her being.

'Natalie? Did you hear me?'

She turned. 'Yes, sorry Toby. I heard you. I'm almost done and then I'll come to the office.'

After checking the function room had been set up properly for a dinner, she paused before heading to the office, steeling herself for being in close quarters with him. He'd said it was only a temporary arrangement to have her desk crammed into the corner of his office, but had it been deliberate? Had he planned for her to share a small, claustrophobic space with him? He'd certainly already made a few inappropriate remarks to her, which she'd had to brush off even though it made her feel like she wanted to wash herself from head to toe.

'Sit down, Nat,' Toby said as she joined him. As always, the room felt stifling even though it was winter. *I wish I was anywhere but here.* How had her life ended up like this? Sometimes it seemed like a living nightmare from the moment she woke up until the moment she slipped into uneasy dreams.

She did as he asked, taking a seat at her desk in the corner, while he turned his own chair around to face her. 'How are you?' he asked. 'Have you spoken to Josh?'

She shook her head. 'I don't answer his calls or messages.'

'Is he hassling you a lot? You could always block him.'

Natalie's stomach churned with hatred. How could Toby care so little about his own stepbrother? Did he find it amusing, this break-up he'd caused? *Of course he does. He found it amusing to taunt him into a suicide attempt. He's a psychopath.*

'He's not hassling me,' she said. 'I haven't heard anything the past couple of days.'

'Has he stopped saying stuff about you? Commenting on your videos and stuff?'

Natalie nodded.

'Well, that's something.'

Is he serious? Anger overwhelmed her. She wanted to leap out of her chair and scream at Toby that she knew he was behind it all, but she held her tongue, her nails digging into the wood grain of her desk.

'And how about your first week at the hotel? How are you finding it?'

'It's good,' she said. This, at least, was true. Aside from the fact she had to work in close proximity to Toby, she did like the job once she was left alone to get on with it. But that was beside the point right now. She had to find evidence of Toby's guilt and she had to do it soon, before she completely lost her mind. She was already distant, distracted, her head frequently pounding with the stress of it all. There was no one she could talk to. No one who could possibly understand the burden of being worried sick about Josh, scared of Toby, overwhelmed by lies, and having to stay in a cramped spare room in somebody else's home. On top of that, even though she liked her new job, there was a lot for her already exhausted brain to take in. If it went on much longer she would start to completely break down.

Toby nodded, looking satisfied that she'd said the job was good. 'Well, I was thinking we could go for a drink later? It's been over a week now since you and Josh broke up. Maybe it would help to get back out there. That would really show him, wouldn't it? You don't want him to think you've let those comments affect you.'

No, her mind screamed, *no, no, no!* The idea of going anywhere with Toby went against her every instinct. But how could she get close to him if she didn't spend time with him? He was giving her an opportunity to do exactly what she needed to do.

'I don't know...' she said. She didn't want to seem suspiciously keen, after all.

'Come on, Nat. I know a nice little place. It'll just be me and you, not a big crowd.'

Just me and you. Did he really think that made it sound better? 'I'm not really in much of a sociable mood at the moment,' she said slowly, 'but I guess *one* drink wouldn't hurt.'

'Exactly,' Toby said, his face lighting up. 'You can't let Josh win. It's a crime for such a beautiful woman to stay hidden away.'

***

The evening passed excruciatingly slowly. Toby was apparently having a great time, chatting away to her animatedly, while she pretended to be interested. After a few drinks, she said she was tired, and although she had to repeat it a few more times before he understood that she wanted to go home, she did eventually find herself outside with him. She glanced around, unsettled now that they were no longer inside the bar where there was a comfortable buzz of noise from other people. The street was empty, and Toby was standing rather close to her.

'I really enjoyed tonight,' he said.

'So did I,' she lied. 'I admit, I thought I wouldn't – not so soon after the break-up.'

'Perhaps you and Josh weren't as well matched as you thought,' he said. 'If you're not feeling that upset. Perhaps it was never meant to be.'

Stepping even closer, he reached his hand towards her arm. He was a good couple of inches taller than her, and she felt suddenly very small. Her instinct was to pull her arm away, but she let his hand rest there for a moment.

'Toby–'

'I know,' he said, 'I know it's soon.'

'My head's still all over the place,' she said. 'There's been a lot of change for me recently, and it's work tomorrow–'

'Well, I guess I should be glad you're so conscientious,' he said.

She laughed at his 'joke', relief flooding through her as he moved away from her. Did Toby have no shame? *Was this his plan all along?* Had he wanted to break up her and Josh so he could have her himself? It seemed far-fetched, but who knew what was going on in his head? And his poor wife, Jodie, did she have any idea how he really behaved?

Toby was giving her a look that made her stomach clench. She was just the latest prize he'd set his sights on – he was eyeing her up like a piece of meat. It was the same way he'd looked at Chantelle that time she'd interrupted them in the conservatory: Toby had barely tried to hide the fact he was staring at the young woman's curves as she'd walked away. No doubt he'd done the same to all the other women he'd driven out of the hotel with his advances, since he apparently thought he was entitled to behave this way. She tried her best to smile, while panic welled up inside her. *He killed Mikayla and he nearly killed Josh. I really have no idea what he could be capable of.*

***

Natalie slipped quietly back inside Rob and Verity's house. She tried to stay out of their way as much as possible now as their questions were too difficult to answer. She took off her coat and her high heels, grateful for the soft carpet on the stairs after a long day on her feet.

As she crept upstairs, she paused in surprise. Verity was crying in the bedroom, and there was the soft murmur of Rob's voice. She quickly made her way to her own room. Was it because of her? Had she been unreasonable, moving in here, burdening their marriage and children with her own problems? *I have to sort things out. I have to get what I need from Toby.*

After a surprisingly deep sleep, Natalie showered and dressed hurriedly, catching Rob in the hall on his way out to work.

'Rob ... is everything okay?'

'Yes,' he said, 'of course it is, what–'

She lowered her voice. 'I heard Verity crying last night.'

He was silent for a long time. 'Nat, I'm on my way out the door, I can't really talk right now–'

'Please, Rob.'

'Verity has been unhappy for a while,' he said reluctantly, as he realised she wasn't going to drop it. 'And this stuff with the business doesn't help.'

'Well, let me look after the kids after school tomorrow,' she said. 'I'm not working, and she could have a bit of time to herself. Maybe you could take her out for dinner or something.'

'You have enough on your plate.'

'I know, but I need to pull my weight – I've just descended on you without warning–'

'You're not the problem,' he said. 'You don't owe us anything, you're family. Of course we want to help you.'

'I'll not be here much longer. I'll sort something else soon.'

A strange expression crossed Rob's face. A sad one, she thought. Bleak. 'Rob, tell me what's wrong, please.'

She trailed off as Verity made her way down the stairs with the two girls in tow, hair freshly plaited and their uniforms particularly neat. 'It's school photo day,' Verity said.

'Oh, lovely!' Natalie said to Daisy and Isabelle. 'You both look very smart.'

Rob had taken advantage of the distraction to scurry out, with a quick goodbye shouted back over his shoulder, and Verity herded the girls towards the door.

'V…' Natalie said.

Verity turned to her, shadows under her eyes.

'Uh, it's nothing,' Natalie said. It wouldn't help to bring it up, not when Verity was busy taking the girls to school. 'It doesn't matter.'

'You on your way out?' Verity said.

'In a minute. I'm just going to grab some breakfast first.'

After Verity left, the house suddenly seemed very quiet. In the past her brother's place had been a kind of sanctuary for her, a dose of normality when her life had felt hectic and ungrounded during her modelling days, and scary after her accident. Now it wasn't like a sanctuary at all. At times the house was as claustrophobic as Toby's office. She sighed. Was anything normal any more?

46

'It was great getting to know you better last night,' Toby told her as she sat down at her desk to catch up on emails. 'I think we have a real connection.'

She turned to him, pasting on a smile. 'So do I,' she said, and turned back to her work. *Please, just leave me alone.* She paused, correcting herself. If he left her alone, she'd just be stuck doing this longer.

'We should do it again sometime,' Toby said.

She paused in the middle of typing. How to play this? She still couldn't seem *too* keen; after all, she was supposed to still be getting over Josh. The subject of an email caught her eye and she clicked on it, scanning the contents. 'Oh, Toby, you'll like this,' she said, amused, and grateful for something to break the tension.

'What is it?'

'Just got an enquiry from a couple wanting to renew their wedding vows–'

Toby rolled his eyes. 'God, isn't going through the whole rigmarole once enough?'

'Well, that's not the interesting thing,' Natalie said. 'They've said it will be ninety guests, or thereabouts, but twenty of the guests are dogs.'

'You what?'

'That's just what it says.'

'Okay.' There was a long pause while Toby's face went through a few different expressions. 'Well, if they have a marquee outside I guess they could bring them. But they can't do it inside the hotel.'

'That's what I thought. But don't you think it's kind of cute, though? What a fun idea.'

He gave her a sickly smile. 'You really see the good in everything, don't you, Natalie?'

'What's bad about a couple wanting to celebrate their love with the ones they most care about?'

Now he laughed. 'You're a breath of fresh air,' he said, 'just what Hartbury needs. You're so perfect for this. I can play at being enthusiastic about people's parties and whatnot, but you actually really care.'

Natalie turned away at his muddled compliment, unsure whether he was genuinely impressed or just making fun of her. It was already perfectly clear that all he saw when he thought of the weddings side of the business was pound signs.

'So, about going out again sometime,' he persisted, getting up from his chair and coming over to rest his hand on her shoulder.

'Toby...' she started, but he quickly cut in.

'I know,' he said, 'I know you feel a bit weird about it. But Josh behaved unforgivably towards you. You don't owe him a thing. You deserve to have fun.'

She nodded. 'I know, it's just—'

'Wednesday,' he said, 'we could go out for dinner? My treat. Surely it's better than constantly being under the feet of your brother and his family, if nothing else? It'll give you all a night off from each other.'

Wow, he really will say anything to try and get what he wants.

She smiled. 'When you put it like that...'

***

Natalie giggled and batted Toby's hand away from her cheek in what she hoped was an endearing and playful way. After another week at the hotel, and a couple of excruciating 'dates' with Toby, it was clear he wasn't happy keeping his hands to himself any more. He'd come to join her as she worked on setting up the conservatory to take new photos for the hotel website, but had quickly become bored of chatting. Now he'd cornered her near the door, the smell of his aftershave overwhelming her. He brought his hand back to her face and stroked the outline of her scar, while her skin prickled with discomfort. 'Nat, come on,' he said, his voice getting a slight edge to it. 'You're driving me crazy. Is this happening or not?'

'It's not happening in here,' she said firmly. It was clear Toby was excited at making advances towards her in one of the public areas of the hotel – her suspicion confirmed as he crudely grabbed her hand and pressed it to the front of his trousers so she could feel his excitement for herself.

'Toby...' she said, trying to stay light-hearted, but his eyes had taken on a clouded look as he pressed her hand tightly against his erection and leant in to kiss her. 'No,' she said, and to her relief, he moved away slightly. 'I think I can hear someone coming,' she lied.

'We'll go back to the office,' he said, and then he whispered to her, 'because I want to hear *you* coming.'

'There's no space in that room,' she said, her nervous laughter hiding genuine fear. If she went into that office with him while he was in this state, she wouldn't be able to wriggle her way out of having sex with him. Not unless she was prepared to completely blow her plan and reveal that all her feelings for him were fake.

'There's plenty of space if we're creative,' he said. 'Or, if you don't fancy that, we work in an entire building full of bedrooms, remember.' He pressed himself against her again, his hand reaching down for the hem of her skirt and beginning to lift it. 'I want to fuck you on every floor of the hotel,' he whispered to her, and then nibbled her ear lightly. 'And the swimming pool,' he added, with relish.

'Toby,' she said, smoothing down the front of her skirt and stepping firmly away from him. 'I ... I want that too, but I don't want to risk it, okay? I only just started here. If people realise something is going on between us–'

'So something *is* going on between us?'

Her chest felt tight. Could she really go through with this? She could walk away right now, and leave the hotel behind. She could just go and tell Josh she knew he was innocent of everything. *But it won't end.* Josh was too tormented by Mikayla's death. He was too convinced that everything was his fault. And Toby had done that to him. 'You know something is going on,' she told him. 'But I just—'

Before she could finish her sentence, his lips were on hers. 'Toby!' she said, pulling away. 'You heard what I just said! Not at work.'

For a moment, Natalie wondered if he was going to try to kiss her again anyway, but then there really was a sound – the unmistakable tap-tap of Angelique's stilettos moving towards the conservatory.

*****

'Gareth, I just want to know how he is,' Natalie said. It had been a long day and her nerves were frayed; memories of Toby lunging at her were spinning around in her mind. Every time she went to her desk, she'd been scared that he would burst in and start pawing at her again, keen to show her the 'creative' ways they could have sex in the office. But thankfully he'd been rushed off his feet since their time in the conservatory and she had not been alone with him again.

'Why do you care?' Gareth said, his voice sharp. Her eyes prickled with tears. If only she could just tell him that she was trying to help. His hostility towards her after what she was putting herself through to help Josh was almost unbearable. She lay down on her bed and stared up at the ceiling. She was getting fed up with spending so much time in the little spare room at Rob and Verity's house. She felt odd and disconnected, uncomfortable with venturing down to the lounge or kitchen where she might have to talk, but sick of staying in her bedroom nearly all the time.

'Look, it might be over between us, but I still think about him sometimes,' she continued. 'I mean, just wondering how he is. I don't want to have anything to do with him, but I want to know he's okay.'

'You mean, you don't want to have his breakdown on your conscience?'

She sighed heavily. 'Is that what's happening? Is he having a breakdown?'

'The last time I saw him this unhappy, he was fresh out of hospital after taking an overdose.'

'Gareth—'

'What do you want me to say, Natalie? He can't even remember writing all that stuff about you. So either he needs a lot of help and support right now, or somebody has really gone out of their way to fuck with his head. Either way, I think he deserves better than what you've done.'

'Please don't be cruel,' she said. 'He's not the only one who's hurt.'

'Well, he's the one I'm worried about.' Gareth said, before he ended the call.

Natalie could have screamed, but instead she just pressed her eyes closed. She opened them to find a message from Toby on her phone.

I can't stop thinking about you and what I want to do to you

Natalie threw her phone away from her. 'Josh,' she whispered, 'I wish you could help me. I wish it didn't have to be like this.' She reached her hand out in front of her face, imagining him reaching back and interlacing his fingers with hers. 'I love you,' she said, and she closed her eyes, a tear spilling down onto her cheek.

Josh

47

Josh paced around the flat restlessly. His head was pounding; he woke every day with a headache, and his nights were long and empty. He'd manage a few snatches of sleep here and there, usually not until the early hours, and he'd get confused and reach out to Natalie, only to find the bed empty. Last night had been one of the worst nights – he'd felt so strongly that she was there beside him, that she needed him, but of course when he'd opened his eyes he was alone, exactly as he deserved to be. He wished his mind would get used to it – that he wouldn't have to keep reliving the realisation she was gone, every time his sleeping mind tricked him into thinking she was there.

He stopped in the bedroom doorway. Natalie had sent Rob around to collect a few more of her clothes and belongings, but her bright yellow throw was still draped over the end of the bed, her mirrored jewellery box on top of the chest of drawers, a few floaty scarves in shades of green, purple and copper hanging behind the door. The time he'd spent in this bed with her had been some of the happiest moments of his life – the times she'd lain beside him, her head on his chest, while he stroked her beautiful soft hair; the times she'd whispered that she loved him; and the pure bliss of her naked body. *I didn't deserve any of it, not one moment of the pleasure and joy she gave me. Not after how I treated her.*

Tears pricked his eyes. She'd told him once that she was his family now. Why had he done what he did? Why had he gone and ruined everything – ruined the best thing that had ever happened to him? A couple of tears fell and he brushed them away. He could feel the darkness creeping up on him again. Nothing felt good any more. He didn't want to do anything. He didn't want to be anywhere. His whole body just hurt.

***

'Josh?' A voice came through the darkness. 'Josh? What's up with you? Wake up! For God's sake!'

He opened his eyes a crack. 'Gareth?' he croaked.

'You left your front door open,' Gareth said. 'I came to see how you are. I'm worried about you. When I saw you like this I thought you might have … done something.'

Josh gestured vaguely at the coffee table, where Gareth took in the sight of various bottles and cans.

'You just drank yourself into oblivion,' Gareth said. 'I guess that's kind of a relief.' He sat down beside him. 'You need to try and get back to normal. I know that's easy for me to say.' He paused as if something had just occurred to him. 'Are you even going to work? The state you're in–'

'Yes,' Josh said. 'I went back straight away. They sent me home for a couple of days, but I've been in since then. Anything to get out of the flat – everywhere I turn in this place reminds me of her. I just needed to block it all out tonight. It's too painful.'

'Yeah,' Gareth said. 'I get it.'

'Have you heard from Natalie at all?' Josh asked. 'You two were kind of friends, weren't you?'

'She did call and ask how you were.'

'When?' Josh said, hope surging through him. She still cared! But what difference did it make? She'd never want to be with him again, and he would be crazy to expect her to.

'She called yesterday,' Gareth replied, 'but I don't think you should get your hopes up. I – look, to be honest I think she just doesn't want to have to feel guilty about messing you up by leaving.'

'Why should she feel guilty? It's my own fault.'

'I know that's what you believe. But whatever the truth is, it's not healthy to dwell on her.'

'Gareth, if you're going to say we should go out drinking to-night–'

'No,' he said. 'I think you've had plenty to drink recently, by the looks of this place.'

'I'll tidy it up in a bit. I – I'll be all right,' he said weakly. 'I'm just having a bad patch.'

Gareth shook his head. 'You don't look all right, Josh. I'm worried about this. I'm worried about you.'

Josh sighed. How could he explain that not having Natalie was a pain that nothing could numb? He kept telling himself that he'd been getting on okay before he met her – at least, he hadn't exactly been happy, but he could function. All he needed to do was try to go back to that again. But now he couldn't go back. He'd always, *always* be thinking about her. *But it's what I deserve,* he reminded himself again. *This is my punishment.*

'For God's sake, at least try and find out who Natalie's troll is,' Gareth said. 'You could hack one of those accounts.'

'Is this some kind of joke?'

'No. I think you're scared. But wouldn't it be better to know? If it confirms it's you then you know you need help–'

'I won't be able to confirm it's me. If I was doing it, nobody would be able to trace it back to me. I would have covered my tracks.'

'But you could confirm it if it was someone else. Unless they're as talented as you are, which I don't believe for a second.'

'Gareth, it *was* me. There was an account open on my lap-top–'

'This is bullshit,' Gareth said. 'You're throwing your life away and you don't even know the facts.'

'I threw my life away at Chedford Lake,' Josh said. 'This has all been borrowed time.'

Gareth opened his mouth to argue but Josh got in first. 'I appreciate you being concerned about me,' he said, 'but you don't need to be. There's no point. There's nothing anyone can say or do that will fix me. There's only one way I can make it right. Tomorrow morning, I'm going to the police station, and I'm going to confess to murdering Mikayla.'

Two weeks after Mikayla's death

48

The door creaked open, startling him from his swirling, depressing thoughts. At a soft footstep behind him, he turned, unsure whether he was glad to be distracted, or exhausted by the thought of another conversation with someone who would never understand him.

'Are you okay?' His mum's voice was subdued as she stepped further inside, reaching her hand out uselessly towards him. It was clear she was suffering. She was still in the same t-shirt she'd had on for days, her eyes puffy as she took in the sight of him. But he was angry and hurt. How had things ended up so bad? Why hadn't anyone seen what Toby was doing to him?

'Leave me alone,' he said, turning back to his computer screen.

'I just wanted to check you're okay.'

'I haven't tried to kill myself again,' he said, his voice catching, 'so you can go.'

She came in and sat on the end of his bed, next to where he sat at the desk. 'I wish you felt you could talk–'

'I've tried to talk! I've tried over and over!' he exploded. 'I used to constantly tell you that Toby did all the things I got blamed for. All the times Gemma got pushed over, or her toys got broken. I've told you that Toby has hit me, and pushed me, and taken my stuff. I told you over and over and no one listened, or no one cared. It was him who pushed me down those steps. He cut the head off of Gemma's cat toy.' He stopped short of saying Toby had given him the pills. He was too ashamed about it – that he'd simply done what Toby had said. He was so angry with himself. 'He makes my life a misery,' Josh continued, 'and I *told* you that when I got back from hospital Toby couldn't be here!'

'Josh,' his mum said slowly, 'we talked about all those things when they happened–'

'And you all decided to take Toby's side. I know.'

'It's not about sides. And Toby *wasn't* here when you got back from hospital. He's been away a couple of days.'

'I meant he shouldn't come back ever again! He's back *now*! It's like you want me to try to kill myself again.'

His mum recoiled. 'How can you say that–'

'Because it's true! It would be easier, wouldn't it?'

Her eyes filling with tears, his mum reached out shakily for his arm. 'Josh, don't ever think that. I love you. So much.'

'Yes, you've said. Over and over. And then you let Toby come back here.'

'Toby wanted to see you. He was worried about you. He saved your life–'

Josh laughed humourlessly. 'Who do you think drove me to it in the first place?'

'Why are you being like this?' his mum asked. 'I feel like I don't know you. But I *want* to know you, Josh, I do. Are you scared about the inquest? Because you know it's not the same as a trial, don't you? They just want to work out exactly how Mikayla died; they're not pointing the finger at anybody. It's just a formality, nobody really believes anyone did this on purpose.'

Josh turned to her. There was an odd searching tone to her voice, like she was trying to encourage him to talk. The realisation hit him. She thought it was him! How could she? She actually thought it might be him, and she was trying to get him to admit it! His anger, which had flared so quickly, subsided to hard, dull pain. Why was he surprised? This is exactly what he should have expected. 'What do *you* think happened?' he asked her tonelessly.

'All I know is that you can talk to me,' she said. 'If there's anything you need to tell me about what happened that weekend, you can. Please, Josh, let me help you.'

He shook his head and looked at the computer screen again. 'Just leave me alone,' he told her, 'nobody can help me.'

***

Josh sat back, awe and horror flooding through him in equal parts as he came to his senses. He'd been completely zoned out from the outside world while he had worked, Linkin Park thundering from his headphones, his mind entirely focused, consumed by his task. Toby had been out all evening with friends, and though he seemed content to leave him alone for the moment, since the conversation with his mum Josh had finally accepted he could rely on no one except himself. To ensure Toby left, he had taken matters into his own hands. After all, how much worse could his life get? Did it even matter if he got caught changing Toby's grades?

But now, his palms began to sweat. He felt sick. Of course it mattered! Terrified, he closed down everything he had been working on and turned the computer off. He hadn't even touched Toby's grades, but he'd got into the exam board's system and that had been enough to give him a cold shower. What the hell had he done? Mikayla's inquest was coming up and now he'd done this! If he got found out, he'd be seen as a criminal right from the start. He stood no chance.

His whole body shaking now, he got to his feet. He had to tell someone about the hacking straight away. It was the only way. He'd say how sorry he was. He'd say he never hurt Mikayla.

As he lurched out of the room and down the stairs, sounds of the TV drifted from the living room. Good. His mum and stepdad wouldn't notice him leaving.

Quietly pulling the front door closed behind him, he slipped out into the darkness, though the evening was still feverishly hot, like the nightmare day when Mikayla – no. Don't even think about it. He walked fast. Then faster, faster, until he ran. He stumbled inside the police station with his heart practically pounding out of his chest. At the reception desk, he opened his mouth intending to confess to the hacking, to explain that all he'd tried to do was help Mikayla, to make somebody, *anybody* under-stand. Instead he just croaked, 'Help me.'

Natalie

49

Bright sunlight streamed down through the trees, falling onto her bare arms, while the light fabric of her summer dress brushed delicately against her legs. Josh walked beside her, but he was facing away from her so she took his arm. 'Josh?'

He turned and beamed at her, his eyes sparkling. 'I wish I'd met you sooner,' he said.

'You met me at school,' she teased him.

'You know what I mean.'

'Well, we've found each other now, haven't we?'

He took hold of her hand. 'Come on, let's go home.'

Her heart skipped a beat as they turned to run back towards his flat, stumbling up the steps to his front door, and once inside he pushed the door shut and pressed her up against it, kissing her so hard it took her breath away. She reached up to slip the straps of her dress from her shoulders, longing for Josh to tear her dress from her body, but he didn't. He stopped kissing her, his lips at her ear. 'Why are you doing this to me, Nat?'

'I'm not,' she said, 'it's all pretend. Please don't stop–'

He was gone. Her eyes snapped open to the darkness of Verity's spare room. She closed them again and tried to get back to sleep, but Josh's wounded voice from her dream haunted her. *Why are you doing this to me?*

Abruptly, she got out of bed, pulled a dressing-gown over her pyjamas and tiptoed down to the kitchen. She couldn't let herself get dragged down by thoughts like that. She had to stay focused.

Just as she finished making herself a cup of tea, Verity appeared in the doorway. 'Oh, hey Nat,' she said, 'couldn't you sleep?'

'I just had a weird dream,' she said as she sat down at the kitchen table. Verity sat opposite her.

'I know how hard you're finding this, but you're doing the right thing,' Verity said. 'I can see you still love Josh, but you can never trust him again after what he did.'

'Yes, I know.'

'Have you given notice to the couple renting your flat yet? You'll be wanting to move back there soon.'

'Uh ... no. Sorry, V, but I promise I won't be here much longer, I'll figure something else out.'

'It wasn't a hint, I just thought it might help to start planning for what's next. And the wedding venue? Have you called–'

'No.'

'I can phone them for you, you don't have to do it yourself. Or at least, I can explain what happened. They might need to speak to you before they can actually cancel. But I can take some of the strain.'

Natalie took a big gulp of tea that burned her throat. 'V ... Rob said you're not having the best time right now. That you're not very happy–'

'Oh,' she said, 'no, it's nothing. He was exaggerating. Yes, I'm a bit stressed about the business but it's nothing compared to what you're going through.'

'I shouldn't be burdening you with all this.'

Verity reached across the table and squeezed her hand. 'Nat, tell me you're not just leaving this stuff like calling the venue because you're considering giving Josh another chance? Rob and I–'

'You seriously think I'd have a relationship with somebody who tried to bully me?' Natalie said, desperate to shut the conversation down.

'I don't know. No. I'm just wondering what's going on with you. It's obvious you're avoiding talking to us, and we're really worried about you.'

'I don't need you to worry about me. I know what I'm doing.' Natalie picked up her tea and made for the door, but Verity stood in her way.

'Natalie, I'm not letting you off that easily. What's going on? I know you're hiding something.'

'I don't have to wear my heart on my sleeve, okay? I really appreciate how much you and Rob have helped me, but please don't worry about me. I will get everything sorted out.'

Verity looked at her strangely, but she didn't press her any further, and Natalie made her way slowly back up the stairs to her grey bedroom.

50

Natalie listened in horror as Gareth told her about the conversation he'd had with Josh the night before.

'I did my best to talk him out of it,' he said, 'but his mind is made up. He's going to turn himself in. I don't think he'll listen to anybody, except maybe for you.'

Her eyes prickled with tears. If she came face to face with Josh, she wouldn't be able to lie to him. He'd find out about her plan with Toby, and he would try to stop her doing it. That couldn't happen, not when it was the one thing that could clear his name forever. 'What will happen to him if he confesses?' she asked.

'I have no idea. Hopefully they'll realise he's not in his right mind and nothing will happen. But do you really want him to take that risk?'

'Gareth, I can't–'

'No, of course you can't,' he snapped. 'You've given up on him like everybody else.'

'It's not like that!' she said. She couldn't help herself. 'You know how much I cared about him.'

'I know,' he said, with a sigh. 'I know. And in your position, I would probably act the same as you are now. But all I can see is how much pain he's in.'

***

'Why on earth do you want to help Josh?' Toby asked her. In desperation, she'd turned to him when she'd arrived for work that morning.

'I don't want him to go to prison for something he didn't do!' she said. 'If you know anything, please, *please*, just help him. Surely you don't want him to end up going down for this? Even if you didn't get on that well when you were younger, you're still family.'

Toby sat down heavily at his desk. She knew it was a huge risk to ask him for help. For all she knew, he would be delighted with this news. But surely it wasn't in his interest to have Josh go to the police and start talking about Mikayla again, especially now Josh knew Mikayla had broken up with Toby mere minutes before she died? If he could just talk Josh out of it … *But if the police believe Josh's confession, Toby will be in the clear. Maybe he'll think it's a good thing, and worth the risk of Josh telling them about the break-up.* She swallowed hard. 'Toby, he said he's going to go to the police today. This morning.'

Toby frowned. 'You mean you want me to drop everything and go round right this second?'

'It's up to you,' she said. An idea struck her, and she touched his arm. 'I just thought you might want to help him. Like you helped me, giving me a job here. You've been so kind. I know you care about people more than you admit.' She took a deep breath. 'I'm sorry I've been giving you mixed messages. I was nervous about sleeping with someone else after what happened between me and Josh. But I can see you're a good man, and that I can trust you. I – I think I'm ready to take the next step with you, but I just need to know that Josh isn't going to end up in prison. If anyone can talk him round, I'm sure you can.'

Sure enough, Toby's expression brightened. Had he even puffed his chest out a little? The man really was like a strutting peacock. But if he went to see Josh perhaps he really would be able to talk some sense into him, or at least make him pause for a moment. And if Toby went out for a good length of time, she could even carry out a search of the office without fear of being discovered. It wasn't likely she'd find anything – after all, was he really likely to keep anything incriminating at work? But it had to be worth a go.

Josh

51

The knock on the door startled him, and he got nervously to his feet. The sound came again as he made his way down the hall, more urgent this time.

'Josh, it's Toby. I know you're in there!'

Josh froze. *Toby.* It just had to be Toby. He was about to leave for the police station, having spent the morning so far steeling himself for what was going to be an incredibly traumatic day. *But I have to do it. I have to pay.*

'Josh! Open the door!'

He did as Toby asked, shrinking back as his stepbrother burst into the hallway. Toby's round face was as pink as a ham, his eyes glittering darkly as he gave Josh an appraising look. 'You look like shit,' he said.

'I feel like shit,' Josh told him. Frankly, he'd say anything to get Toby to leave. He couldn't deal with this right now.

'Josh, I'm just going to say this once. Leave the past in the past. You're driving everyone nuts. You've destroyed your relationship with Natalie already. Don't start being ridiculous by going to the police. You know as well as I do that you're barely capable of hurting a fly, let alone Mikayla. The only way you could ever attack someone is behind a keyboard, like you did to Natalie. Like a coward. You know, that woman is worth ten of you. Telling her she's ugly, saying things about her scar. You're a disgrace.'

'I'm not listening to this,' Josh said. 'Just let me go, this is nothing to do with you.'

'That's where you're wrong. Natalie still seems to care what happens to you – God only knows why – and she wanted me to come here and talk some sense into you.'

'You've been talking to Natalie?'

'Course I have. Oh, that's right, you don't know. She's taken a job at the hotel. She's our events manager. I think she wanted to throw herself back into working to take her mind off the fact she was in the middle of planning her wedding to a man who has done nothing but try to hurt her.'

Josh froze. She was working at the hotel? Even knowing how Toby had treated him in the past. He swallowed hard. 'Is she okay?'

Toby gave him a withering look.

'I'm worried about her.'

'Look, we all just think you need help. You need to talk to somebody. Do you ever suppose that when everybody is telling you you've got a problem, they might actually be right?'

Josh was silent for a moment, taken aback by the idea.

Toby shook his head. 'I don't like seeing you like this. Believe it or not, I really was pleased for you and Natalie. I thought you deserved to be happy. But you need to accept that you completely blew it with her. Trying to get attention isn't going to help, and this little stunt of yours, going to the police, isn't going to get Natalie to come running back.'

'That's not why I'm doing it.'

'Well, whatever your reasons are, you're not thinking about what's best for anyone other than you. You're doing it to make *yourself* feel better.'

Natalie

52

Natalie paused for a moment, frustrated with herself. She'd quickly darted across to Toby's desk once he had left to see Josh. He was still logged in at his computer, but there was nothing incriminating in his recent emails or browser history; no sign that he had been the one trolling her. Neither was there anything untoward in his well-organised desk drawers, and now she was stumped. *Think! You might have to wait ages to get another good chance like this.*

Her eyes fell to his coat hanging on a hook – in his haste he'd forgotten to take it with him. She peeked out into the hallway. There was no sign of anyone coming, but that could change at any moment. Quickly, she started searching through his pockets … only to jump out of her skin when the door opened.

Angelique was startled too, her eyes fixed on Natalie's hand which she'd quickly snatched from Toby's pocket.

'What are you doing?' Angelique said.

Flustered, Natalie babbled some nonsense about having lost her car keys and checking whether Toby had found them and picked them up.

'He won't like it if he realises you are going through his things,' Angelique said. 'He caught a girl stealing once and he hit the roof.'

'I'm not stealing!'

'I know that. But –' Angelique gave her a concerned look. 'I've seen how he looks at you. Be careful, Natalie.'

'I – what did you need, Angelique? Can I help?'

'No, I need to speak to Toby. But it's not urgent.'

'Okay.'

Angelique hovered in the doorway for a moment, looking pointedly at her.

'… You don't need to worry about me,' Natalie said. 'I'm not going to get involved with Toby. I really am just looking for my keys. Maybe you could keep an eye out? They're on a key ring with a big pink pom-pom on it.'

'Like that one,' Angelique said, pointing to the key ring sat right in the middle of Natalie's desk.

She left without saying anything further, and Natalie let out a noise of frustration and anger at herself. Angelique probably wouldn't say anything to Toby about what she'd seen, but she couldn't be certain of that. Still, she couldn't give up now. She carried on searching, but there was nothing.

Eventually, admitting defeat, she sat down at her desk. She wasn't going to find anything here. She either had to get Toby to trust her so much that he opened up to her about Mikayla, or she'd have to get into his house and search there. But would that really help?

The photos. The thought suddenly struck her. *The photos he took down from the hall. Maybe it wasn't just about wanting a change. Maybe there was something more to it.*

And where would he have taken the photos? He probably wouldn't have got rid of them – he was too proud of his pictures for that – and they couldn't have contained anything seriously incriminating to have been displayed so long in public. But maybe there was something not immediately obvious, yet still a clue that could be pieced together if somebody knew what they were looking for. He'd have taken the photos back to his home, no doubt, and put them away in some box somewhere. *His house. I have to go to his house.*

***

'He is just impossible!' Toby announced as he burst back into the office.

Natalie turned, trying not to appear overly worried. 'Did you manage to talk him out of it?'

'Who knows? I told him he was being selfish, that he was going to the police to get attention. But maybe it would be good if he *did* go to them. Perhaps then he could get the help he so obviously needs.'

He strode over to stand behind her with a sigh, and his hands slithered over her shoulders, playing with the neckline of her shirt.

'Thank you for trying, Toby,' she said, trying not to stiffen as his fleshy fingers slipped inside her shirt, his hands soon finding her breasts which he squeezed as though he was testing the ripeness of a piece of fruit.

'I don't know what you saw in him,' he said, as he bent down so that his head was beside hers. She turned towards him and their lips met, while he continued rummaging around in her bra. *Just put up with it,* she willed herself. *I can bear this for a minute or two if it gets me closer to saving Josh.*

'Was everything okay while I was out?' he asked, abruptly breaking off their kiss and taking his hands off her chest. Relief flooded through her – thank God he was distracted enough by work not to want to take things further.

'Yes. Angelique wanted to speak to you, I don't know what about.'

'Course she did,' Toby muttered, 'I leave this hotel for five minutes and the whole bloody thing grinds to a halt.'

He was still complaining to himself under his breath as he left the office, and Natalie hurriedly readjusted her bra and did up the buttons on her shirt almost to her throat, the touch of his fingers on her skin still lingering. She had to press her hand across her mouth to stop a sob escaping. God knows if Toby's words would prevent Josh turning himself in, and she'd had to endure his thick tongue in her mouth and his hands groping at her chest. A wave of nausea washed over her, so strong it almost had her running to the toilets down the hall, but she managed to calm herself. *It really will be over soon. I will find what he's hiding.*

By the end of the day, Toby's irritation with Josh had lifted and his mood had improved considerably. He managed to catch her coming down the corridor and cornered her. 'Jodie and the kids are going to stay with her parents for the weekend,' he said, his eyes sparkling with delight. He leant close to her and draped her neck with a few cloying kisses, while she looked nervously about in case they were spotted.

'Oh, that's nice for them,' Natalie said, panic descending and making her prattle on as she tried to process what this meant. *I have to go to his house to find those photos. But what sort of price will I have to pay?* 'My nieces absolutely adore going to see my mum and dad,' she continued, 'they get spoilt rotten.'

He laughed. 'I think it's us who are going to be spoilt,' he said, 'a whole night to ourselves.' He stroked her cheek. 'I can't wait. You'll forget all about Josh after a night with me, I can promise you that.'

'I'm looking forward to it,' she told him, and he smiled with satisfaction before making his way down the corridor. Once he was out of sight Natalie sagged against the wall, her legs weak.

53

The days until the weekend passed excruciatingly – the time moving simultaneously fast and slow as she dreaded having to go to Toby's house, yet equally couldn't wait for the whole thing to be over. Once she'd found out whatever it was Toby was hiding, she could use it to make everything stop. She could tell Josh he was definitely innocent, she could move back into his flat, and Toby would get whatever justice he deserved. Cold dread seeped through her at the thought of what she might discover, and the thought of what she might have to *do* to discover it, because Toby wouldn't be put off from claiming his prize much longer. But she had to use that to her advantage. It was pretty obvious that Toby had no genuine feelings or respect for her. Having slept with her once or twice, he would likely lose interest in her entirely, but while he was chasing her she had a unique opportunity to get what she needed, and she had to make the most of it. But if Toby had actually killed Mikayla, and he discovered her snooping around in the house…

'I'm so sick of people's attitude here sometimes,' Toby said as he thundered into the office. 'Little details. I tell everyone constantly. It might seem like nothing to them, but a little dust and grime here and there can completely change how our guests see us!'

'Toby–'

'No, don't try to tell me everyone makes mistakes. It's laziness, pure and simple.'

Natalie got up and touched his arm. 'It's great how passionate you are about this place,' she said, 'but we do have some really good people here. Not everyone has a bad attitude.'

'Yes, you're right,' he said, but then his face clouded again. 'If I catch that new girl Becky on her phone again when she's supposed to be working–' He left his threat hanging. *Has he tried it on with her too?* She could easily believe it. Pursuing her and Becky simultaneously would just be an extra thrill for him.

'So, did Josh turn himself in, do you know?' Toby asked her, surprising her out of her thoughts. She had messaged Gareth to ask the same thing, and to her relief it seemed that he had decided against it.

'I don't think so,' she said. 'Whatever you said to him must have worked.'

'I don't know why he was so obsessed with that girl anyway,' Toby said. 'I know you're not supposed to say stuff like this about the dead, but Mikayla wasn't really anything all that special. I swear he was only interested in her because she was going out with me. That's just the kind of thing he would do – making everything all about him.'

Natalie twitched with anger, but she forced herself not to show it. 'Well, we've all seen what sort of person he is from what he did to me,' she said. She leant forward towards Toby as he sat down at his desk. She had to focus. He'd brought up that weekend without her needing to prompt him. Perhaps if she could keep him talking, she'd find out something useful. 'He must have been very jealous of you and Mikayla,' she said.

'He was. But he never said anything much about it. He was always just behind a screen in his own little world. Apart from when he was with Gareth, and God knows what the two of them used to talk about.'

'He wouldn't have acted on it, though. His jealousy.'

Toby shrugged. 'Only a weirdo like Josh would start winding himself up about something that happened so long ago and is already resolved. Why can't he just trust what the police con- cluded? And how he can think he did something and then forgot? It makes no sense to me at all.'

'Could you ever imagine it,' Natalie asked. 'Being *that* jealous? Because it can happen, can't it, feelings getting out of hand like that?'

Toby gave her an odd look. 'Nat–'

'I didn't mean–' She laughed uncomfortably. God, she was bad at this. What a stupidly suspicious thing to ask him. 'I had an ex once who was a pretty jealous type,' she lied quickly. 'I vowed to myself I'd never end up with a creep like that again, but after this stuff with Josh, I worry sometimes.'

'You're asking me if I'm a creep like Josh and your other ex?' Toby asked. Luckily, he'd found the question more amusing than offensive.

'No, of course I'm not. It's just ... I don't know. You know what I mean, don't you? It's hard to really know people. And besides, don't you feel bad about Jodie?' The words were out of her mouth before she could help herself. She felt awful for Toby's wife.

'I don't feel about Jodie how I feel about you,' he said. 'Me and Jodie have been together a long time. Stuff changes. But what she doesn't know can't hurt her.'

54

By the time the weekend rolled around, Natalie felt sick. Aside from the awful prospect of taking things further with Toby, how on earth was she going to find the old photos? What if she got into the house and they just weren't there? What if she never even had an opportunity to search? What if Toby discovered her? The what ifs filled her mind, and she could barely concentrate at work. More than once she had to flee to the toilets to hide away and take some deep breaths.

Saturday was busy at the hotel, as usual, and it was late before she could leave. She hadn't seen much of Toby all day, apart from when they'd briefly crossed paths earlier in the afternoon and he'd checked she was still coming round, telling her how excited he was and giving her a little pat on the bum when he thought no one was watching. Natalie's hands were shaking as she arrived at Toby's house. How much more of this could she take?

But when he opened the door, she was surprised to hear a child crying somewhere inside.

'Nat,' he said, 'I tried to call you—'

She took her phone from her pocket. 'The battery's dead,' she said. She'd been so distracted she'd forgotten to charge it the night before.

'Katy's ill,' Toby said. 'She's got a fever and Jodie thought it was better to come back home. Katy managed to get a little sleep in the car, but now she's screaming—'

'Toby?' Jodie's voice called from upstairs. 'Who is it?'

Natalie's heart was pounding. If Katy was ill, most of the family would probably be at home for the next day or two at least. How on earth was she going to get a chance to snoop around the house?

'Can I do anything to help?' she asked, once Toby had called up to Jodie that the visitor was 'nothing important'.

'I don't think so,' he said. He reached out and stroked her cheek. 'Another time, okay?'

Natalie's heart sank. How long would this go on for? She'd been in pieces all day worrying about this night, and now it wasn't even going to happen! The horror was just delayed, and she couldn't bear it. It had to be this weekend. She had to make it stop.

Suddenly, her gaze fell on a row of little hooks on the wall by the door. House keys! Lots of them – they clearly had a couple of spare sets. If Toby turned round again, she could grab one without them even noticing it was missing.

Toby leant in to kiss her, pulling her towards him. As quick as she could, she reached her hand around, trying as gently as possible to grab a set of keys. They jangled softly, but he was apparently too caught up in the moment to care. Jodie called him from upstairs, and he quickly pulled away from her, his face a little flushed. Natalie smiled at him, her pulse thundering so hard she felt faint. But she'd done it! She'd got the keys.

'I hope Katy feels better soon,' she told him, before turning and making her way back towards her car.

Instead of leaving, she drove a little down the road and parked again. The lights were on upstairs in the house; there would be no chance of her getting in right now. She'd have to wait. But even then, the situation was hopeless. She couldn't let herself into the house while the family were still inside, could she? Even if she was confident they were asleep, surely she couldn't prowl around silently enough not to wake them. And with a feverish toddler in the house, no one was likely to be sleeping soundly that night.

She sighed as she plugged her phone in to the car and waited for it to power up. This was a nightmare. But once her phone had finally woken up, the nightmare only deepened. A message from Gareth.

Josh has turned himself in. I just hope they don't take him seriously.

A small cry escaped her. She hadn't acted fast enough! She couldn't let Josh put himself through this – she *had* to find something that would clear his name once and for all. She tried to take heart from Gareth's words, but her mind teemed with awful possibilities. The police probably *wouldn't* take Josh seriously if he walked in and confessed to a crime he couldn't remember doing. But if he thought one of the nightmares he had about killing Mikayla was the truth and told them that version of events, who knew what could happen?

She was startled out of her thoughts some time later as the door to Toby's house burst open. The whole family spilled out onto the street, Finn in pyjamas and a dressing-gown, while Jodie was in leggings and a long sweatshirt, a small bundle in her arms that must be Katy. They all got into their car and quickly drove away. Natalie frowned. Where were they off to? Then it struck her – they must be taking Katy to hospital. She vaguely remembered from when she and Josh had gone round for dinner that Jodie had said she couldn't drive. The whole family must have gone as Jodie probably couldn't bear to be parted from Katy if Toby took the little girl on his own.

She picked up the house keys. The idea of going into the house was still nerve-wracking, but at least now it felt possible. She'd have the whole place to herself, with virtually no risk of being discovered.

It was now or never.

55

Natalie sighed as she put yet another box of photos aside. She'd gone to the computer in the upstairs study first to look for evidence of Toby trolling her, but that had been fruitless, so she'd turned her attention to the photos. It had been easy enough to find where he stored them all – there were boxes and boxes inside a cupboard next to the desk. Unfortunately, Toby wasn't as well organised at home as he was at the hotel and the collection wasn't labelled, so going through them was slow and laborious. Eventually she came across a wallet of photos that looked to be from the right time period, and her breath caught in her throat as she flipped through the stack of images. But, no. Nothing from Chedford Lake.

She put the photos carefully away again, and started on another set, and then another, until the sight of a familiar image nearly made her drop the whole pack. The photos he'd taken down from the hotel, and with them, all the other pictures from the lake! She flicked through them feverishly, trying to look for every detail in the images, the tiniest thing that seemed strange, any faces that didn't seem to fit. She shuddered at a horrible image Toby had taken of Josh being sick, and quickly flicked that to the back of the pile. Toby really was a pig. But before she knew it, she was staring at that same photo again. She'd gone through the whole lot! And there was nothing – nothing at all that was related to Mikayla's death. No strangers; the teenagers in the pictures were clearly all one group. Some of the photographs were really beautiful, showing the lake at sunset, but half of them were just embarrassing pictures of drunk kids.

Maybe there were more. *Or maybe Toby hid the incriminating ones somewhere else.* The thought made her pause. If there was anything truly incriminating, why would he even keep it? If he had any sense, surely he'd just throw it away, no matter how proud he was of his photography.

She sat back with a sigh. What on earth was she doing? This was never going to work. She'd broken into the house of a family with a sick child, started looking through their possessions, and for what? There wasn't even anything here! Tears stung her eyes. She'd been such an idiot! How had she ever thought this would work? It was just sheer desperation.

She opened another wallet full of photos, though she could barely see them through her tears, and forced herself to focus. More images swam before her eyes. These pictures weren't even of Chedford Lake. But then an image made her pause. A run-down house – it looked virtually abandoned – except for the fact there was a woman standing in the doorway. She was angry, her arm outstretched as she pointed her finger at Toby accusingly. Her hair fell in a messy dark blonde tangle around her shoulders, and she was wearing a bright pink cardigan covered with blue flowers which stood out oddly – a flash of colour against the grim, creepy house. Behind her the hall was just visible, piled high with boxes and other junk.

This was Gareth's house! This was when Toby had found it and upset Gareth by taking photos. Natalie stared at the woman's face. How difficult it must have been for both her and Gareth to live this way. And how cruel of Toby to laugh about it.

She was so absorbed in her thoughts that she jumped out of her skin at the sound of the front door slamming shut. Feet thundered upstairs. She leapt to her feet, trying to kick the photos under the desk as she ran across to close the door and turn the light off. But the person was already upstairs, and from the sound of the heavy footsteps it had to be Toby. If she closed the door he would notice. All she could do now was try to hide, and Toby would hopefully assume the light had been left on by mistake when he had left the house earlier. She tucked herself away beside the storage cupboard where the photos were kept. It wasn't a great hiding place, but she wouldn't be visible from the hall. As long as Toby didn't come inside the room and start looking around she would be safe.

For a brief, heart-stopping moment, she thought she had got away with it. The footsteps passed by the doorway, and on down the landing. But then they stopped. Natalie squeezed her eyes closed in fear, not that it helped. What was Toby doing? Had he stopped to look at the study? Was he wondering why the light was on?

The room exploded with jangling sound, making her jump out of her skin. For a moment she couldn't understand what it was. As realisation struck her, she fumbled her phone from her pocket. Toby's name was on the screen. He'd stopped in the hall to call her. And there was no way he couldn't have heard her phone ringing.

56

'Natalie?' Toby said, once his eyes had fallen on her in her hiding place. His face was confused rather than angry. But why would he be angry yet? He had no idea what she'd been up to.

'Toby, I–' she rushed to speak, but she couldn't finish her sentence. She'd been so confident no one would come back before she finished what she was doing that she hadn't even tried to think of an excuse in case she was discovered! But what excuse could she possibly give, anyway? Her presence here made absolutely no sense. Instead of explaining herself, she wriggled out from beside the cupboard, straightening her clothes primly as if the whole situation was completely normal.

'Are you okay?' he said. 'You look like you've been crying.'

'I–'

'How did you get in?'

'The door wasn't locked,' she lied. 'I don't know why I came here. I didn't know where else to go, I guess.'

'Have you fallen out with your brother? I thought you were staying with him?'

'How … how's Katy?' she asked. Her mind raced. She shouldn't even know that the family had gone anywhere – she only knew that because she'd been keeping watch on the house, and she could hardly tell Toby that. 'Where is everyone?'

'We took Katy to hospital. They've checked her over, they're just keeping an eye on her now, but it looks like she'll be completely fine. Finn fell asleep on Jodie's lap, and I just came to pick up a couple of things because I think we might still be there a little while.'

'I'm … I'm glad she's okay.'

Toby's expression hardened. 'I don't understand why you came here. Jodie and the kids are still around this weekend – what did you think you were doing?'

As he waited for her to answer, his eyes fell on the photos she'd tried to kick under the desk.

'Toby–' she started, as understanding bloomed on his face. 'I was just–'

He went across and picked the photos up. 'Is this … is this what I think it is?'

Sheer panic overtook her. 'Josh has turned himself in,' she blurted. 'I'm just so worried–'

'But you and Josh are over,' he said, unconcerned by her news.

'I know,' she said, still trying to play along. 'But he's obviously not thinking straight. Even though it's over I don't want him to suffer. I thought maybe I could find something to help. I saw that you all went out, I'd taken some keys from beside the door earlier and I let myself in. I'm sorry, Toby. I didn't mean to deceive you, I was just trying to help Josh, but I knew you wouldn't like it.'

'There's nothing here to find,' he said.

'But you said how you didn't want the photos up in the hotel any more–'

'I just don't like thinking about it right now!' he said. 'Not when it's all been brought up again. I just wanted to get some bloody peace and get rid of any reminders!' He narrowed his eyes at her. He was standing in her way, so she couldn't dart past him to the door. *He knows. He knows I'm lying.*

'Did Josh ask you to do this?' he said heavily.

'No. I told you, it's over–'

'Is it?' he said. 'Because you are doing a lot for someone who has treated you so badly.'

'Toby, just let me go home. This has all been an awful mistake.'

He reached out a hand towards her. 'Kiss me,' he said.

'What?'

'You heard me. We've got the place to ourselves right now, haven't we?'

'Because your daughter is in hospital!'

He nodded slowly. 'There's always something, right? Not at work. Not right now, even when there's no one here to see.'

'Surely you're worried about Katy—'

'She's fine, Natalie. She just picked up some bug at nursery that's given her a rash, but the doctors aren't worried about her. They're just being cautious.'

'I just can't right now,' she said. 'I don't think I'm ready for a new relationship. Me and Josh have only just broken up, my head's been a mess—'

'Or,' Toby said, his eyes fixed on hers, his voice low and menacing, '*or*, this whole thing has been fake.' He ran a finger down her cheek, along her scar and around her chin. His touch was so soft that she broke out in goosebumps. He was looking at her differently now: not as a new conquest to drool over, but as a person. And he could see her, because when it came down to it, she was no good at hiding. If he hadn't been so blinded by his lust he probably would have seen through her right from the start.

'No,' she said helplessly, as he moved himself more firmly in front of her. 'You said it yourself. Josh has treated me badly, I'm not still interested in him—'

'Then there's nothing standing in your way from being with me, then, is there?' he said, a slow smile spreading across his face.

He knows full well I'm lying. He knows, and now he's playing with me like a cat with a mouse.

57

Panic flooded her. No one was likely to be coming back to Toby's house any time soon. She was alone.

'Toby,' she said, 'not like this. This is all wrong.'

'I just want to know if this has ever been real,' he said. 'You've always been blowing hot and cold with me, playing silly games. I've put up with it long enough.'

Natalie tried to squirm past him but he grabbed her arm. 'I thought you cared about me,' she said, pulling her arm free and rubbing it pointedly so he could see he'd hurt her. 'I thought this meant something to you.'

'Don't be so deluded,' he said, 'you knew exactly what this was. This never *meant* anything, Nat. It was just sex. And *you're* the one who's really at fault here. You're the one who is being dishonest. Just tell me the truth.'

'Please, let me leave,' she said, trying to keep her voice calm. 'This whole thing has been one huge mistake.' She took a deep breath. 'I'm sorry I misled you. You're right, I'm the one at fault here, and I – I'm sorry.'

He snorted. 'I don't get you at all. You must be mental to be helping Josh when he's tried to drag you down the way he has. He said awful things about you.'

Natalie stared at him. Was he serious? Was he still going to try and maintain that *Josh* did all of it?

'I've lost all respect for him now. He–'

'*You've* lost all respect for *him*?' Natalie exploded. 'After you have been trying to cheat on your wife with your stepbrother's ex-fiancée? After how you treat the women at the hotel?' She jabbed her finger at him, anger temporarily burning away her fear. '*You* wrote that stuff to me! You wrote it, and you framed Josh for it that afternoon you came to visit me at the flat! Just because I haven't managed to prove it yet, doesn't mean I don't know for certain it was you! And you know what else? I'm going to tell Jodie exactly what you've been up to. I'm going to tell her the second she gets home, unless you help Josh right now by telling the truth about exactly what you know, and exactly what you've been up to!'

'What?' Toby said, taking a step back. 'I don't know what the hell you're talking about! You and Josh, the pair of you deserve each other, you're both completely insane!'

'Then I will tell Jodie! I'll tell her that you tried to sleep with me, that you hassle all the female staff at the hotel, so much that they leave after just a few weeks–'

His face turned thunderous, his eyes popping. 'Those stupid girls brought it all on themselves!' he said.

Natalie shoved him out of the way, hard. 'You're a pig,' she said. 'The way you treat women is disgusting!'

'And what about the way they treat me?' he yelled. 'Jodie's not the same since we had the kids, we hardly ever have sex–'

'She's probably exhausted!' Natalie said. 'Kids are hard work. Do you really think that gives you the right–'

'Well, at least I'm not deluded,' he snapped back. 'Running around like this after a man who tried to ruin your self-esteem just to get you to stay with him, or whatever the hell he was trying to do? It's pathetic, Natalie. I thought you were made of stronger stuff than this! Josh doesn't deserve–'

'Josh deserves justice!' she yelled. 'You gave him pills and told him to kill himself. You should be ashamed! But you're not, are you? All you care about is your own ego. That's why you couldn't handle it when Mikayla said it was over, could you? When you heard she'd found someone else.'

He nodded slowly. 'You think *I* killed her?'

'Did you?' Natalie said. Fear was prickling down her spine now. Toby was still standing in her way.

'No!' he said.

'I'm going to tell Jodie,' Natalie said, though her voice was smaller as she realised what a mistake she'd made threatening Toby. Her words sounded stupid now. Would he even care if she spoke to Jodie? But apparently he did, as he said, 'You're really willing to destroy a family over this?'

'What, like you tried to destroy me and Josh?'

'I am not letting you tell Jodie,' he said. 'You are going to stay here, and we are going to talk this through until you come to your senses.'

'Let me go.'

'You're not leaving until we've sorted this out.'

She tried to dart past him and he grabbed both her arms. In a blind panic, she threw her head forward, smashing it against his with enough force that he let her go and staggered backwards. Natalie didn't waste a second. She dashed out of the room towards the stairs, but as she started to sprint down them, Toby's footsteps weren't far behind her.

58

Natalie let out a scream as he grabbed her shoulder at the bottom of the stairs. 'I am not letting you destroy my family!' he said. 'You're not leaving this house until you've calmed down and started thinking straight.'

He was holding her tight. But she wasn't far from the front door. If she could just get him to let go, she would be able to get out. 'Toby,' she said, 'just tell me the truth.'

'If I had killed her, I'm hardly going to tell you and let you walk out of here, am I?'

His small blue eyes were fixed on hers, but she couldn't read them. 'I'm pleading with you,' she said. 'Surely there's some part of you that doesn't want Josh to suffer. If there's something you know, just tell me.'

Toby's grip softened. 'It won't help,' he said. 'It's like Josh wants his life to be bad. If it's not this, it'll be something else, and it's not your responsibility or mine to help him if all he wants is to self-destruct.'

'Well, I'm not going to kick him while he's down,' Natalie said. 'Not like you did. I'm going to do my best to help, and maybe a little kindness for once is what he needs.'

A flash of pain crossed Toby's face and he was silent for a moment. 'What is it you think I know?' he asked eventually.

'I don't know,' she admitted. 'Maybe what Mikayla did straight after breaking up with you. Did you see anything unusual, or any*one* unusual? People are saying there was someone else there that day – did you see anybody? Was it the other guy Mikayla liked? Did she call him?'

He shifted uncomfortably. She was right! He did know something. 'Toby,' she pressed him. 'Please. Just tell me.'

'Okay,' he said. 'Okay. But if I do, you don't talk to Jodie. That's the deal.'

'Yes. I won't talk to Jodie.'

He held her gaze for a moment, as if checking she was telling the truth. Satisfied, he began to speak. 'I followed Mikayla, just for a minute or two after she split up with me. I stayed hidden, and once she thought I was out of earshot, she called him – this guy she was into. I didn't hear his name. I hardly heard anything, really. She was upset. She was crying, she said she wanted him to come and pick her up.'

'Do you think he did come to get her?'

'I don't know. I was so angry that she had called him, I just turned around and ran the other way. That's it, though, Natalie. That really is all I know. I'm telling you the truth.'

Natalie was silent for a moment. 'You need to tell the police that,' she said. 'Now that Josh has turned himself in, you need to go and tell them what really happened that morning. It could help him.'

'No.'

'Why not?'

'Do you really think the police didn't check who she'd called on her phone that day? They would have known exactly who this guy was. If they were suspicious about him, they would have arrested him at the time. Nothing I have to tell them will make the slightest bit of difference. All it will do is make *me* look suspicious.'

Natalie took a step towards the door, and Toby stepped closer too, trying to position himself between her and the exit, but she was too quick for him. He hadn't locked the door behind him when he'd arrived home and it opened easily when she pushed down on the handle. In her eagerness she practically fell out into the street.

'Natalie, stop!' Toby shouted, as she struggled to regain her balance. Then he lowered his voice to a hiss. 'You cannot go to the police about this.'

One look in his eyes was enough to tell her that it was time to go. Time to run.

59

She burst through the door into Rob and Verity's house and almost collided with Rob in the hall.

'Natalie? What on earth–'

She quickly turned back to the doorway, peering outside into the street. Could Toby have managed to get to his car fast enough to follow her as she drove? She hadn't seen his car behind her, but that didn't mean he hadn't. Adrenaline was still pounding through her after her desperate flight from Toby's house. Had she not managed to dart across the road just before a car sped past, blocking Toby's path, he would have caught up with her. As it was he'd been forced to pause, giving her enough time to dash to her car and speed away.

Rob helped her inside and pushed the door closed, and she sank back against the wall, her breath coming in jagged gasps.

'Natalie?' Rob said, taking hold of her as she sagged down to her knees. 'Take some deep breaths.'

She did as he asked, but when she breathed out it turned into a low moaning sound as the terror of the last hour or so overwhelmed her.

Rob held her as she cried a few huge, frightened sobs, and then she pushed him away. 'It was him,' she said. 'It was Toby.'

'Natalie, look at me,' Rob said. 'I don't know what you're talking about. Has Toby done something to you? Has he hurt you?'

'You don't understand,' she said, 'you don't understand!'

'No, I don't.'

'There's no time!'

She tried to stand but she couldn't, and Rob took her hands. 'There's time for you to tell me what this is about. You're frightening me.'

Rob listened to her as she choked out the whole story, his face filling with increasing horror as she outlined her plan with Toby and her belief that Josh was innocent of everything.

'But now he's turned himself in, and I need to help him, but I have no evidence it was Toby who killed Mikayla! I couldn't find anything. The only thing that convinced me was how he reacted to me running away from his house, how he said I couldn't go to the police about it—'

'Natalie, you're telling me that you believe Toby killed Mikayla and yet you have been getting close to him, putting yourself at risk, for the sake of helping Josh?'

'Toby said himself that he was angry Mikayla called this other guy she had feelings for at the lake. He must have snapped and drowned her out of jealousy. Or maybe this guy she phoned came to the lake and that's when things turned nasty. If I only knew who he was—'

Rob let go of her hands and stood up abruptly. 'I'll make you some tea.'

She struggled to her feet and followed him into the kitchen. What else could she do? Her nerves were shredded and she needed to think.

She sipped her tea slowly, while Rob sat opposite her, his eyes dark and troubled.

'I don't know what to do,' she said softly. 'I'm frightened. It's been ... it's been so hard.' She covered her face briefly with her hands. She was physically, emotionally and mentally exhausted. She'd pushed herself to breaking point with her subterfuge, and it had come to nothing.

'Listen, there's...' He sighed, and the look on his face sent chills through her. 'There are things you need to know.'

'Please, I can't think about anything other than this—'

'It's about this. It's about the lake.'

At these words, she stared at him in astonishment. What could Rob possibly know? But there was clearly something – he looked as though he had the weight of the world on his shoulders, his eyes haunted as he met her gaze. 'What is it?' she asked, her voice almost a whisper. 'Tell me.'

He was silent for a long, excruciating moment, and then his words, when they finally came, were not at all what she was expecting.

'It was me,' he said. '*I'm* the person Mikayla called.'

Natalie's mind buckled at his bizarre statement. What on earth was he talking about? Was this some kind of joke? Was he playing with her?

'I don't understand,' she said at length. 'You didn't know Mikayla.'

'Yes, I did,' Rob insisted. 'She had a Saturday job at that pet store where I used to help out in the holidays when I was back from uni. She had a crush on me. I didn't encourage her, or anything.'

'So you were the person she called that morning!' Natalie said. Her words came out broken: odd, faltering sounds as her mind still refused to take in what he'd said.

'Yes,' he said. 'I – she kissed me once. I got talking to her one day, and she lunged at me. I didn't push her away as quickly as I should have. That's all it was. But she read a whole lot more into it.'

'Rob, why didn't you just tell me?' Natalie exploded. 'Why did you keep it a secret when you knew what people were saying about Mikayla's death? When you knew Josh was upset about that day?'

'Because I feel ashamed!' he said, 'and embarrassed. And guilty.'

'Why?'

'Because I was twenty and she was only sixteen. I shouldn't have kissed her back and I shouldn't have let her think I was interested in her. But I didn't think it was a big deal at the time. I guess I felt flattered. I kind of liked her attention.'

'So, you made a mistake–'

'And she called me in tears and asked me to come and get her from the lake. And I said no.'

'You said no?'

'I didn't want to get involved.'

'So you weren't there?'

Rob took a deep breath and let it out as a sigh. 'I changed my mind in the end and I did drive there – she was only young and she was obviously upset. I wanted to take her back home to her parents. She shouldn't have been out there on her own feeling like that.'

'And what happened when you got there?' Natalie demanded. 'Josh has gone to the police and turned himself in for killing her. He was so upset by what people have been saying he started to believe it! So if you know anything–'

'I never saw her. I – I chickened out.'

Natalie stared at him. 'You chickened out. What do you mean?'

He didn't meet her eyes. 'That's why I feel guilty. If I had gone there earlier, if I had actually bothered trying to find her…' He shook his head. 'But I saw the ambulance and the police cars and I just left again.'

Tears stung Natalie's eyes. 'How could you spend all these months saying nothing? You know how upset I've been.'

'I didn't know you were investigating Toby! I didn't know you were putting yourself through all of this.'

'Why doesn't anyone care about the truth? Why is everyone happy to make Josh the scapegoat?'

'I'm sorry,' he said. 'I'm so sorry. But it makes no difference. I can't help Josh.'

'Of course you can! You can tell the police exactly what happened in that phone call!'

Natalie waited, boiling with impatience, while he got up and took her empty mug over to the sink. 'Do you want another?' he asked her.

'No!' she said. 'All I want is for you to tell the police–'

'There's nothing to tell,' he said heavily as he sat back down at the table. 'They already spoke to me at the time because they know she called me. I just told them she was upset and wanted me to come and get her. She didn't really even tell me what she was upset about, just said she needed me. That's all there was to it. I have nothing new to tell the police.'

But when Natalie scrutinised his face, she could tell that was *not* all there was to it. From the deep lines across his forehead to the pained look in his eyes, it was obvious there was much, much more.

For a moment they sat in oppressive silence, the air thick with unspoken words, until Natalie couldn't bear it any longer. 'What else aren't you telling me?' she asked as calmly as she could. 'I know there's something.'

He shook his head, and in her desperation she wanted to reach across the table and give him a slap. Why was he drawing all of this out so much? Didn't he understand what she was going through? Couldn't he see she was in hell? She jumped as her phone began to ring, the pealing sound fraying her nerves afresh.

Toby. She rejected the call with a shiver of fear and focused on Rob. 'Tell me!' she said, her voice high and strained. 'Can any of this really get any worse?'

'Yes,' he said. 'It can.'

'Well, there's no way out of this thing now,' she snapped. 'I just have to carry on. I have to make sure the right people get justice. If I can't do that, Josh's life is ruined, and mine too. I don't even have a job to go back to. I can't go back and work for Toby – I'm sure he won't let me set foot in the hotel even if I wanted to. No doubt he'll do his damnedest to make sure I can't get work anywhere else as well.'

'Nat, it's–' Rob's shoulders shook, and she got up and went around to his side of the table, placing her arm around him. 'Look, I'm not angry any more,' she said, taken aback by his display of emotion. 'I wish you'd told me earlier, but we can't change that now.'

'It's … it's Verity,' he said.

'What about Verity?'

'She's gone. She's taken the children.'

'*What?*'

'And it's my fault.' He buried his face in his hands. 'All of this – it's all my fault.'

60

Natalie sat back down opposite him as Rob started to speak. 'I slept with someone else,' he said flatly.

'When?'

'A couple of years ago. But Verity didn't find out straight away. It all came out not long before you went to that school reunion.'

'Rob ... how could you do that?' Natalie asked, her voice low.

'I don't know what I was thinking,' he said miserably. 'It was a huge, huge mistake. I regret it more than I can even say.'

'How did Verity find out?'

'I told her. The guilt was eating me up, I couldn't bear lying to her. One night I just crumbled. I thought it was the right thing to do – she could tell there was something bothering me.'

'Being honest *is* the right thing to do, surely,' she said.

'I don't know. I'm beginning to wonder.'

Natalie's head was pounding, and while Rob collected his thoughts she got up and filled two glasses with water. He gulped some down, while she sipped hers slowly, her mind reeling as she tried to take everything in.

'She took it really hard,' Rob said.

'Can you blame her?'

'No, of course not. I know this mess is all my fault. Verity has always been a bit insecure–'

'Seriously?' Natalie said incredulously. The vivacious, optimistic Verity she knew had never seemed insecure.

'About her appearance,' Rob said. 'She hides it well, but she said she's always been that way, so hearing about what I did really wrecked her confidence. She could hold it together at work and put on a brave face, but when she was alone with me she was very hurt and angry. She didn't want us to separate because of the girls, and of course I didn't want to – I still love her, that's never changed. But ever since then life has just been unbearable. She never lets me forget it. Every day she wants me to see how much I've hurt her, and I've apologised so many times the words don't mean anything any more. They're just useless sounds.'

'Oh, Rob,' Natalie said. She couldn't think what else to say.

'She threw herself into the business, she started spending a lot of time working in the evenings. I thought she did it because she just didn't want to be around me, and I guess I couldn't really blame her. She stopped letting me help her with the business accounts–'

'Why?' Natalie asked. Verity had made no secret of how much she hated doing the business accounts and how glad she was to have an accountant husband.

'I thought she was just doing it out of spite. I said it was ridiculous, she was clearly cutting off her nose to spite her face, but I just let her get on with it.'

'She spent a lot of money around then on advertising and refurbishing the shop,' Natalie said. 'I thought it was a bit risky.'

'Well, after she let you go, it kept bugging me. She said there wasn't enough work and she couldn't afford to pay you, but she's been snowed under. And she seemed really negative about you and Josh. I mean, I thought she was justifiably worried to begin with, and when it seemed like he was behind what was happening to you online–'

'*Toby* was behind that,' Natalie insisted. 'And Rob, I really do want to support you with this, but I'm so worried about Josh, I can barely think about anything else right now–'

'You don't understand!' Rob insisted. '*Verity* was behind it! Toby had nothing to do with it. It was Verity who said all that stuff to you.'

Natalie stared at him, floored by yet another mental blow. But this one couldn't be right. It made no sense. 'That can't be true,' she said. 'I don't believe you.'

'It is true. Earlier today I decided to look at her accounts. I was really worried about the business, and I wanted to help her, even if she made it clear she didn't want anything from me.' Rob paused for a second. 'When I looked at the accounts, I saw that she had every reason to be anxious. She'd clearly spent a lot of money on advertising and things like that, but there were other chunks of money coming out of the business that didn't make a lot of sense.'

'So what was happening to it?'

'That's what I wondered,' Rob said. 'I decided to try and work it out, and that's when I stumbled across all her other social media accounts. The ones she was using to terrorise you.'

61

Tears stung Natalie's eyes, and she got up from the table, walking aimlessly around the kitchen. 'She hates me,' she said, resting her elbows on the worktop, head buried in her hands. 'She must actually hate me.'

'I confronted her about it earlier this evening,' Rob said. 'I could barely believe it. I still hoped there was some other explanation.'

'What did she say?' Natalie asked, her voice virtually a whisper.

'She went completely berserk. She was screaming that I always take anyone's side but hers, that it wasn't fair you were in some fairy-tale relationship when you're – and this was her word not mine – disfigured, while she was married to a man who cheated on her. She was so angry that you have all these followers online who love you, and that you have the confidence to do your vlogging at all. She said that she had tried to help you after the accident, giving you a job, and that you'd repaid her by taking over – that her clients would come to the shop and ask for you instead of her. She said your life had ended up better than hers, that you were just a parasite feeding off of her kindness. I was so angry and disgusted with her, and that just made her worse. She was so full of spite and hate ... and *she* framed Josh. She said she visited you at your flat that day, and she had a brief chance to use Josh's laptop to set him up.' Rob gulped down the rest of his water, avoiding Natalie's eyes. 'She said she was taking money from the business to try and save up to have cosmetic surgery, and that it was my fault for making her feel so bad about herself that she needed to do that. Then ... well, then she said she was leaving and she walked out with the girls. I don't even know where she went.'

'My God,' Natalie said. 'I'm so sorry.'

Rob paused for a moment, as if to try to stop himself breaking down again. 'The thing is, that's when it hit me. *She* knew that I knew Mikayla. And she knew that I went to the lake that morning. She's pretty much the only person who does know that. I confided in her about it not that long after we got together. When we started getting serious.'

'Rob—'

'So she wasn't just saying stuff about Mikayla online to hurt Josh and you, she was doing it to hurt me, too. That "stranger at the lake" stuff that came up, that was her. I couldn't understand where you had got that from, when you told me you'd heard about it. Nobody – *almost* nobody,' he said, stressing the word in a way that made her frown, 'knew I was there. But when you first started getting trolled it wouldn't have crossed my mind to suspect Verity. I thought it really was some silly rumour, nothing to do with me at all.'

'You mean someone apart from Verity *does* know about it?' Natalie said. 'You said *almost* nobody knew you were there …' She paused, and then light dawned. 'Toby! He overheard the call between you and Mikayla. Did he see you when you drove there?'

Rob looked startled. 'Toby? No. He didn't see me. At least, I didn't see him.'

'Then who?'

'Natalie, I've never told anyone this. Not Verity, not the police when they questioned me. Nobody.'

'Rob, you're frightening me,' she said, as cold goosebumps broke out over her skin. 'What are you talking about?'

'There really was a stranger there. A woman. And she was acting sort of … odd.'

Natalie listened closely as he explained to her about the woman he'd seen at Chedford Lake, her mind searching for anything that could help – any clues to her identity.

'You're sure?' she said. 'Messy light brown hair, and a bright cardigan with flowers on it?'

'Yes,' Rob said. 'I never forgot what she looked like. I've never been able to forget her at all. Nor the way she burst out of the trees, almost running straight in front of my car. I had to slam on the brakes and I got out to check she was okay.'

'And she said, "that poor girl,"' Natalie asked, repeating what Rob had told her.

'That's right. I was going to ask if she needed a lift somewhere – not that I really wanted her in the car with me – but it seemed wrong to just leave her. But she dashed off again. After that I didn't want to be there any more. I turned the car around and drove back home.'

His eyes had a faraway look as the memories played out. 'She … she frightened me, Natalie. She really frightened me.'

***

Up in her room, Natalie paced about restlessly. *Verity* had been the one trolling her. And Rob had known Mikayla. There *had* been a stranger at the lake. As the thoughts whirled, she stopped for a moment to sit on her bed, only to stand up and pace, then sit again as she tried to process it. Admittedly, there had been some odd moments in the shop from time to time with Verity – the way she'd tried to suggest a venue far bigger and flashier than Natalie and Josh had wanted for their wedding, and with a price tag to match. The look that had flashed across her face when one of their brides, Carmel, had been in tears and looked to Natalie rather than Verity for help. Not to mention how Verity and Rob had ambushed her about Josh, which had clearly been her idea.

But the way she wrote about me. About my scars. About Josh. It was twisted. It was *evil*. Anger flushed Natalie's cheeks. Verity had made her life a living hell! She'd made all this happen! And she'd driven Josh to breaking point with her callous, selfish words. No matter how much pain she was in herself, how dare she do this to make herself feel better? And to pretend to be concerned and sympathetic – all the while gloating at the misery she'd caused?

And Rob. He'd lied too. He could have told her months ago that he knew Mikayla. But he hadn't bothered. He'd been more concerned about saving himself a little bit of discomfort, without considering that Natalie or Josh might have liked to know the truth.

Nobody gives a shit about Josh! The only person who gave a damn was Gareth. The only person who had been honest was Gareth – though he hadn't exactly covered himself in glory by keeping Toby and Mikayla's break-up hidden so long. But at least he'd done it out of compassion for his friend rather than any selfish reason.

In a fit of anger she pulled her suitcase out from under the bed and started stuffing in her clothes. She couldn't stay here a moment longer. Rob and Verity's house wasn't a safe place for her any more – it was as poisonous and untrustworthy as everything else in her life. She'd suffocate if she spent one more night in this room. She packed her clothes so badly that she couldn't do up the zip on her suitcase and she yelled in frustration, whacking it several times until her hand hurt. What was she going to do? She might have all this new information, but what good was any of it? She'd been looking in all the wrong places – making a fool of herself and letting everyone else take her for a fool as well. No wonder Toby thought she was crazy when she started saying he'd been trolling her. But he had gone mad at her in the house when he realised what she was up to. He'd terrified her. He might be innocent of the trolling, but he was behind Mikayla's death, she was sure of it.

And there was a stranger at the lake that day. There were things going on that weekend that the police don't know about.

Oh, Josh, I wish you were here. She checked her phone, but there was nothing – no news about him. *He's going to go down for this.* She pushed down as hard as she could on the suitcase and managed to force the zip closed. There was nothing left for her now. She'd find somewhere to stay for the night, and then she'd go to the police station and see Josh in the morning, if they'd let her. Perhaps if he was lucky they would release him before then, though what sort of man he would be after this ordeal, who knew. He still wouldn't have got any closure.

But the police still don't know about the break-up between Mikayla and Toby. Sure, Josh might have told them, but it wouldn't be as powerful coming from him – it was just hearsay. They needed to hear about it from the person who witnessed it. It might not prove anything on its own, but maybe, just maybe, it would be enough to get Josh released, and once they started investigating Toby again, Mikayla would finally get the justice she deserved.

***

'Gareth, I need you to help me,' she said urgently. She spoke quickly, the phone pressed against her ear, as she dragged her suitcase out onto the landing.

'Are you okay?' he asked. 'What's happened?'

She took a deep breath and put her case down at the top of the stairs before plonking herself on top of it. It would be hard work to explain it all again, but she had to do it. She had to stay strong. 'I need you to tell the police about the argument you overheard between Toby and Mikayla, and the break-up,' she told Gareth. 'It's the only way we can help Josh. I've been on his side all along. I've been trying to find evidence it was Toby–'

'What?' he said, 'you've been doing what?'

She hurriedly tried to outline her plan and her reasoning behind it, while Gareth listened in silence. 'I didn't find anything at his house,' she said finally, 'but it *was* him, I know it was. If we can at least give the police some reason to doubt Josh's confession and to start looking at Toby–'

'Your break-up with Josh was all pretend,' Gareth said, softly. 'You never lost faith in him.'

'Of course I didn't. I love him.'

Natalie dragged her hand through her hair. Adrenaline was pounding through her again. All that mattered now was getting Josh home safe, and giving some meaning to the hell she'd been through.

'I can't believe you did all this for him,' Gareth said. 'I'm so sorry for the things I've said to you. I've given you such a hard time.'

'It doesn't matter now. Gareth, I've burned so many bridges. And I thought … for a few moments I thought I wouldn't get out of Toby's house alive after he found me with all the old photos. We have to get the police to see it was him, even if I didn't manage to find any evidence.'

'Natalie, without any evidence, what can you really tell them?'

'Well, *you* can tell them what you overheard at the lake that morning. And I've found out something else, too. There *was* someone else there. A woman. Nobody knew that. She said "that poor girl" so she must have seen what happened!'

The image flickered before her eyes, and suddenly she gasped. The woman standing in the doorway of the hoarded house in Toby's photo. Gareth's house! Gareth's mum, in that bright, jazzy cardigan.

Messy light brown hair, and a bright cardigan with flowers on it. That's what Rob had told her about the woman he saw at the lake. It must have been her. *But how did she come to be there? Why?* But it didn't matter any more. She was certain.

'Who told you there was a woman?' Gareth asked.

'My – my brother.' She did her best to outline what Rob had told her, and after a pause she said, 'The woman, was that… was it your mum, Gareth?'

Gareth was silent for a moment and she tried to calm down and get control of her racing thoughts. Had she gone too far? Was she adding two and two and coming up with five again? But Rob had been absolutely clear about his description and it matched the photo so precisely. The police wouldn't be able to speak to the woman, of course, she'd been dead for many years, but maybe she'd confided in Gareth about what she'd witnessed that day.

'Have you heard anything from Josh?' she asked, trying to backtrack a little when Gareth still didn't reply. His mum was a tricky subject. 'Anything at all?'

'Nothing. And his phone is off.'

'Gareth ... please, you will help me, won't you? We need – *you* need to tell the police what you know. I'll come with you to support you. Once they see that it is down to Toby–'

'Yes,' he said at length. 'Okay. In fact, I might have something that can help, but we should meet in person. I can't tell you over the phone. And you can tell me more about this woman. What exactly did she say to Rob?' He paused. 'Hold on a second, I've got another call. It might be Josh–'

'Then go!' she said, 'answer it!'

'I'll text you my address,' he said quickly, 'come round later, and we'll make a plan.'

Josh

62

'Josh?' Gareth's voice was filled with relief as he answered the call. 'What's happened? Are you okay? Have they let you go?'

Josh sighed. 'They let me go hours ago. They never took me seriously; they just tried to encourage me to get help.'

'They let you out *hours* ago? And you only just thought to tell me? I've been worried sick!'

Josh sat down heavily on a bench at the side of the road. He'd been wandering aimlessly in the dark for hours. What had he been doing? What had he been thinking about all that time? He could hardly remember. 'I'm sorry,' he said. 'I was so embarrassed.' He realised as he spoke that he'd wandered near to his childhood home. In fact, there was the railway bridge Toby had dangled his head over once. He shuddered. *Maybe it would have been better if Toby had let me go.* After all, he'd done nothing with his life other than fuck it up. Even worse, he'd hurt Natalie.

'Okay, well, as long as you're all right,' Gareth said. 'Where are you? It doesn't sound like you're at home.'

'I'm not. I've just been walking.'

'I'll come and get you as soon as I can. It shouldn't be too long. Just tell me where you'll wait for me.'

After the call ended, Josh sat silently, staring at the railway bridge. He could almost hear the train thundering by below his head, and feel the air rushing by. He lost himself in dark memories until finally he turned at the sound of his friend's footsteps. 'Gareth, I'm sorry,' he said. 'I've dragged you out in the middle of the night–'

'I offered to come, you didn't tell me to. And I don't mind helping.' Gareth sat down beside him. 'Josh, this is just a really rough patch right now. It might feel like it's going on forever, but it won't. It'll get better.'

'I hope you're right,' Josh said.

'I am right. You just need to go home. Get some rest.'

Back at the flat, Josh unlocked the door uneasily. He hadn't wanted to come home – not to the place where there was a ghost of Natalie around every corner. Gareth followed him inside, and Josh was glad to have him there. He wouldn't have been able to hold it together if he'd arrived back on his own. He swayed slightly and clutched at the wall, weak and dizzy, his legs like jelly.

'When did you last eat or drink anything?' Gareth asked.

'I don't know. Just some water when I was at the police station.'

'Right. I'll make you a sandwich.'

Josh was about to say he could do it himself, but the words died on his lips. Even doing something as simple as making a sandwich felt out of reach right now. When Gareth went into the kitchen he let out an exclamation of surprise, and Josh rushed to his side.

'Josh,' he said, 'what – what is this?'

Josh stepped closer reluctantly, afraid to see whatever it was Gareth had found. When his eyes fell on the bizarre display, he stepped back in horror. All the knives had been removed from the knife block, and placed in a circle around a photo of him and Natalie, taken from a frame in the living room. Natalie's face was scratched out.

'I know you're angry about Natalie,' Gareth said, 'but stuff like this isn't going to help.'

'I didn't do it,' Josh said automatically. But then he paused. It was in his flat. Who the hell else could have done it? He could barely remember what he'd done before heading to the police station – there was every chance he could have done it. Just like all the other stuff he'd done and then forgotten. He picked up each knife and thrust it quickly back into the knife block. As he picked up the defaced image of Natalie, his fingers shook, and he threw it unsteadily in the bin.

'What's happening to me, Gareth?' he said.

Gareth looked up from buttering bread. 'Well, for one thing you're hungry.'

Josh let out a hollow laugh. 'Hungry? That's what you think my problem is?'

'Right now, yes. You're not going to figure anything out on an empty stomach, are you? Go and sit down. Then you need to eat this, and go to bed. I'll come back and see you again in the morning.'

'Gareth?' Josh said.

'Yeah?'

'Thank you.'

Gareth shrugged as if it was no big deal. 'I know you'd do the same for me,' he said. 'And besides, I've got something that will cheer you up. I'll show you.'

'What is it?' Josh asked. He wasn't particularly hopeful, but Gareth's eyes were glittering with mischief and even through his state of numb despair he was slightly curious.

'Turns out,' Gareth said, 'that Toby isn't as squeaky clean as he likes everybody to think. He has a profile on Hearts.' To prove it, he took out his phone and showed Josh Toby's profile.

Josh groaned. 'Is that it? That's what will cheer me up? He's probably just window shopping. It doesn't exactly present him in the best light, but I'm sure plenty of people do it.'

'He is not just window shopping. He is well behind the window. Handling the merchandise.'

'So he's cheating on Jodie?'

'If that's his wife, then, yeah.'

'Why would that cheer me up?' Josh asked.

'I don't know. I guess I'm just trying to make you see that you're not the bad guy, Josh. Other people do bad stuff. And I mean actually do it, not just thinking they do it.'

Josh sighed. 'If you say so,' he said. 'I'm just tired, Gareth. I'm so, so tired.'

***

A sound woke him, and he sat bolt upright on the sofa. He looked around him – it must be morning – the first light of dawn beginning to creep through the curtains. The knock came again, and he got to his feet, exclaiming in surprise as something smashed. His sandwich plate had fallen on the floor. He must have gone to sleep with it still on his lap.

'I'm coming, I'm coming,' he said, as there was a third knock.

When he saw who it was, he tried to close the door again, but Toby put his foot in the way.

'You're here,' Toby said. 'I was worried you would still be at the station.'

'They didn't take me seriously.'

'Of course they didn't,' Toby said. 'You don't remember hurting her. Because you didn't do it.'

'If you've come to tell me I'm crazy, you can save your breath,' Josh said. 'I know I need to get help.'

'No, I didn't come to say that. I came to tell you the opposite. I think there *is* something going on here. And I think I know who's behind it all.'

Josh was so taken aback that he let Toby inside.

'Let's go and sit down,' Toby said. He paused and looked more closely at Josh. 'You don't look well.'

'I don't think I've been well for a while.' Sighing, he let Toby follow him through to the living room. 'What is this about, Toby?' He didn't believe for a second that his stepbrother really had anything useful to tell him. He'd probably just come to rub more salt into Josh's wounds.

Toby looked around at the mess in the darkened living room, and strode across to open the curtains. Josh sank down onto the sofa and winced at the bright light. Outside it was a sunny, crisp February morning. The daffodil bulbs in Natalie's planters on the roof terrace now had fat buds that would soon burst into a riot of cheery yellow. He turned away from the sight. He didn't want sun. He wanted to stay in his pit.

'You know Natalie came to work at the hotel?'

'Yes,' Josh said. He could hardly have forgotten.

'It was all an act. She thinks *I* framed you for posting all that stuff on her vlog. She thinks I know something about Mikayla's death, or even that I might have had a hand in it, and she's been trying to find evidence.'

Josh sat bolt upright. Natalie had been helping him? He couldn't let himself believe it. But if it was true, where was she? Why had she lied to him?

'She had to make you think it was really over between you to make sure *I* believed it,' Toby said, as if he'd heard Josh's unspoken questions. 'I think she was hoping either that she could get me to tell her something, or that she'd stumble across some kind of evidence. I found her in my house last night, rooting through old photos of Chedford Lake. I – I got pretty mad at her. She was threatening to tell Jodie–' Toby paused. 'I was – I'm not particularly proud of myself for this – but I was hoping something might happen between me and Natalie. She said she'd tell Jodie about it, and I was scared. I tried to stop her, and she ran away, terrified. It's crazy, but she seems to think I'm some kind of murderer.'

Josh was speechless, his eyes fixed on Toby. Was this some sort of joke? Or a trick? Natalie had been prepared to put herself through all of this for him? It couldn't be true. But Toby wouldn't lie – not about this. Not when it showed him in such a negative light.

'Where did she go after she ran from you?'

'I don't know. Josh, I – I'm sorry I tried it on with her. I thought you'd said all those awful things to her and that you didn't deserve her–'

'I don't care about that right now!' Josh said. 'Where is Natalie? What did she do, after she left you? Did she go to the police?'

'I have no idea. I'm sorry.'

'Then what do you mean about knowing who is behind everything? Is Natalie in danger?'

'I don't know,' Toby said helplessly. 'It really depends on what she did next. On where she went, and who she spoke to.'

63

Josh jumped as his phone started to ring, and he was surprised to see it was Rob. He answered tentatively, his fear growing as he listened.

'Natalie's bed wasn't slept in last night,' Josh told Toby once he'd ended the call. His words came out sounding hollow and frightened. 'He said she packed a suitcase but she just left it in the house and went out somewhere. And now her phone is off. So you'd better tell me everything you think you know, Toby.'

Toby looked at him closely. 'Can you really not see it for yourself?' he said at last. 'Who's the other person who has been involved in this whole thing? Who told you about me and Mikayla splitting up?'

'Gareth?' Josh said. 'That makes no sense. I know you hate him, but–'

'Listen to me!' Toby said. 'I know there's something not right about him. You haven't seen the side of him that I have. When he came and threatened me after Mikayla died, saying he would go to the police about me if I didn't agree to leave you alone, he was being really weird. He was asking me what I thought it would have felt like for her when she drowned. He seemed really fascinated by it.'

'He had a difficult childhood. How do you think you would end up, if you'd been through what he had?'

'You're not hearing me!' Toby said. 'Why was he so keen to throw the spotlight back onto me when all of this came up again, telling you that Mikayla broke up with me?'

'Because he was trying to show me that it wasn't me! This is crazy, and it's not fair on Gareth. I mean, he hardly knew Mikayla, so he can't have been involved. It's laughable.' Suddenly, Josh felt utterly furious. 'You hate him because when he was around, bullying me never seemed to work out so well. But for most of my life Gareth has been the person – the *only* person who gave a shit about me!'

'And that's what this is about, is it?' Toby said, his voice rising too. 'You're not going to listen to me even when I might be able to help Natalie, just because I gave you a hard time when we were teenagers?'

'A hard–' Josh stopped, speechless. Was that all he thought it was?

'All right, look, I know it was a bit more than that.'

'A bit?'

Toby's face began to redden. 'What is it you want me to say? Fine. I made your life hell. I know I did.'

'I almost died.'

'And I said sorry.'

'No, you didn't. You came to the hospital and you said, "I didn't think you'd really do it."'

Toby looked taken aback for a moment. 'Is that all I said?'

'Yes. I can remember it like it was yesterday.'

'I … okay, I guess at the time I thought that was an apology. But Josh, we don't have time for this right now. This is about Nat, and I have a really bad feeling–'

'If you had anything sensible to say about Nat, I'd listen. This is just a hunch, based on nothing more than the fact you don't like Gareth. I'm going to go out and look for Natalie. You can help me if you want. Or not.'

'Did Rob say anything about where he thought she might be?' Toby asked. 'Anyone she could have talked to?'

'You mean did she go and see Gareth?'

Toby's silence was enough to answer that question, and Josh lost his temper again. 'Just go!' he shouted. 'I don't want your apology, not that you've really given one. I don't want you pretending you care all of a sudden. You've already told me the first thing on your mind after hearing Natalie left me was getting her into bed. Just leave me alone!'

Toby stood up. 'Gareth is not who you think he is,' he said, his face reddening. 'The guy is weird, Josh! He's wired all wrong.

He doesn't have anyone's best interests at heart, no one's except his own.'

'You're a fine one to talk about that! When have you ever given a shit about anyone else? You're even cheating on Jodie!'

'Me and Natalie, it wasn't real, we never–'

'I'm not talking about that! I've seen your profile on Hearts.'

Toby was stunned for a second, and Josh expected him to bluster his way through a denial. Instead, he nodded slowly as though another piece of the puzzle had slotted into place. 'On Hearts?'

'Yes.'

'And who owns Hearts, Josh? Who could have made that profile, shown it to you, and then deleted it, so that you end up sounding even crazier than everyone already thinks you are?'

In a fit of anger, Josh got to his feet and faced Toby, his hands itching to give him a shove. 'I am not letting you do this!' he shouted. 'Gareth has always tried to help me. He couldn't do anything more for me if he tried.'

'And you think he's got nothing back? What about all the free labour he got you to do on Hearts? I know it was basically you that built that thing. And what have you ever got for it?'

'I don't *want* anything! He's offered. He's tried to give me money more times than I can remember, and I always tell him no. I'm not having this conversation with you. I trust Gareth completely. One hundred per cent.'

'You're wrong, Josh,' Toby said slowly. 'You're wrong about me not giving a shit about anyone. No matter what you might think – and God knows I've given you enough reasons to doubt it – but I do give a shit about *you*. Look, Gareth isn't the only one who had a bad childhood. I know you did too, once I was in your life, but things had been bad for me as well, for years. My parents were at each other's throats for as long as I can remember. They were toxic for each other, constantly arguing. My dad – well, I mean, you know what he was like. He always tried to be reasonable, and fair, but my mum would just push his buttons. Then all of a sudden he was leaving, he wanted to be with *your* mum. He was supposed to be the one who held everything together, and then you came along and tore everything apart!'

Josh was too shocked by his outburst to react straight away. 'Toby—' he started.

'I don't know why, but I decided it was your fault. I couldn't really punish my dad, or your mum, or my mum. They were adults. They were untouchable. But I could punish *you*. I could control your life, the way I couldn't control anything in mine. It made me feel powerful. I – I liked it.' Toby paused briefly. 'I spent so long telling myself that I hated you and I wanted you to just go away – even though it made no sense. It wouldn't have made anything better if you went away. But there was nothing logical about it. And then I gave you those pills, and you took them, and I thought you might actually die—' His voice caught. 'I was in tears when I found you passed out in our room and called the ambulance. It wasn't Gareth's stupid blackmail that made me stop hassling you. It was because I didn't want you to be gone. It was because I saw what I'd done, and I was so ashamed. I couldn't – I never wanted to talk about it. I wanted to pretend it never happened.'

'So you let me carry on being the one who is cut out of the family. Better not invite *Josh* to things, because it's too awkward.'

Toby couldn't meet his eye.

'I've lost out on so much. But I've accepted it. I've accepted that there's nothing I can do to change any of it. I've accepted my family want nothing to do with me. Even Gemma, and you know how much I cared about her.'

There was a long silence before Toby spoke again. 'Gemma still asks about you, you know. Even though you left for uni when she was little, she remembers spending time with you before that.'

'She does?'

'Yes. And I'm not going to be selfish enough to ask you to forgive me. If I was you I wouldn't forgive me. I've tried to say I'm sorry, and I guess this is my one last shot at it. I really am sorry, Josh. And if you never want to see me again, that's up to you.' He walked up to Josh so that they were face to face. 'But please, if there's one thing you'll let me do for you, believe what I am saying about Gareth. I think he has some other agenda here. I don't think he's on your side.'

64

Josh walked away and opened the doors to the roof terrace, welcoming the cool blast of air as his mind reeled from everything that had been said. When he glanced back over his shoulder Toby was clearly impatient, striding around the flat until he stopped by the sofa and bent down to pick up the pieces of broken plate with an irritable sigh. Josh stepped back inside and closed the doors, before trying Natalie's number. Her phone was still off and fear rippled through him, but still he couldn't bring himself to take Toby's accusation seriously.

'Look, Gareth has done nothing but try to help through all of this,' he said, as Toby stood and dumped the pieces of plate he'd collected down on the coffee table. 'He came and picked me up late last night after the police let me go, and he stayed until I fell asleep. I don't know what I would have done without him.'

'Or,' Toby said, '*or* he's trying to stay close to the situation. Making sure he knows exactly what's going on.'

'Why?' Josh said. 'Gareth had nothing to do with Mikayla! That's completely insane.'

'Well, why was he sneaking around following me and Mikayla that morning?'

'He just did it for a laugh,' Josh said. 'He wasn't exactly your biggest fan either. I think he thought it would be funny to overhear you arguing. And besides, have you ever really explained what *you* did after Mikayla broke up with you? Does anyone know?'

'I told Natalie, I just ran away from Mikayla after she called the other guy she liked. I was angry and hurt, and I wanted to get away from her. I know that doesn't help, but I'm not the only one whose movements that morning aren't fully accounted for.'

'I know exactly what Gareth and I were doing.'

'Do you?'

'He overheard you and Mikayla arguing, then he came and woke me up. I'd fallen back asleep in the tent.'

'Think about it! You have no idea how long after overhearing us that he came back, because you were asleep. Yeah, it could have been straight away. It could have been thirty minutes later. More.'

'Gareth had no reason to hurt Mikayla. None at all. He barely knew her.'

'Really? She saw his house. She saw him shoplifting. You know what she was like about getting involved with people's lives. Trying to "help".'

Josh was too infuriated to answer. What the hell was Toby going on about? Why was he talking all this nonsense while Natalie was missing and needed help?

'When did you see this profile of mine on Hearts?' Toby asked.

'Last night.'

'And Gareth went out of his way to show it to you, did he?'

Josh's lack of response gave Toby the answer he needed, and he stabbed furiously at his phone screen for a second. 'Here!' he said. 'I downloaded the stupid app, because I don't even have it on my phone. And I am not on it. There is nothing here.'

Josh looked at Toby's phone. He was right. There was no profile. An unpleasant prickling sensation worked its way down his spine. He had definitely seen Toby's profile mere hours ago when Gareth had been at the flat. He went to the kitchen bin and took out the defaced picture of him and Natalie. 'This was in my kitchen yesterday,' he said, 'with all my kitchen knives around it.'

'What do you mean? You mean someone put them there?'

'I'm losing my mind, Toby. I thought I saw your profile on Hearts. And I don't remember doing this with the knives, but it all must have been me. It's not Gareth—'

The colour drained from Toby's face. 'The knives,' he said. 'Where are they now?'

'I put them back in the…' Josh's eyes fell on the knife block, and a cold chill spread through him. 'It's empty.' He picked it up to show Toby. 'Look.'

'The knives were out,' Toby said slowly, 'you picked them up with your bare hands and put them away, and now they're gone?'

'Yeah.'

'And Gareth was here last night, and didn't leave until you fell asleep on the sofa?'

'Well … yeah, but–'

'Josh… we need to find Natalie. Right now.'

Seven hours earlier

Natalie

65

Natalie started driving towards the address Gareth had given her, but as the directions took her away from town and into the countryside, she grew confused. He lived in a flat in the middle of town, didn't he? She was sure that's what Josh had said. She called Gareth again. 'Did you move house?' she asked. 'This address you gave me isn't where I thought you lived.'

'It's my second home,' Gareth said. 'Sometimes I need to get away for a bit and clear my head.'

Natalie glanced at the map on the car's navigation. She was almost there. The house was right out in the countryside; all that surrounded her as she drove was darkness. She could see why it would be a good spot to think, but it was surprising that Gareth had a place like this. He didn't seem like somebody who wanted to go away to think in a secluded place, surrounded by nature. He seemed like a city person. 'Okay, well, I'm almost there,' she said.

Pulling in to the drive, Natalie found an old brick cottage, not particularly large, but homely, from what she could make out in the light of her car headlights. She got out and picked her way down an uneven path towards his front door.

'You found it okay then,' Gareth said as he opened the door.

'Yes,' she said as she stepped inside, glad to be in the warm. She looked around briefly, trying to stop herself from demanding Gareth tell her what he knew that very second. The front door opened straight into a living room, the walls painted a warm terracotta, with a couple of armchairs facing an open fireplace.

She took her coat off and Gareth hung it up. 'Come inside,' he said with a smile. 'I'll make some tea.'

'This is a nice place,' she said, forcing herself to make at least a little small talk. 'I'm sorry to come here practically in the middle of the night—'

'I was hardly likely to sleep anyway, what with what you told me earlier about your plan with Toby.'

'I'm sorry if I worried you. But I think I really am onto something.' Her voice wavered a little, and she paused. The past few weeks had put her under so much strain it was all she could do to stop herself grabbing Gareth and trying to physically shake the answers from him.

'Sit down,' he said, 'I'll bring the tea.'

'Thank you, but I'm really just here to sort all of this out. I'm worried sick about Josh.' She took out her phone. 'I should message him, or call him, he needs to know—'

'Leave that for a minute. We need to talk first.'

She put her phone away and followed him through into a cosy snug, with a mustard-coloured sofa and a fluffy rug on the floor. Had he decorated this place himself? It had a lovely feel to it; so warm and inviting. Maybe all that activity he had on Hearts had led somewhere after all – perhaps he didn't come here alone to think. He didn't stop in the snug, but led her through into a dining room, and then to the long, narrow kitchen at the back of the house.

'Okay,' he said, as he started filling the kettle. 'So what exactly did your brother tell you that made you think my mum was there? I know you tried to tell me earlier but it was a lot to take in.'

'He said he saw a woman there, and his description matched almost exactly with a photo I saw at Toby's house. It was a picture he took of your house with your mum in the doorway. She ran out in front of Rob's car, and when he stopped she said, "That poor girl."'

Gareth listened intently as she spoke, his expression impossible to read.

'Was it your mum?' Natalie asked tentatively. 'It was, wasn't it? And she saw what happened to Mikayla.'

He gave her a long, hard look. 'It's such a shame,' he said. 'I was hoping, really hoping, that it wouldn't come to this.'

'What? Was it your mum who was there? Did she tell you what she saw that morning? Is there anyone else she could have told–' She trailed off as he placed his hands around the handle of a large, heavy saucepan that sat on top of the range cooker.

'Gareth, what are you–'

The last thing she saw was him whipping the pan off of the stove. Then he sent it smashing into the side of her head.

Seven hours later

Josh

66

'We need to call the police,' Josh said, dread beginning to seep through his body. Toby's suspicions about Gareth were finally sinking in, and he was terrified for Natalie. 'If you're saying what I think you're saying.'

'I don't know what the hell we'd tell them.'

'Neither do I. But if you're right...' Josh trailed off, his conviction faltering. What was he saying? Toby couldn't be right, surely? This couldn't really be happening.

'Gareth is the most logical person for her to have gone to. She was still determined all this was down to me when she left my house. But the only person who really has anything on me is Gareth. Because he heard the argument and he knows about the break-up. If she wanted to expose me, she must have gone to him.'

'Then what do we do? I don't know what to do. But we have to help her!'

Toby was silent briefly. 'Look, let's just go to Gareth's flat and see if Natalie is there. If we can't find either of them, or we think she's there and in danger, we'll call the police then. We're just going to sound crazy otherwise.'

'Okay.' Josh said, trying to stop himself shaking. 'Okay, let's go.'

Josh drove in silence through the early-morning commuter traffic while Toby fidgeted at his side, checking his phone, and turning his wedding ring round and around on his finger. Josh tried to ignore him. He had to stay focused.

Toby thinks Gareth took my knives.

He glanced around at Toby, who had gone back to checking his phone again.

He thinks Gareth is going to use them on Nat.

Josh's chest grew tight. Tears prickled his eyes, and his heart beat so fast he began to shake again. Why would Gareth do this? Gareth didn't *hurt* people – he'd always been disgusted by Toby's bullying.

Finally, Gareth's modern apartment block came into view. 'I can't see Natalie's car here,' Josh said, 'can you?'

Toby looked around quickly. 'No. What about Gareth's?'

'His isn't here either.'

Josh quickly parked in a visitor's space near the entrance and they managed to slip inside the building before sprinting their way up to Gareth's door on the second floor. But once there, Josh didn't know what to do. He turned to Toby.

'If I knock, won't it just alarm him?'

Toby crept closer, until he was pressed up against the door trying to listen. 'I can't hear anything in there,' he whispered.

'Their cars weren't here,' Josh said, with a flicker of hope. If they weren't in the flat, maybe Natalie had met him somewhere public. Maybe they had had a few drinks, and Toby's suspicions were all just nonsense. But why hadn't she gone back to Rob's house afterwards? It was morning now, and her bed hadn't been slept in.

They both jumped at the sound of a voice behind them. 'Are you looking for someone?'

At the top of the stairs stood a young man, eyeing them curiously.

'Uh … yeah,' Josh said. 'Gareth Rennox, I'm a friend of his. I'm a bit worried about him–'

'He's not here much,' the man said. 'I live next door to him. He used to be here most of the time during the week and not so much at the weekends. Now he hardly comes here at all.'

Josh stared at him. 'Where does he go?'

One of the man's eyebrows rose. 'If you're his friend, you're more likely to know than me.'

'Yeah. I – thanks. We'll figure it out,' Josh said.

They stood out of the way to let the man get to his own door. Josh's mind was racing. Where the hell did Gareth go all the time if it wasn't to his own flat?

Josh took his phone out. 'I'm calling Hearts,' he said.

They made their way back down the stairs as he waited for an answer. Finally, as he was about to hang up, someone picked up, and Josh asked her about her boss, listening in growing horror.

'She said he's barely been there for days,' he told Toby. 'She can't get hold of him either.'

'Right. We're calling the police. But we'll carry on looking for her ourselves as well. We might have more chance of figuring this out quickly than they do. Do you know anywhere else he could have gone? Is there anywhere that means something to him? Anywhere significant, any places he likes?'

'I don't know,' Josh said, his panic rising. 'I don't … I mean, he's my friend but I don't really know him that well. I have no idea what he does apart from work. I don't know who he hangs out with, where he goes, I don't know anything.'

'You must know something.'

Josh wracked his brain. Why *didn't* he know anything? Suddenly, he grabbed Toby's arm. 'Hearts. He uses Hearts.'

'He uses Hearts himself?'

Josh thought for a moment. Something was nagging at the back of his mind, but he couldn't put his finger on what.

'Let's go back to your place,' Toby suggested. 'I'll call the police while you drive, and say Natalie and Gareth have both gone missing.'

Josh was shaking as his mind rattled through a hundred awful possibilities. 'Toby, you don't really think he's going to hurt Natalie – he wouldn't, would he? What if he–'

'Don't waste your energy on panicking. We just need to find her, Josh.'

Natalie

67

She woke with a cry, trying to reach up to wipe the cold water from her face, but she couldn't move her hands. She tried again. No. Her wrists were tied behind her, and she tried to stand, but her ankles were bound too, attached to the legs of the chair she was sitting on. Gareth came into view, holding an empty glass. 'Hello again,' he said, 'sorry it was a bit of a rude awakening.'

Natalie blinked the water from her eyes, each movement causing fresh bursts of pain in her head. What the hell was going on? How had she ended up like this?

'Gareth?' she said, in utter confusion. 'What's happening?'

'Ah, well, that's the question isn't it?'

Fear gripped her. Why did he look so calm? Happy even? Something was clearly wrong here, badly wrong. Why wasn't he worried about the state she was in? Why wasn't he helping her? She struggled more violently against the chair. She was in the dining room, the chair in the middle of a large plastic sheet covering the carpet. The sheet hadn't been there when she'd arrived earlier. Had he put it down just because he was going to throw water on her? She tried to move her hands again, realisation dawning on her through the pain in her head. Gareth had tied her up. He wasn't going to help her. He had done it. 'Gareth, let me go,' she said, her voice rising. 'Let me go, now!'

He pulled up another chair and sat directly opposite her. He ran a hand through his dark hair and smiled at her, but his smile made her skin crawl. What was up with him? This wasn't the Gareth she knew. 'That's not going to happen,' he said. 'I'll get to why eventually. But since you're here, and you're something of a captive audience –' he chuckled to himself '– let's have a chat.

Firstly, I've been curious to know, what's Josh like in bed? He's so uptight, I think it must be one extreme or the other; either deathly boring, or he's into something super weird. Which is it? Obviously I hope it's the latter.'

Natalie winced as a wave of pain washed over her. What the hell was Gareth talking about?

'I'm going to have to insist you answer,' he said. 'You're in my house, so we're going to play by my rules.'

'Let me go,' she said again.

'Oh dear,' Gareth said. 'You are not making things better for yourself. Why not just answer me? It's an easy enough question. Boring, or weird?'

'Neither,' she croaked out.

'Is that right? So Josh is better adjusted than I thought. You know, I assumed he'd stay tragically alone for the rest of his life. His first few relationships were a disaster, after all, and then he all but gave up on trying. I think it's because of what Toby did. Really fascinating, the effect that had on him. What do you see in Josh anyway? I'd love to know. I just cannot see the appeal myself.'

'You're his friend,' Natalie said, unable to put her thoughts together any more coherently than that.

Gareth got up and went into the kitchen, where he refilled the glass with cold water and threw it over her, before clapping his hands loudly and saying, 'Wake up, Nat. It's no fun talking to someone half-comatose.'

'You can't do this—'

'Yes I can. Now, I know what you were getting at. I'm his friend, so I should be talking about him nicely, right?' He didn't wait for her to answer. 'Yes, I do like Josh. He's amusing. Useful, too, for Hearts. It doesn't mean I can't talk about his flaws. I would go through *your* flaws, but I guess someone made those pretty well known online.' He grinned at her. 'Oh, the fun I had reading all of that. Whoever was behind it, I've got to hand it to them, it was great entertainment.'

Anger and disgust surged inside Natalie. 'You really think I let that stuff bring me down? After what I went through in that car accident? How I nearly died? Those stupid comments are nothing compared to that.'

'I think you did let it get to you, though. The "right thing" is to say it doesn't bother you, right? To rise above it? But you can't. Not when it's day in, day out. Not when I'm sure it's things you think yourself, on your dark days.' He paused briefly. 'But anyway, this is all beside the point.'

'Gareth, you need to let me go. Please. I can carry on talking a little, if you want, but please untie me at least–'

He pointed his finger at her. 'You are pissing me off!' he shouted, the suddenness of his outburst making a little noise of fear escape her. But then he smiled again. 'It was weird when someone framed Josh for all that. Brilliantly twisted – I didn't see it coming. But the thing is, your troll, they caused me a lot of bother. Bringing up the lake like that, it was inconvenient.'

'Let me go,' she repeated, her voice unsteady. The lake. Why did Gareth care what anyone said about it?

'I can't,' he said. 'I'm sure you can see why. My mum might be dead, she can't say what she saw, but you have put too many pieces together. I don't want anyone out there knowing about a connection to me. And from how you described your conversation with Rob, you didn't tell him your suspicions about who she was. So it's just you. You, and me, and this secret that should never have seen the light of day again.'

'It can go back to being that way,' Natalie said. 'I don't have to tell anyone about this–'

'No. No, it *can't* go back to being that way. You are a loose end. A blemish on my perfect world.' He laughed and gestured at her face. 'Well, you know how it feels to have blemishes. I bet you'd do anything to make yours go away. Fortunately, for me it will be quite simple. Very neat. I think you'd be impressed – that's if you were around to see how it all plays out. '

Josh

68

Josh paced around his living room, his mind on fire, though he could think of no answers. 'How can I not know where to look for them!' he exploded. 'I need to do something. I don't even know where he really lives! He must have somewhere else that he goes, and his flat is just – I don't know! It's just a front, or something. It's all fake. And now Natalie ... and it's all my fault. It's all my fault!'

Toby put his hand on Josh's arm. 'We *will* figure it out. Or if we can't, the police will. They're going to come and speak to us later this morning.'

'But are they even going to take it seriously? We can't prove she's in danger! How can I explain what Gareth's been doing in my flat with the knives? And he must have had a key, there's no sign that anyone ever broke in.'

'I'll be here to back you up. They'll have to take it seriously if I'm also saying the same thing.'

'He took my *knives*, Toby.'

'He might just be trying to scare you. Look, he just wants everyone to drop this Mikayla stuff, right? There's no reason to think he'll hurt Natalie, it's just a threat–'

'You don't believe that!' Josh stopped in his tracks. 'Hearts! Why didn't I think of this already?' He grabbed his laptop and Toby sat down by his side. 'What are you–'

Josh held up his hand to silence him. 'Hearts knows where its users are when they log in,' he explained. 'If he has Hearts on his phone, I can find out where he was when he last logged in.'

'You're going to hack his account?'

'I don't need to. I helped Gareth with a security breach at Hearts not so long ago. I have an admin account there, I can get straight into their system…'

Toby watched him silently while he worked. 'Well?' he said after a while. 'Don't you need his username, or something?'

'No. He probably signed up with his phone number.'

Josh's heart skipped a beat at the information that came up. 'Look at this!'

Toby peered over his shoulder. 'Gareth Chedford,' he read. 'That's not his name, right?'

'No. He's put the name of the lake as his surname.' Bile rose in Josh's stomach, and he forced himself to swallow it back down and carry on working.

'Okay. Here are his most recent logins–' He stopped talking.

'What? What, Josh? Where–'

Josh shoved the laptop away from him with a cry of horror.

***

'It was here, near your flat,' Toby said quietly.

Josh nodded once he'd taken a moment to recover. 'He was here last night after I called him, but before he picked me up. He came and set up the knives ready for bringing me home.' His stomach churned as the full horror of it dawned on him. 'He really did do all of this. He really did do it.'

'Is there anything on Hearts that could help us work out where he is right now?'

Josh shook his head as he picked up his laptop again. 'He hasn't logged in again since. He's not stupid. He knows how his own app works, he won't use it if he doesn't want to be found.'

'Isn't there anything–'

'Wait,' Josh said, as he spotted something else. 'This doesn't make sense.'

'What is it?'

Josh rubbed his forehead. This was a nightmare.

'Tell me what it is! What have you found?'

'Gareth doesn't have any logins earlier than a month or so ago, but he was using Hearts way before that.'

'You must be looking in the wrong place–'

'I am not looking in the wrong place! According to this, Gareth wasn't using Hearts until three weeks ago! Unless he has a second account...'

Josh scanned through the login dates and times. The nagging feeling returned. 'No,' he said softly. 'This can't be.'

'What is it?'

'I should have seen this,' Josh said. 'I knew it was weird...'

'Josh, what are you talking about?'

'He has no logins before the date of the security breach I told you about. I've always found that whole thing odd.'

'I don't know what you're getting at.'

'*Gareth* has been deleting his own records from Hearts.'

'Why?'

'There's only one reason anyone could possibly want to. He's doing something he shouldn't be, and he's changing his records to hide it. And he was brazen enough to get me to come and help when he slipped up and almost got caught!' Josh thought back. 'He was worried, though. But he wasn't worried about his users, he was worried about getting found out!'

'You think he's, like, assaulting women he's met on there, or something?'

Josh stopped and put his hands over his face. 'Josh,' Toby said. 'Are you okay?'

He took his hands away shakily. 'This is wrecking my head, Toby. Gareth ... Gareth wouldn't do this. I know him. I couldn't have got him this wrong–'

'This isn't your fault; nobody could have seen this coming. Even I only just thought of it and you know I think he's a tosser. We'll tell the police what you've discovered–'

'No, *I* should have seen this! I was there, looking into it, and I didn't see it. I was only considering possibilities I've seen before. *Motivations* I've seen before. It would never, ever cross my mind to think he'd done it himself. And then to get me to help! Why would anybody do that?'

'I don't know. But you need to keep digging. There must be some clue somewhere.'

Josh tried to concentrate. His vision swam, and he shook his head to focus on the screen. 'Here!' he said, 'this must have been him. All the stuff from his account before the security breach was downloaded. There's a cached copy of it still on the server.' Josh opened it and began to scan through what he'd found. 'These are his messages. He must have exported it all before he got rid of it. Saved a copy.'

'What for?'

Josh's blood turned to ice. Toby kept pressing him, but he didn't speak until he'd checked a few more things, his horror growing at every turn.

'Josh, you're scaring me. Why did Gareth want a copy of the very stuff he wanted nobody to find?'

'For a souvenir,' Josh said, his voice barely above a whisper.

'A what?'

'I just searched Hearts for this woman he was talking to, Avril. She doesn't have a Hearts account. But she did when these messages were sent.'

'He's deleted her account too?'

'She's dead, Toby.'

'She's … what?'

'Well, she's missing. I found her full name, and look at this.' He turned the screen towards Toby.

'Appeals for information,' Toby said.

'He's killing them,' Josh said, his voice trembling. 'He must be. He killed Mikayla, and he's using his own dating app to find more victims. He's … he's killing them, Toby!'

'Christ.' Toby sat back heavily on the sofa, running a hand through his hair and tugging at it, hard. 'You don't know that for definite. He'd have been caught, surely, if he was meeting them on Hearts–'

'How? There's no record that this woman had anything to do with him. Even if she'd told someone she was going on a Hearts date and the police came to the Hearts office, what are they going to do if she has no account? They can't find out who she was speaking to or who she met, and I'm sure Gareth wouldn't leave her phone lying around to be found. He could be specifically targeting new users, too, women who've not had any other interactions on Hearts. And Avril didn't live locally. He's travelling to meet them to cover his tracks.' Josh paused for a moment. 'He was always going away over the weekends – he must have been going to meet women all over the country! But why involve me? Why get me so close to this?' He carried on scrolling through the messages, though he could barely take in the words. Reaching the bottom, his eyes settled on the very last letters typed by Gareth, many hours after his last communication with Avril, and he cried out in horror. 'No,' he said, 'no, no, no, no!'

He closed his eyes but when he opened them, the words were still there.

Well done Josh.

69

'This was part of his game,' Josh said eventually, pushing his laptop away from him and pressing his fingers against his temples. '*I* was part of his game. That's why he got me to come in to Hearts. He wanted me to come and work on the breach because having me there made the whole thing more exciting for him. He *wanted* me to figure it out.'

'He can't want to get caught, surely?'

'Maybe not, but he's flirting with the idea of it. He must have been imagining what it would be like if I found this, or why would he have written that message to me? He's like a killer who follows the police investigation into their own crimes.' Josh's voice was choked with emotion. 'He made me part of his sick little world. He probably laughed at me for not being able to see what was right in front of me.'

'Wait, what's this?' Toby said, grabbing Josh's arm. He'd picked up the laptop and scrolled back up through the messages. 'This is an address. It looks like Gareth and Avril met up a couple of times and it went well, so he's inviting her to stay at his house.'

'We've already been to his flat—'

'This isn't his flat. Look.'

Josh read where Toby was pointing. 'This must be his other address!' he said breathlessly. 'This is where he is! This is where he's taken Natalie.'

Natalie

She shook with fear, but she shouted at him angrily. 'Let me go!' she said. 'Let me go, let me go!' She screamed the last words at him, and he shouted back in irritation. 'Shut up! Just shut up and listen.'

She did as he asked, and he sighed, as if he found the whole thing incredibly tiresome. Then she realised that the room was lighter than it had been when she'd first awoken. It was morning! *Hopefully someone has realised I never went home last night. Hopefully Rob has realised I need help.*

'This isn't how I like to do this,' Gareth said. 'This is all wrong. You and Josh are spoiling everything for me.'

'We've done nothing to you!'

'Nothing?' he said. 'Digging up all this shit about Mikayla? Winding Toby up? Threatening to go to the police? Josh turned himself in to the police, for fuck's sake – he made them think about this whole bloody business again!' He gave a humourless laugh. 'They thought he was nuts. But I can't carry on like this. I need to shut this down. I need to shut *you* down. You're the problem. Josh will solve the rest of the problem himself. He's his own worst enemy.'

'Look, I'll stop with the Mikayla stuff,' she said, her voice shaking with desperation.

'Do you think I'm stupid?'

'No. But you can trust me–'

'You do think I'm stupid then. I'm a joke to you, right? The guy with the dating site who's always single.'

'I never saw you as a joke.'

'I don't like relationships, Natalie. No. I don't like them at all.'

'Not everyone does,' she said. What the hell was he going on about? She struggled against the bonds tying her wrists behind her back. But they were strong.

'I don't like *anybody*, really. Except for Josh. I like Josh, or at least I *liked* Josh. He's so tragic. He makes me laugh. And you, I used to find you tolerable, at least. You and Josh, you were my social circle. I liked that. That worked okay for me. You were my social people. Then there's work people. Family? No. I've got none of that. But there are rules. The different circles, they don't mix. Especially not with the most important circle.'

Natalie stayed silent. What could she even say? He was crazy. She couldn't make sense of it.

'Ask me about the most important circle.'

She swallowed. 'What's the most important circle?'

'The women,' he said with a grin. 'Mikayla first. Then none for a long time. Then, some. More recently.'

'I don't want to know about this,' she said, her voice barely above a whisper.

'They're in the garden now. Not Mikayla, obviously. But the others.'

Her body turned to ice and she didn't think she could speak. She could barely breathe. 'Gareth,' she said finally, her voice weak, 'I don't need to know this. Let me go. Me and Josh, we'll both leave you alone. You leave us alone, we'll leave you alone. And your... circles.' Her body felt weak and cold. Nobody knew she had come to this place. She'd given Rob no hints about who she was going to meet; she'd just rushed out of the house without even a goodbye. Gareth's cottage had no neighbours, no traffic coming down the lane outside, absolutely nobody. Even if she had access to her phone, it would almost certainly have no signal, and she had no idea where Gareth had put it.

'Natalie, I know why you're saying all this. But you *won't* leave me alone. You've already gone way too far. You've invaded my privacy. You've messed up my life.'

'I told you, I'll back off!'

'Stop saying that,' he said calmly. From his pocket he took a pair of gloves and pulled them on, and then he walked over to the dining table behind her and picked something up. Having settled himself back in his chair, he placed the bundled tea towel in his lap. Slowly, with relish, he unfolded it, revealing a full set of kitchen knives.

'Now, these are Josh's,' he said, 'complete with fresh fingerprints. I don't usually kill with knives, but, like I said, the pair of you are determined to fuck with me. You've forced me to have to kill somebody that is not my type, that I didn't meet the way I like to meet my special girls, that I'm going to have to kill in a way that I don't enjoy so much. I can't even put you in my garden. But then again, you don't deserve to go in there. Only the special ones go in there.'

Natalie began to shake all over. 'You… you're trying to frame Josh, aren't you? They'll know he didn't kill me. They can tell all sorts of stuff. Forensics. They'll know…' She desperately struggled for words. She could barely string a sentence together.

'Maybe you have a point,' he said, 'but you're forgetting something. When Josh finds your body in his flat, covered in stab wounds, he'll think he did it himself. I've been setting the scene for him. He's starting to unravel. He'll confess. Everything already points to him.' Gareth laughed, with apparently genuine humour. 'He made it so easy! He called me and said he'd been wandering around since the police let him out. All I had to do was drive to his flat, set up a nice little display for him to enjoy, pick him up and take him home. Getting inside was no problem. One morning after I took him out and got him drunk, I took his keys and got a copy. I told him I just went out for coffee. It was just a kind of insurance policy then. I had no particular plan, but I didn't like the way things were going and I like to have options.' Gareth looked down at the knives. 'What's the best way of going about this, then?' he said. 'I guess "frenzied" is the look I'm going for.'

'You don't have to do this, Gareth.'

'Maybe I'll let you choose,' he said. 'Which knife do you fancy?'

He started to close his gloved fingers around one of them when she didn't answer, placing the rest of them, still bundled in the tea towel, down on the floor. 'It'll be over soon, Nat. I'll get Josh out of his flat somehow, and get your body inside.'

'You think you're really clever, don't you?' she said, trying to avoid looking at the knife. She recognised it; it was the one she always used to tackle butternut squash for her veggie curries.

'Yes and no. I mean, I've killed five women – six, in a minute – and no one has the slightest clue that I have anything to do with it. So, yeah, I'm not doing too bad.'

He got up and stepped towards her with the knife. She had to get him to stop, to buy herself time, at least. He seemed to enjoy talking, so if she could keep him talking, just a little longer…

Then what? After all, no one knew she was here.

He reached out and stroked her cheek. 'I'm the last person you're ever going to see,' he said. 'I like it when they realise that. I like it when they realise they're going to die.'

He pressed his finger against her lip, then let it go, and smiled at her. 'Maybe this will be fun after all.'

He began to raise his hand, so she said urgently, 'Why do you do it?'

'Because I like it,' he said, as if she had asked a stupidly obvious question.

'And why … why Mikayla?' Natalie asked, panic making it hard for her to form the words. 'She was your first. She must be special to you. Tell me about her. Tell me what you get out of it.'

Gareth cocked his head to the side. 'Okay,' he said. 'I'll tell you about her. I'll tell you about all of it, if it'll make you happy. I guess you deserve to have one last wish, after all.'

The day of Mikayla's death

Gareth

70

The heat was like a wall as Gareth made his way along the path, following the route Mikayla had taken after her argument with Toby. How interesting it had been to hear them fight. Very few things were interesting, but that had been, briefly. Perhaps Mikayla was crying somewhere. That might be funny to see.

He stopped in his tracks when he entered a clearing by the water's edge. Mikayla! She was peeling off her t-shirt and denim shorts. Okay. Now he *really* liked the way this was going. He strode boldly out towards her, and she jumped when she heard his footsteps.

'What the hell do you want?' she asked, swiping angrily at her face like she'd been crying.

'What are you doing?'

'Going for a swim.'

'You're not supposed to swim in there.'

'Gareth, leave me alone. I don't want to talk to anyone.'

'Why don't you go home, then?' he shot back.

'I've called someone to come and get me. But he doesn't want to come. I thought he cared about me, but—' She shook her head. 'Will you please just leave me alone?'

He sat down on the grass and she made a sound of exasperation.

'Gareth—'

'I'm tired. I just need to sit down, I won't talk to you if that's what you want.'

'You know, I'm going to tell my mum about your house and how you're living. You shouldn't be there. One of my mum's friends is a social worker–'

'Has anyone ever told you that you're an interfering bitch?' Gareth asked casually.

'At least no one can say I'm a freak,' she spat back. 'Not like you. I'm only trying to be kind. How do you expect anyone to help you if you throw it back in their face?'

'I don't need help from you. I don't need help from anyone.'

She laughed. 'Really?' she said.

'Are you going to swim, then? Or maybe you're so perfect you can just walk across the water.'

With a furious glance at him, she turned her back and then sat down on the bank, slipping her feet into the water. Gareth watched her closely. He had the feeling that if he hadn't been there she would have thought twice about her swimming idea, but with him watching, she inched her way further in, finally flinging herself away from the shore and gasping as the water covered her body.

Gareth stood up. 'Come on,' he said, 'it's too cold. I'll help you get out.'

Once she'd stopped gasping, Mikayla choked out, 'I'd rather drown than have *you* touch me.'

I'd rather drown than have you touch me. It was obvious Mikayla was still drunk and emotional to have said something so stupid. But the words set a flame flickering inside him. The same flame that shoplifting had used to set alight, though the excitement of that had long since dulled.

Gareth stripped off his own clothes, down to his underwear, as Mikayla stubbornly thrashed her way further from the bank. He wandered down to the water, watching her closely. She had swum further out, her black hair fanned out around her. But then she started struggling, her head dipping below the water for a moment.

'Help,' she gasped as she bobbed up again. 'Help me!'

He jumped in and swam awkwardly over to her. He'd never learned to swim very well, and the water was bloody freezing. It took his breath away, and he was alarmed to find his feet couldn't touch the bottom. Mikayla had bobbed below the surface again, and then she popped back up as he reached her. She tried weakly to put her arms around him, but he stopped her. Their eyes briefly met, terror and panic filling hers as he gently pushed her shoulders into the water, down until her head went below. He was getting pretty cold and scared himself now, but the excitement was stronger than all that. Her struggles were weak, and his body hummed with electricity. And besides, she didn't *want* his help. She'd rather drown than have his help. Isn't that what she'd just said? Just like his mum would rather drown in her piles of festering junk than have Gareth help her.

Abruptly, he grew scared. His head whipped round to the clearing. Could he have been spotted? Nobody was there. No, wait. There was movement. He froze, then choked as the icy water rose up to block his mouth and nose. Was that – Mum. His mum was there. Only for a fleeting second, and then she disappeared again. Excitement surged through him, taking him aback with its force and intensity. *Now she knows what she's turned me into.*

He kept his hands on Mikayla's shoulders a moment longer, but she began to float away from him. She was gone. A tingling thrill swept through his body, but equally strong was the cold seeping into his bones. The water seemed to be trying to grab him, to pull him down too. He quickly thrashed his way towards the shore, and heaved himself out onto the bank. While he pulled his clothes back onto his body, the electric feeling surged back again as he relived the moment; that moment when she'd realised he wasn't going to help her. That moment she'd realised she was going to die. He couldn't help but grin as he stuffed his numb feet into his shoes, and then he ran back to the path, and towards the campsite.

Natalie

71

'Your mum saw you do it?' Natalie said.

'She did. I'd told her I was going to leave home and she was so upset she came to the lake to talk me out of it, but instead she saw me with Mikayla. Not that we ever spoke about that. But she was always nervous around me. She turned away when I looked at her. She never questioned me, or tried to get me to do anything, she just left me alone.' He laughed. 'Perhaps she knew I was going to kill her too. Because I did. Not until a good few years later, but she got what she deserved.'

'I'm sorry,' Natalie croaked, her mouth drying, 'about what happened with you and your mum when you were young.'

'Are you?'

'Yes,' she said. 'I told you before. You shouldn't have gone through that.'

'I shouldn't have gone through that,' he said, turning the words over as if he found them quite intriguing. 'What should I have gone through?'

'I just – your mum wasn't well. It wasn't good for either of you. But you were only a child, it was a lot for you to deal with–'

At this Gareth grabbed her by the throat. 'Don't you dare,' he spat into her face. 'Don't you dare try to tell me about my own life. You don't have a fucking clue.' He let go of her abruptly and sat back down, crossing his legs and leaning back comfortably. 'I can tell you about my life, though, if you want. Would you like that, Natalie?'

'Yes,' she said. Anything to buy some time.

He nodded indulgently. 'Where should I start? Well, Josh thinks his family was bad. And it was. But I think I could make a good case for mine being worse. I think things were always weird. You don't realise when you're a kid how weird stuff is, not until you get older and realise other people's lives aren't like yours. I used to be pathetic like my mum. We'd just hide away amongst all the crap she bought, like we were in some sort of nest. It felt nice, and cosy, and safe. Or she'd take me to the shops, and she'd be so excited. So ridiculously excited – like buying this one more thing would change our lives. But it's all an illusion. My dad would come back, and our nest of belongings couldn't protect her from him, could it? He'd get so furious with her about the state of the house. About how she'd never sort anything out. About how she was spending all of their money on stuff we didn't need.'

'I didn't realise–' Natalie said.

'Why would you realise?'

'I just mean, I didn't know quite how bad things were.'

'Neither did Josh. This was before I knew him; before I moved to his school. We lived in this nice house – it should have been nice, anyway. It was nice to me, I didn't know any different. I knew it was hard to play or to get around, or find anything, but like I said, it was our nest, and I was just a little kid. And there was this big garden that wrapped round three sides of the house. I could run wild in there. Anyway. One day my mum took me out after school and bought a load of stuff for redecorating the living room; paint, curtains, a new lampshade, cushions. She was on such a high. I was excited, too, because she said I could help. But when my dad got home from work and found all of our supplies, he went mental; he said she would never actually do the redecorating – which was true, of course, she never actually *did* any of these little projects. And he started taking things out and throwing them in the street outside – new stuff, old stuff, he didn't even look at what he was grabbing. Things were smashing and breaking. My mum was terrified. Crying. Screaming. I didn't want him to keep upsetting her – like I said, I was still a bit soft back then, I guess I was only about seven, maybe six. I picked up one of the pots of paint by its handle and just swung it into him while he was going out of the front door to chuck some more stuff into the street. It hit him somewhere stupid like his arm, nowhere that could do him any damage, but it caught him off balance, and he fell over and hit his head on the ground.'

'Gareth–'

'I didn't really know what was going on. There was all this blood, and his head was messed up, and Mum was hysterical. But I don't think I really felt anything about it. I never meant to kill him – I didn't get into any trouble, obviously, I was only little and everyone knew he was a nasty piece of work. I was only trying to defend my mum. Only, Mum wasn't grateful for the fact I'd tried to help her. She hated me, because the old bastard was the love of her life. She never outright said it, but I knew she blamed me. Somehow she forgot all the bad shit he used to do, and she'd go on and on about the handful of nice or romantic things he did, even though it really was just that – a handful.'

Natalie's skin prickled. 'Wasn't there anyone you could talk to?'

'Anyway,' he continued, ignoring her, 'I got pretty used to life by myself. She loved the stuff far more than she loved me. I learned that the hard way.'

'Gareth, you know that's not–'

He held a finger up. 'Just shut up and listen.'

'I need the toilet,' she said. She did, a bit, and maybe if Gareth took her to the bathroom there was something she could do to escape. Could she hit him? Or if he left her alone, could she get out of a window? But she wasn't surprised by his reply.

'Good job I've put the plastic down then. There's going to be all sorts of spillages.'

'Gareth, please,' Natalie said, 'killing me isn't going to make anything better.'

'Well, I'm sure you can guess what else happened after he died,' Gareth continued, ignoring her again. 'Not a single thing he ever wore, owned, touched, could ever leave. She told me eventually that she first started hanging on to things after she had a baby that died – a baby that would have been my big sister.

Hoarding all her baby things was when she started getting bad. So of course when she lost somebody else, it just spiralled. We ended up having to move, she couldn't afford the nice house on the nice street – she hated that, having to leave her home. But all the shit came with us. And then it wasn't even logical any more. She just kept everything. Even rubbish, sometimes. She injured herself falling in the house and couldn't work any more, so she'd spend all her time combing through charity shops, day after day, building up her hoard.

'The house soon got pretty fucked up. She couldn't get in and out very easily, so she stopped the charity shopping and started ordering stuff from catalogues, and online. People barely saw her. I think some people even suspected she wasn't there at all, with how the house looked from the outside. She barely spoke to me, unless I threatened to throw some of her shit out. She'd get up from her filthy old armchair and talk to me then. I suppose, to give her credit, there were some times she said she regretted how things were, or she'd make a show of asking me about my day, about what I liked, who my friends were, or she'd remind me how close we used to be. But I'd shut her down pretty quick when she started that. I started to think perhaps it would be good to kill her. Not by accident, like my dad. On purpose. I could be, like, a self-made orphan. I thought that would be pretty cool.

'The thing was, it was risky. She still took care of some stuff, and the school would realise. She needed to put in an appearance occasionally. Sometimes people serve functions. I was smart enough to realise that. Like Josh. Once I'd met him, he was a good distraction for me. I liked the whole thing he had going on with Toby. Not the way Toby treated him, I thought that was distasteful. Just a bully, like my dad. But I liked trying to get inside Toby's head and weird him out. Those were some good times. Then, later, of course, there was Hearts, and Josh came in very handy for that.'

'What about Mikayla?'

'Mikayla was just there. Right place, right time. I had to kill *somebody*. I thought about it all the time. Day and night. I knew it couldn't be Mum; not then. I was going to get away from her anyway when I eventually managed to move out, so I knew I could bide my time on that one. But Mikayla just made it so easy. She was irritating, interfering, and she would have had no idea it was coming. The buzz from it lasted me for years. It was incredible.'

'And then?' Natalie breathed, a chill making her shiver. How long could she keep him talking for? She'd been gone hours. She closed her eyes briefly. *Just keep asking questions. Keep him talking.*

'Well, then the buzz ran out, several years ago now. I knew I was entering a new phase. I planned for a time, and then when I was ready, I went back to where it all started. I turned on the gas on Mum's old deathtrap of an oven and I blew the whole thing off the face of the earth, her included. Then, I really got down to business. That's when I started looking for my special girls. The ones I found on Hearts.'

Josh

72

'That's her car!' he said, as they drew close to Gareth's house.

Josh stopped a little way away, keen not to be spotted, and parked in a muddy clearing in front of a farm gate. Toby had called the police on the way and told them the address, but they both immediately got out of the car and crept towards the house, not wanting to leave Natalie in danger a moment longer.

'How should we do this?' Josh whispered. 'If we make any noise trying to get inside he'll just realise we're here.'

'Get as close as we can, and try to look through some windows,' Toby suggested. 'Perhaps we'll be able to see where they are and what's going on.'

Josh nodded. 'Okay.' Slowly, they picked their way towards the house, Toby going around the right hand side, while Josh went left.

Josh soon came to a window near the back of the house where the curtains were drawn. He crept closer. Could he hear voices inside? He couldn't make out the words. But if they were talking, that meant Natalie was alive!

He jumped as Toby appeared around the back of the house, and quickly made his way over. 'Are they in there?' Toby whispered.

'I can hear talking.'

'So she's alive?' Toby asked urgently.

'Yes. She must be.'

'How can we get inside? He's going to hear us—'

At that moment, the voices inside stopped abruptly and then, piercing through the silence around the house, Natalie screamed.

Natalie

'No!' she shrieked as he lunged at her. 'No, please, no!' In her violent struggles, the chair overturned and she crashed onto the floor, narrowly avoiding Gareth's attack. Hysterical now, she carried on screaming and crying, thrashing uselessly as he grabbed her, until they both heard a loud crash from the kitchen. Gareth's head whipped around in shock. Knife in hand, he made his way towards the kitchen door, only to be thrown backwards as it burst open and Josh and Toby were there. She let out a huge sob of relief. *Thank God, thank God!*

Gareth was so taken by surprise that Toby managed to hit him before he could react, and Josh made a grab for the knife, cutting a huge gash across his palm in the process. Running to her, he used it to cut the tape from her wrists and ankles, before throwing the knife well out of Gareth's reach. Toby hit Gareth again, sending him crashing into the dining table, where he then flopped down to the floor.

'Nat, are you hurt?' Josh said quickly, checking her body for wounds. 'Did he hurt you?'

'Just my head when he hit me,' she said. 'Get me out of here, Josh. Get me out of here!'

Toby and Josh helped her up between them, leading her away from Gareth's crumpled body. 'You're going to be okay,' Josh said. 'It's over, Nat, it's over.'

Just as they were making their way out into the living room and towards the front door, Toby cried out, and they turned. Gareth was holding the knife he'd stabbed Toby with, blood dripping down the handle. 'Oops,' he said, flashing a smile. 'I have *all* your knives, Josh, remember? Looks like you're going to be responsible for a massacre.'

Josh lunged at him, but Gareth took a swipe with the knife, narrowly missing cutting Josh's face.

'Why are you doing this?' Josh cried, his words full of fear and betrayal. 'What's wrong with you?'

'Because I know the truth, Josh. People are nothing. Family is nothing. Relationships are nothing. The only thing that's real is when you have someone in the palm of your hand and they know that it's up to you whether they live or die.' He laughed. 'My mum would stress for months over whether to throw away a piece of rubbish. I can decide in a heartbeat to take somebody's entire life. And it is *never* a difficult decision. It's no different to when I used to go shoplifting, only to throw away everything I stole. Nothing means anything. Only the thrill means anything. But you know how it is, Josh. Diminishing returns. The risk has to get bigger, and bigger, and bigger. On the topic of which, did you find my message for you?'

Natalie stared at Josh, while Toby sagged against her. 'Josh!' she cried, seeing that he was getting sucked in, desperate to understand the actions of his former friend. 'Don't listen to him!'

Josh turned to look at her, and Natalie screamed as Gareth took the chance to grab him and hold the knife against his cheek.

'Let him go!' Natalie screamed.

Gareth cried out suddenly and dropped his knife, blood streaming from his hand where Josh had bitten him. Josh lurched over to her, taking Toby's weight from her. 'Go,' he told her, 'open the door, I've got him.'

'What are you doing, Josh?' Gareth asked. 'Helping *Toby?* I've done you a favour! Let him die.'

Natalie paused. Josh and Gareth's attention was fixed on each other, Gareth looking triumphant, proud, thinking he had won, while Josh was angry, heartbroken and sickened. His eyes were shiny, but his face was set hard with fury.

'I thought you hated how Toby picked on someone weaker than him,' Josh said. 'And yet, you're using Hearts—'

'The women I meet on Hearts aren't weak like you are. That's why it's fun. They're strong. They think they're out to have a good time. And they do, right up until I decide it's time for *me* to have *my* fun.'

'I don't understand,' Josh said. 'This isn't … this isn't you.'

'Yes it is. Maybe it wouldn't have been, if you hadn't betrayed me.'

'What?'

'We were supposed to leave Wayfield *together,* remember?'

'Yes, and we couldn't, because of the inquest.'

Gareth pushed his excuse aside with a wave of his hand. 'No, you gave up, Josh. You were the one thing that mattered to me, and after Mikayla's death you took those pills and you tried to kill yourself. That's when I truly stopped caring. About anything. That's when I knew I had to take a different path. If I couldn't trust you, I couldn't trust anyone.'

Natalie's heart was in her throat as she slipped past them both. Toby wouldn't last much longer, but Josh was too transfixed by Gareth, too desperate to understand. The two men were oblivious to her, so she grabbed the chair she'd been tied to, and with a cry of rage she smashed it over Gareth's head. He dropped like a stone. She pulled the tea towel from under the remaining knives on the floor, running back over to Toby and pressing the towel against the wound in his side.

'You're going to be okay,' she said, her voice trembling. 'You're going to be okay.'

The colour had drained from Toby's face, but he managed to press the tea towel against the wound himself. Josh, snapped out of his trance now that Gareth was unconscious, ran over to help and they dragged Toby outside.

'Natalie—' Josh said, 'I'm so … I'm so glad you—'

'I know,' she said, 'I know, Josh.'

He touched her cheek softly, 'I could never have imagined—'

'It's over now,' she whispered, 'it's over.'

'Help,' she and Josh both cried in unison as a police car rounded the corner and Toby's legs sagged. 'Help us, please!'

Epilogue

'I'm so glad Toby's nearly recovered,' Natalie said, as she leant against Josh's shoulder. They were sat outside on his roof terrace, spring sunshine warming their faces.

'Me too. I'll invite him round for dinner soon, and Jodie and the kids too.'

'Josh, regardless of what he did to help me, he still made your life hell when you were younger. And he tried to sleep with me. If you still couldn't face seeing him, I don't think anyone could blame you.'

'I ... I don't really know how I feel about that yet,' Josh said at length. 'But I do know that if it wasn't for him, you wouldn't –' his voice wavered '– you wouldn't be sitting here now. And he really does seem different. He's lost that arrogance he used to have. He seems to actually see the people around him now. It's not just all about him any more. And he and Jodie seem stronger than ever. Opening up and admitting to her how he was behaving with you and with these women at the hotel has really worked out for him. I can't imagine many people would be as understanding as Jodie, though.'

'Well, he never actually cheated by the sound of it,' Natalie said. 'Not one of the women he came on to at the hotel ever responded the way he wanted. I'm still uncomfortable about how he behaved with me, but you and him, you saved my life. I'm so – I can't stop thinking about that moment I saw you both. I've never been so grateful for anything.'

Josh kissed her head. 'You don't have to keep thanking me. Especially not after what you did for me. I'm in awe of you. You put yourself through hell.'

'Well, I got it all wrong anyway. I put all my focus on the wrong person.'

'You didn't get it as wrong as me. I've known Gareth for years, but if Toby hadn't made me see who he really was...'

'Let's not think about that.'

'To be honest, I think Toby only realised because he knew none of it was down to him.'

'Some of it was Verity,' Natalie said. Her heart still hurt whenever she thought about the actions of her sister-in-law, and she'd tried to contact her a few times to get some kind of explanation. It had seemed hopeless, until earlier that week she had got a reply:

I've been too ashamed to speak to you until now. I feel sick every time I think about the things I said to you. It was like I was a different person – it didn't feel real. I was just pouring out my own hurt. Trying to get a reaction from you turned into an obsession, maybe even an addiction. But I never want to go back to being that person again. I know you probably can't forgive me, but I truly am sorry. I just want you to know that.

Josh gave her a squeeze. 'I know how much it still hurts, Natalie. She meant a lot to you.'

'Rob told me they're working through things. He says the marriage counselling is going well. At least, he says *some* of the sessions have gone well. It's still pretty turbulent. But he says he won't give up, and they both want to make it work, by the sound of it.'

A light breeze played with Natalie's hair, and after a few moments of silence she said, 'Gareth was completely crazy, Josh.'

'I know.'

'I don't know how somebody could end up like him. He said all this stuff about his past, but he was so – I don't know. I don't think he saw any value in life at all.'

'He'll be in prison for the rest of his life,' he reassured her. 'You'll never, ever, see him again.'

They were silent for a long time, until she spoke again. 'I had a call out of the blue from my modelling agency this morning – the one I was with when I was still modelling, anyway.'

'Oh yeah?'

'She said there's a job that would be perfect for me. A TV ad, for skincare products.'

'I thought you didn't want to do that any more.'

'I used to feel that way. But this company, they want to do a campaign that celebrates real women. Not just women that have been made to look flawless and perfect. Women like me.'

Josh thought for a moment. 'It's up to you, Nat. You've been through such a lot, but if you think this would be good for you, of course I'm behind you.'

'I think I will do it,' she said at length. 'I think I need to. Gareth called me a blemish – he wasn't really talking about my face – but to be honest, with what Verity was saying about me, I had started to feel pretty low again. But then I thought to myself: I stopped a man who would have gone on to kill who knows how many more women. I put myself in horrendous danger when I started down this path to clear your name. Perhaps it was a crazy thing to do, but it's made me feel like I don't want to hold back on anything now. I want to grab every chance I get to do something exciting.' She paused briefly. 'And besides, I'm only working part time at Hartbury Hotel, I'm sure I can make it work.'

He smiled down at her, and she kissed him, before snuggling against him with the sun on her face.

If you liked Into The Lake and you're keen to read more of my books in the future, I invite you to subscribe to the LK Chapman newsletter. I send only occasional emails with information about new releases and offers – no spam. You will also be able to download a free copy of my short story about a one night stand gone wrong, 'Worth Pursuing' (a prequel to my No Escape series), when you sign up!

Visit my website, www.lkchapman.com, or any of my social media pages to sign up to the reading group.

Thank you so much for supporting me by buying my book, it means a lot to me, and I hope you enjoyed reading Into The Lake. Please consider leaving a rating or review wherever you bought this book, to help other readers to discover my books!

Information about issues covered in Into The Lake

UK
Information about hoarding & suicidal feelings:
mind.org.uk, samaritans.org or call **116 123**
Access information on bullying & cyber bullying:
bullying.co.uk

US
National Suicide Prevention Lifeline:
suicidepreventionlifeline.org or call **1-800-273-8255**
Information about hoarding:
hoarding.iocdf.org
Information on bullying & cyber bullying:
stopbullying.gov

Other books by LK Chapman

No Escape series:
Worth Pursuing (short story)
Anything For Him
Found You
Never Let Her Go

Psychological thrillers/suspense
The Stories She Tells

Sci-fi thrillers
Networked
Too Good for This World (short story)

Connect with LK Chapman

Keep up to date with the latest news and new releases from
LK Chapman:
Twitter: **@LK_Chapman**
Facebook: **facebook.com/lkchapmanbooks**
Subscribe to the LK Chapman newsletter by visiting
www.lkchapman.com

Acknowledgements

Into The Lake certainly turned into a more complicated project than I expected. I began writing it in 2019, thinking it would be published in 2020. I think it's safe to say that 2020 wasn't a year that anyone could have foreseen, and there were many distractions with my young son in the house more than usual! Nevertheless, I got there in the end, and as always I would like to thank my husband Ashley for his support through every stage of the writing process.

For her brilliant feedback on early drafts of Into The Lake, thank you to Lucy Dauman, and for helping me whip Into The Lake into shape when it wouldn't behave itself, thank you to my wonderful editor Carrie O'Grady. For yet another fabulous cover thank you to Stuart Bache at Books Covered.

A big thank you to my readers, and to all my family and friends who support me. It means such a lot to me to have people believe in me and in my books.

Also, as most of the work on this book took place during the coronavirus pandemic, I would like to include a special thank you to all of the key workers who continued going out to work during the pandemic.

About the author

LK Chapman writes psychological thrillers and suspense. She published her first psychological novel, Anything For Him, in 2016. A chilling thriller about obsession, jealousy and revenge, Anything For Him has now become a three book series with two sequels (Found You & Never Let Her Go) creating the No Escape trilogy. She has also written two standalone psychological novels, The Stories She Tells, and Into The Lake.

LK Chapman's books are inspired by her studies in psychology, and she has always been fascinated by the strength, peculiarities and extremes of human nature. As well as working as a psychologist, Chapman volunteered for mental health charity Mind before starting her journey as an author. It has been an incredibly exciting journey and she is so grateful for the support of her readers! In 2020 she moved to Somerset with her husband and young son, and when she's not writing she enjoys walks in the woods, gardening, and spending time with family and friends.

You can find out more about LK Chapman by visiting her website **www.lkchapman.com**.

The Stories She Tells

A psychological page-turner by LK Chapman
A heartbreaking secret. A lifetime of lies.

When Michael decides to track down ex-girlfriend Rae, who disappeared ten years ago while pregnant with his baby, he knows it could change his life forever. His search for her takes unexpected turns as he unearths multiple changes of identity and a childhood she tried to pretend never happened, but nothing could prepare him for what awaits when he finally finds her.

Rae appears to be happily married with a brand new baby daughter. But she is cagey about what happened to Michael's child, and starts to say alarming things: that her husband is trying to force her to give up her new baby for adoption, that he's attempting to undermine the bond between her and her child, and deliberately making her doubt her own sanity.

As Michael is drawn in deeper to her disturbing claims, he begins to doubt the truth of what she is saying. But is she really making it all up, or is there a shocking and heartbreaking secret at the root of the stories she tells?

No Escape Series

Anything For Him (Book 1)
Vulnerable and alone after the tragic loss of her parents, Felicity finds herself in a relationship with volatile and troubled Jay.

Against her better judgement, Felicity allows Jay to draw her in to a twisted revenge plan against his former best friend. Soon Felicity becomes trapped, and as Jay turns increasingly controlling and abusive, she questions everything he has told her about his past and his former girlfriend, Sammie. But when she tries to expose the truth, she comes up against an even greater threat. Someone obsessed and dangerous. Someone who has always been in the background of Jay's life. Someone who will do anything for him.

Anything For Him is the first book in the chilling NO ESCAPE psychological thriller trilogy. It can also be read as a standalone psychological thriller.

Found You (Book 2)
She escaped. But he's coming to get her.

After her imprisonment at the brutal hands of her ex, Jay, Felicity is slowly putting her life back together. She's got a new name, a new hairstyle, and even a new partner: strong, supportive Scott, whose down-to-earth nature makes him the perfect stepfather to little Leo. Though the nightmares still haunt her, she's starting to feel that her struggles are over; that she may, finally, be safe.
But Jay is still out there somewhere.
And Felicity can't shake the feeling she's being watched.

Never Let Her Go (Book 3)
All he wants is his family…

After escaping her ordeal at the hands of her obsessive ex, Jay, Felicity thought she was safe, building a new life with Scott and son Leo in a seaside town. Little does she know that Jay has tracked her down and wormed his way into the confidence of Vicky, a woman from Scott's past who has her own very sharp axe to grind…

In the gripping final book of the No Escape trilogy, Jay's obsession with Felicity pushes him to ever more desperate lengths to get her back. Felicity soon discovers that he'll stop at nothing, and history begins to repeat itself as she finds herself terrified, alone, and at Jay's mercy once again. Can she escape him before it's too late, or will she be destroyed by his determination to never let her go?